RISKING IT ALL

A Taboo Romance

LINZVONC

Copyright © 2021 by Linzvonc

All rights reserved.

No part of this book may be reproduced in any form or by any electronic or mechanical means, including information storage and retrieval systems, without written permission from the author, except for the use of brief quotations in a book review.

This is a work of fiction. Names, characters, places and incidents are either the product of the author's imagination or are used fictitiously, and any resemblance to actual persons, living or dead, business establishments, events or locales is entirely coincidental.

Cover Design: Getcovers.com

Editors: S.Glide & L.Carter

Beta readers: A.Fernandez, J.Cormack and J. Hoppe-Williams.

❀ Created with Vellum

Dedication

For Sam and my husband, for telling me I would do a taboo relationship like this justice.

I hope I have.

Foreword

This story is purely fictional.

I must warn you that it is a taboo romance and of mature nature. Things in this book may offend you or make you uncomfortable, but that is for you to decide.

This is for the readers that want to explore what happens when you fall in love with someone both society and your family declare inappropriate and wrong.

If you are sensitive to such themes (taboo and heavy sex) then this book isn't for you.

But if you are inquisitive and beyond curious, then read on.

I'm only just dipping my toes into the realms of what is truly taboo.

If you choose to read on, please remember my warnings.

If you've got any doubt, don't read it.

THEN AND NOW

"ELLA, LOOK AT ME."

Tears streamed down my face when Franco knelt in front of me, brushing my hair out of my eyes.

"What's happened?"

"Ben Calladine wrote on Ella's locker that she's a frigid bitch." Maria sang, dancing around us in circles.

"Fuck *off,* Maria!" I yelled as Franco cringed.

"I'm telling Papa you swore!" Maria shrieked, her lower lip trembling.

"Hey, if you can keep it a secret, I'll give you five bucks." Franco grinned, fishing a crumpled bill from his pocket.

Maria gazed at it, her eyes flickering over to me.

"And Ella says sorry."

Franco turned back to me, his delicious brown eyes pleading with me.

"Say sorry, El, come on."

"Sorry, Maria."

"Hmph. Cash," Maria smirked, holding her hand out

to Franco, who dropped the money into her hand, turning back to me as she scurried off.

"I don't think we were that savvy at thirteen."

"I wasn't that fucking emotionally challenged either." I snapped, wiping under my eyes with my sleeve. "It doesn't matter, Franco, I'll be alright. Just a shitty day, that's all."

Franco studied me, his hair falling in his eyes.

God, he was handsome.

"I'll be the judge of that. What happened?"

Franco fell back on the grass, gazing at me as I shrugged, wishing my little sister hadn't opened her mouth.

"Just some dick at school."

"How old is this dick?"

"He's my age."

"Sixteen?" Franco asked, sipping from the soda can beside him.

I nodded, playing with the hem on the bottom of my skirt.

"He called me frigid, but I don't know why that upset me so much. Maybe it's because I am, but I'm proud of that, you know?"

I could tell Franco anything.

"Little fucker. I'll sort it out. I know Calladine thinks he's the fucking man," Franco growled, staring at me. "I'm glad that's your reputation, Ella. Rather that than a slut."

Like his girlfriends, I thought, chewing on my lip.

At twenty-one, Franco was living my dream life. He rented a house not far from here and had landed a job in the city for a huge financial company doing god knows what.

All I knew was he worked hard and played hard, as my dad often said.

"Are you still with what's-her-face?"

"Who?" Franco laughed, tilting his head at me. "I'm

not *with* anyone. But, listen, I've gotta get home. I've got stuff to do for work. So ignore the pricks at school, yeah?"

My eyes followed him to the gate, as he called goodbye to my dad and Maria. He turned to me with a grimace.

"They're arguing again."

"Great."

"Chin up, beautiful."

THREE YEARS LATER

"Daddy, you've got to stop getting Grandpa drunk," Maria whined, rolling her eyes at Grandpa trying to do the hokey-pokey.

"He's having fun, Maria. Stop being a spoilsport," Dad said with a yawn.

I glanced at Grandpa from my schoolwork, shaking my head when he slapped his leg heartily.

"Come on, dance with me, Maria!"

"Hey, you remember that song your mother used to sing to you?" Dad smiled, waving his finger in the air. "The one with the guitar? Maria, Maria...you remind me of a Westside story...now who sang that?"

"Santana, old man." A voice boomed from the doorway as I turned to see my Uncle Franco standing there.

"Francesco!" Grandpa cried out, bumping into the table on his way to greet his youngest son.

I smiled, dropping my pen onto the paper as I rose to greet him, my eyes drinking him in like they did *every damn time*.

"Give me some sugar, Maria." Franco grinned, ruffling my sister's hair. "Jeez, you've been growing again?"

"It's only been two weeks, Uncle F."

As usual, Franco's eyes met mine, the twinkle in them telling me I was in for a hug.

"Here she is, the beautiful Ella."

He strode toward me, pulling me into his arms as I rested my head on his chest, feeling at ease immediately.

"How was Mexico?" I asked, pulling away as he held me at arm's length, studying me.

"*Hot*," Franco smirked, causing my cheeks to burn.

"You've got a great tan," I said, fanning myself.

"Nah, I've got great genes," Franco corrected me, nodding at my dad, who was dozing in the chair. "How much has he had?"

I glanced at my dad, heaving a sigh.

"I don't know, but they've been at it all afternoon. I've got this essay to do, and they won't stop interrupting me."

"Poor baby," Franco teased, leaning over to twist my essay toward him, his eyes scanning it. "Shit, heavy stuff for a Friday night, babe."

"I know. It's due on Monday."

"You've got two days. Chill."

"You should be at parties. That's what I'll be doing when I'm nineteen." Maria piped in.

Three voices answered her in unison.

"No, you won't."

Maria rolled her eyes, grinning at Franco.

"Uncle F will take me to a party, won't you?"

"Hell no, I won't. I'll take *you* though, if you fancy it, Ella?" Franco winked, nudging me.

"Ew, with you and your old friends?" I shot back, enjoying the annoyance on his face.

"Babes, five years older than you. When you're eighty, and I'm eighty-five, that will mean fuck all."

"I'll be dead!" Grandpa hooted, lifting a fresh glass of wine to his lips.

"Let's get you home, Grandpa," Maria said, nudging Dad with her foot.

"Huh? Yeah, home. Let's get you home," Dad yawned, lifting to his feet. "What time is it? I'm wiped."

"Nine." Franco laughed, his gaze on me. "Past your bedtime, old man."

"Listen, pipsqueak, you may be twenty-odd years younger than me, but I will still kick your ass," Dad warned, helping Maria guide Grandpa out the door.

"So, Ella," Franco yawned, dropping to the chair opposite me. "What have you got to tell me?"

I scribbled a note down before I forgot, shrugging my shoulders.

"Nothing, I've just been at school."

"Any boys' asses I need to kick?"

I rolled my eyes, gathering my papers together. There was no way I would be able to get anything done with him here.

"None as handsome as you, Franco." I winked, enjoying the flash of mischief in his eyes.

"Still no girls prettier than you either, Ella."

I poured a glass of filtered water from the fridge, our playful banter suddenly seeming inappropriate considering how hard my heart was hammering in my chest.

"Not even in Mexico?"

Franco turned to look at me with a sigh.

"Not even in Mexico. The girls are just so eager. They love my Italian good looks and American accent."

"Lovely." I forced a smile. "I'm going to watch a movie in the den. Are you waiting here for Dad or…"

"What movie?" Franco asked, lifting his brow. "Wait, let me guess."

"Nightmare on Elm Street." I laughed, ruining his moment. "I love scary movies."

"To be fair, I'd have gone with the Godfather. Lord knows you've got a soft spot for cute Italian guys with an attitude."

I avoided his gaze, turning toward the den so he couldn't see my eyes.

Because it's precisely what I like, and he comes in the shape of my fucking uncle.

ONE

ELLA

JACKSON PRESSED me up against the lockers, his hips thrusting against me as his tongue stroked mine, his hands squeezing my ass.

"Come and see me later, Ella."

"Jackson...I can't. My uncle just got back from Mexico and—"

"Fuck your uncle. I've got something better for you right here," Jackson growled, burying his mouth into my neck.

"Fuck my uncle? You need to watch your mouth," I huffed, pushing him away from me.

Jackson held his hands up, looking at me through big baby blues.

"Sorry, baby—"

I scowled at him, hoisting my bag onto my shoulder.

"Yeah, you are. Don't ever cuss my family again."

"Jeez, I wasn't—"

The door slammed behind me as I shook my head, wondering why I kept kissing the cheating jock from school.

I was a college girl now. I shouldn't be fucking with what should be ancient history.

I'd always had a little crush on Jackson, his loud mouth and cocky attitude had attracted me along with his ripped body.

He had a girlfriend, but he was the one that had committed to her, not me.

Besides, I wasn't sleeping with him.

I wasn't that stupid.

DAD:

Are you out tonight, Ella? DAD XX

My dad still insists on putting his name at the end of text messages regardless of telling him I've got his number stored.

I was out tonight, but I wondered what my dad wanted.

ELLA:

What's up, Dad? I've got plans, but I'm curious what you need me for 😂

DAD:

The weather is glorious, baby, and your old man bought some steaks from the Italian market in town. Maria is at a sleepover. Didn't want you to miss out. DAD XX

. . .

"Ella!"

I shielded my eyes from the sun, grinning when I saw Vanessa and Avery striding towards me. Vanessa threw her silky black hair over her shoulder, her scarlet red lips pulling into a smile.

"Gah, girl, you've got Jackson Miller written all over your face."

Vanessa reached out to squeeze my cheek, her dark brown eyes squinting in the morning glare.

"You know if his girlfriend finds out you're dead," Avery said with a sigh, holding her books to her chest. "You need to be careful."

Vanessa rolled her eyes, linking her arm with mine. "Are you kidding me? My girl?" She pointed at me with a snort. "She can handle herself."

"Hey, if his girlfriend has a problem with Jackson kissing other girls, she's got a lotta girls to get through before she gets to my name."

Avery chewed on her lip, shaking her head.

"Still—"

"Ave's. It's all good, don't worry yourself. How's Nate?" I said, watching her face change from panicked to relaxed and gooey.

Avery and Nate had been best friends for as long as I could remember, and recently he'd moved to go to a college on the West Coast.

"He called me last night, and he sounds so happy. He wants me to visit as soon as possible, yay!"

"Do I hear a road trip?" Vanessa winked, nudging me.

"Urgh, I've got to get to class. I'll catch you later?" I held up my hands apologetically.

"Party tonight, don't forget!" Vanessa yelled after me.

"I won't!"

. . .

ELLA:

I promised Vanessa I'd go out with her tonight. Do you want me to cancel? Don't want you on your own. 🩶

DAD:

It's okay. Franco is coming around to watch the game. That boy would never turn down a steak. DAD XX

My stomach jolted at the thought of Franco being in my house, especially when I was going to a party. He'd no doubt give me shit about my outfit and insist on waiting up for me. In some ways, he was way worse than my dad, who just wanted me to be safe and have fun.

I wish Mom were here.

My heart ached at the thought of my mother, but I knew that I'd been lucky enough to have her as long as I did. Unfortunately, poor Maria can't remember her as well as I can.

My memories were faint, but I remember that she loved me fiercely, the way a mother should love a child.

Still, my dad had done well with us as kids, but the dynamics changed so drastically that it meant I had to grow up quickly.

Most kids do chores around the house, but mine often involved getting my sister ready for school. I made sure our uniforms were pressed and our lunches were made.

Pretty shitty when you're eleven years old.

I peered at the mirror, my heart thumping in my chest, when I heard Franco's stentorian tones announcing his arrival.

"I'm famished, brother."

My dad responded to him, and I returned my attention to the mirror on my desk.

The photo of my mother smiling down at me caught my eye, and I gazed at it, wondering what she'd say to me now.

She'd probably tell me to 'knock them dead' or something equally confident.

"I will, Mom," I promised her, dabbing my lips with the peachy nude lipstick I adored.

I'd gone for minimal makeup, and as I knew there would be no way I'd get out of this house in any kind of skin-revealing outfit, I'd gone for a dress that clung to my curves, hugging my legs together and stopping mid-thigh.

I slipped my ballet pumps on, refusing to wear stilettos.

I need comfort.

I stopped, examining my reflection and groaning.

I needed heels. I was so fucking small.

Begrudgingly, I slipped my peep-toe heels on, satisfied they made my legs look a little longer. I grabbed my bag, stuffing my phone and pepper spray inside.

No one fucks with a Russo girl.

I threw my hair over my shoulder in a side parting, strutting down the stairs carefully.

The last thing I needed was to trip and fall at the feet of—

"Fuck me."

Franco stood before the open fridge, his eyes balking at my outfit. He had a thin t-shirt on, revealing his muscular tattooed arms.

Help me. Anyone.

I wished Maria was here for once, for her mindless chatter would fill the awkward silence that fell between us.

"Hey, Franco." I smiled, walking into the living room. I looked out of the window for Vanessa and Avery's cab.

"Where are you going?"

This came from Franco, and my dad grinned at me, knowing the score between Franco and me when it came to me going out.

"Out."

"No, really?" Franco gasped, shaking his head. "Seriously. Where are you going?"

He sipped his beer, his eyes slowly journeying down my body as I pretended not to notice.

"A party."

"Whose party?"

"Oh, Francesco, leave the girl alone. Tell her she looks beautiful and let her have a good night, eh?" Dad groaned, pointing at the screen. "The game's about to start."

Franco gazed at me, licking his lips as he did.

"She *knows* she looks beautiful."

"I do," I answered honestly, doing a little twirl. "But I hate these heels. I wanna wear my sneakers."

"So wear them then," Franco suggested. "No one is forcing you to wear heels, babe."

"I'm too short. If I don't wear them, I get lost in crowds," I joked, grabbing my bag when a horn honked outside.

"Jacket." Franco stopped me as I passed him, his dark eyes boring into mine. "It's fucking freezing, Ella."

"It's a house party. I'm good. Alcohol warms me up anyway."

Franco scowled at me, following me to the door, closing it behind us.

"*Ella.*"

I turned to give him an exasperated look, wondering why he insisted on raining on my parade every time.

"Yes?" I asked in a clipped tone.

"I'll wait up. Be good."

He waved to the cab behind me, his fingers rubbing his chin as he examined me.

"Fucking *hell*. My *niece*, ladies and gentlemen."

He turned and walked back into the house, my head spinning in confusion.

What did he mean by that?

"Ask Franco to come to the party, oh my god, *please*!" Vanessa screamed out of the cab, her boobs pressed against the glass.

I rolled my eyes, strutting to the cab as I shivered.

It *was* bloody cold.

"Shut up with your crush on my uncle. It's weird." I snapped, climbing into the front seat beside the driver. "God, I need a drink."

TWO

FRANCO

ELLA HAD BEEN GONE for fucking hours, and I hadn't stopped thinking about her in that dress. Not that it made a difference; the girl looked hot in a fucking trash bag.

It's your niece, you dick.

It made no difference how many times I told myself this. It didn't stop me from wanting her as I did.

"I'm heading to bed," my brother declared, looking down at me through tired eyes. "You waiting up?"

"You know I am."

"I'm lucky to have you, and so is Ella." He patted my arm as he moved past me, my eyes closing, guilt ripping through me again.

If Christopher knew the thoughts I was having about his daughter, he would kill me; of that, I had no doubt.

But he didn't know.

No one did.

I must've dozed off, jumping when the door opened; the sound of girls giggling woke me up.

"Fucking hell," I muttered when I squinted against the bright light that filled the room.

"Oh, it's your sexy uncle," Vanessa purred, coming to sit on the sofa across from me.

Another hot girl, but this one wasn't off-limits.

"You're drunk. Go to bed." I yawned, watching as Ella threw her heels off, falling onto the sofa beside me.

"Rub my feet, Franco," Ella purred, her eyes half-closed, her feet pushing onto my lap. "Please, they've been trapped in those fucking things all night."

She stretched, wriggling her toes as I tried not to stare at her fucking legs.

"Ella, I need to sleep," Vanessa whined, stumbling to her feet. "I'm going to bed."

My heart rate increased at the thought of being alone with Ella, drunk.

Nah.

"Ella, bed." I tapped her feet, but she groaned, moving her feet against me.

"Please rub them."

"Oh, for fuck's sake," I cursed, grabbing her foot and kneading it with my fingers. Her toenails were a glossy red, and I tried to pay attention to the television. Fuck knows what sales channel was on, but I tried my hardest to find it interesting whatever it was they were selling.

"Mmm, that's so good."

I froze, allowing my head to drop back on the sofa.

She's your niece.

Every one of my friends had tried it on with her.

She turned everyone down, too.

"Go to bed then, El," I swallowed, knowing if I continued stroking her soft feet like this, I was going to get myself into a state.

"Why? Don't you like sitting with me?" Ella said, her voice all croaky.

"I love sitting with you."

"Shall we play a game?" Ella sat up, her eyes wide.

I tore my eyes away from her, patting her leg.

Her fucking thigh.

"No," I said firmly, pushing her feet away from me.

"Franco." Ella pouted. "Is it better if a guy kisses you fast or slow?"

Please, God.

"How the fuck am I supposed to answer that?" I scoffed as she tucked her legs beneath her, cozying up next to me.

Sweet vanilla perfume.

"I kissed this guy tonight, and it was so fucking slow. Do you kiss slowly?"

"Fuck, Ella, why are you kissing random guys?" I snapped, scowling at her.

"Because I'm nineteen, single, and ready to mingle!" Ella giggled, pushing her hair to one side.

"You should be careful, Ella."

"Stop being so grumpy. Why are you so grumpy, Franco?"

I was struggling with this. Ella's long legs peeked out from beneath her dress that was riding up her thighs, her eyes sparkling as she teased me.

"Go to bed, sweetheart," I murmured as she gazed at me, her eyes locking onto mine.

"Do you?" Ella asked, trailing her finger down my arm, a shiver shooting down my spine as I turned to her with annoyance.

"Do I what?"

"Kiss slowly."

"I don't kiss myself that often. You're drunk." I sighed, hitting the off button on the remote.

"I kiss like I want to fuck, apparently."

I stiffened, turning to stare at her lips, swollen and bare like she'd been kissing someone hard.

"Who told you that?"

"Jackson. But he just wants to fuck."

I want to kill the prick.

"Is that who you've been kissing tonight?" I stared straight ahead, rubbing the bridge of my nose. "Jackson?"

Ella laughed, biting her lip as she frowned. "Um, no. This was some guy from a different college."

The slice of envy that ripped through me was enough to make me scrunch my eyes shut as I exhaled through my nose.

"I'm going, Ella. Go to bed."

I went to stand up when Ella caught my hand, pulling me close to her. She licked her lips, gazing at me with her huge eyes.

"Are you mad at me, Franco?"

"No." I lied, closing my eyes when she tilted her head, trailing her finger down my jawline.

"You're so gorgeous. Vanessa wants you."

"Good for her," I muttered, pushing myself up by my hands, ignoring the way she made me feel.

"Don't you want her?" Ella breathed, hooking her arms around my neck, tugging me back to her level.

What the fuck was this girl doing?

"Ella, let go." I barked, moving back.

"Fine, go." Ella pouted, staring up at me with a challenge in her eyes. "I thought you'd want to stay with me."

I paused, momentarily perplexed.

"Why?"

"Because it's us," Ella said, rising to her feet, still loads smaller than me. "It's us, Franco," she repeated, giving me a sad smile as she gathered her hair into her hands, her dress riding up to expose more of her thighs. Her neck was exposed, and I couldn't take my fucking eyes off her.

She knew too because she smiled, striding toward me with her arms outstretched for a hug.

"Whoever we end up with will be fucking lucky, Franco," Ella purred into my ear, her lips brushing against my ears as I refused to hug her back, knowing to do so would be fucking suicide.

Then she shocked the fuck out of me.

She pressed her lips against mine, pulling away ever so slightly, her eyes searching mine as I pushed her gently away, walking past her.

"Goodnight, Ella."

I had to get away from her before I did something both of us would regret.

THREE

ELLA

VANESSA WAS ANNOYING me with her incessant chatter about Franco, and there wasn't much rationality to my reaction.

"Just set me up on a date with him," Vanessa stretched out on my bed, revealing her toned stomach. "He's a God, and I need him, El."

You're not the only one, except I'll burn in hell for my thoughts alone.

"He's not interested." I shrugged as I finished braiding my hair for work. "He said so the other night."

Vanessa shot up, her mouth forming a perfect 'O' as she gaped at me.

"As if he did!"

"He did. He's not into younger girls."

More lies.

"Well, maybe I can convince him otherwise." Vanessa chuckled, chewing on her lip. "Have you heard from Jackson?"

I had, he was burning up my phone with dick pics and filthy texts, but I hadn't replied.

"Fucking Jackson," I muttered, coating my lashes with mascara. "He's dumped his girlfriend."

Vanessa clapped her hands together excitedly. "Yes, because he wants you."

I stared at her in the reflection, my stomach twisting in knots. The great thing about hooking up with Jackson was that he was taken; it meant things could never progress between us. Now? I shook my head, pushing the bronze eyes away that sprang into my mind, the feeling of his lips against mine making me shiver.

Shiver? I needed to get a grip.

"I'm not getting involved with Jackson, Vanessa." Straightening my blouse, I shrugged. "What about you? Don't say Franco."

"Poo. I was going to say, coffee-deprived Franco. Can I come for dinner the next time he's here?"

The thing that bothered me the most was that I couldn't tell anyone, not even my best friends, that I'd kissed Franco. It didn't matter that it was a peck on the lips—it was electric between us; whenever he was around me, I felt giddy. But he was my uncle, even though we'd never acted like uncle and niece—that's how we knew each other.

"The guy you made out with at the party was super hot," Vanessa mused, leaning forward to slip her feet into her shoes. "What was his name?"

"I didn't get his name," I replied, grabbing my purse. "And you know you're always welcome for dinner."

"Ooh, let me know then," Vanessa giggled, biting her lip. "The things I would do—"

"V." I held my hand up, shaking my head to stop the torrent of filth that would've left her lips had I not interrupted her.

"Sorry. It must be so weird having a sexy uncle that's pretty much your age. I'm so glad it's not me."

"Yep. I need to go to work."

"Can I grab a coffee?" Vanessa asked, grinning at me. "A spiced pumpkin latte?"

I worked at the coffee store in town, and Vanessa was a coffee addict. So some days, she would laze on one of the tables with Avery, both of them slurping free lattes and admiring the men that came in.

"We aren't doing that right now, and you know this." I laughed.

"You must have the stuff in there somewhere."

"I don't! We only have it during the Fall."

"Oh, poo!"

"Do you want a lift home?" I sighed, tugging on my jacket. "Dad's taking me to work."

Until I passed my test, Dad's taxi was my go-to mode of transport.

"No, I'm good. Avery is picking me up." Vanessa tapped away at her phone, yawning.

Twenty minutes later, I strode into the coffee store, waving at Ria, who beamed at me over the line of coffee-deprived souls waiting to get their daily fix. I hurried into the back, sliding my jacket onto a hook, noticing the new schedule on the wall.

"Morning, Ella," Ethan, my boss, drawled from his desk behind me. "You alright?"

"Morning, Ethan. I'm all good, thank you, you?"

I dragged my phone out, snapping a photo of the schedule.

"Yeah, I need to speak to you about Ria's birthday." Ethan grinned, his brown eyes glinting with excitement. "You know how she's always wanted to go skiing?"

"Yes." I pushed my phone back into my bag, folding my arms.

"Well, there's an indoor ski area not far from here. Do you want to try that?"

"That's a great idea!" I agreed, glancing back to the line of customers. "Just let me know where and when." I tugged my apron over my head, fixing a smile on my face as I joined Ria, scribbling someone's order onto the paper cup.

"Hey, yeah, can I get a..." said a husky voice, causing both me and Ria to glance at the owner with interest. Curly black hair fell over his forehead, his deep blue eyes staring at me with recognition. "Oh, it's you!"

Oh, God. It's the guy from the party, the one I spent most of the night kissing slowly. My cheeks colored as my pen hovered over the cup I'd selected, aware our conversation intrigued the surrounding people.

"Hi!" I said brightly, nodding at the cup in my hands. "What would you like?"

My mystery man winked at me, his lips curving into a smile. "Well, how about I take you for a drink sometime?"

The businessman beside him looked up from his phone with a grin, watching my reaction.

"Uh, sure, but I meant to drink?" I shot back as he nodded.

"Just an espresso, please. School is killing me today."

I nodded, scribbling on the cup. "Name?"

"Don't you remember?" he teased, enjoying the way I squirmed beneath his gaze.

"I'm afraid not." I shrugged, scribbling down John Doe. "I'll just make one up."

Sniggers came from the line; people were enjoying our banter.

The guy craned his neck to catch a glimpse of my

scrawl, but Ria had it in her hand. Her peach-colored lips pursed together as she bit back a smile.

"Three eighty, please."

I avoided his eyes, smiling politely down the line of people as he scanned his phone to pay.

"Great, just wait down at the end, and Ria will get your drink ready for you."

"Thanks, Ella," John Doe drawled, striding toward where Ria was preparing his drink, his eyes on me as I took the following order. He was pretty cute.

Sometime later, the line had died down, and I grabbed myself a bottle of water, tipping it over ice.

"This is for you," Ria announced, holding out a ripped piece of paper. "From Cruz."

"Cruz?" I echoed, unfolding the note.

Ella, this is my number. I'm sorry I'm not John, whoever he is because I'm jealous of you writing his name. Cruz.

"Holy shit, he's smooth," Ria said over my shoulder, shaking her head. "Cute, too. Dalmont University too."

"How do you know that?" I laughed, studying the note again before pushing it into my pocket.

"He had a hoodie on with it written on."

Delmont? That's where Franco goes.

"So, what are you waiting for? Text him!"

I shrugged, knowing full well why I wasn't texting him. But it wasn't proper or healthy to have thoughts like this about your father's brother.

"I guess…" I muttered, sipping on my ice water.

"He's cute and funny. Come on, Ells!" Ria grinned, leaning on the counter. "How did you meet him?"

"At a party," I replied without emotion. "He was a slow-ass kisser."

"Haha!" Ria belly chuckled. "You want hot and fast,

huh? Like that guy from your high school, what's his name?"

"Jackson."

"That's it," Ria clicked her fingers. "You're so lucky. You can have anyone you want."

Not anyone.

FOUR

FRANCO

I WOKE up to the winter sunshine burning my eyelids, forcing me from my slumber. Typical that it was sunny on the day I wanted to stay in.

I'd been working like a demon all week, and today was the start of my three-day weekend. Dragging myself out of bed, I dressed for the gym, seeing no point in showering if I would get all hot and sweaty. I brushed my teeth and grabbed my gym stuff, jogging down to the kitchen.

A cup of coffee and a banana later, I was in my car. It looked sunny, but it was fucking freezing. I passed Ella's house, glancing up at her bedroom window with a sigh.

Since that kiss, I'd not seen her. I'd purposely avoided her because it was just too fucking weird.

Not too weird, though, because I can still remember what her breath felt like against my mouth.

It was torture. That's what it was. I tried to push thoughts of Ella out of my mind, eyeing up the hotties training in the window of the university gym. I nodded at my buddy, Kellan, who was killing it on the weights. He was ripped as fuck, because he didn't miss a day at the gym. He earned that shit.

"Russo." He grunted out, the veins in his face popping when he dragged the weights towards his body, releasing them slowly. "Thought you were dead."

I chuckled, wrapping my hands before hitting the punch bag. I needed to get rid of the pent-up tension and aggression, but nothing helped. I hit the bag with three punches, one after the other, as the sound of my knuckles pounding into the leather echoed around me.

"Maybe you should get laid," a voice suggested from behind me. I glanced at Cruz, someone I'd barely known until we'd got talking here.

"Sex doesn't solve everything," I muttered, switching my feet so I could attack from a different position.

Now I was thinking about sex with Ella.

Holy shit. It's getting worse.

"Rochelle is having a party tonight; you should come. The girls got more money than sense, and you know there'll be plenty of free beer."

My chest ached as I began to pant, my knuckles aching from the beating they were getting. Being a smoker wasn't the best plan, but I didn't give a shit. Everyone had their vices; smoking and wanting to fuck my niece was mine.

"Stop by," Cruz said, dropping onto the rowing machine.

"Hey, did that girl get back to you?" I asked, remembering Cruz telling me about some girl he'd met at a party, then he'd seen her in a store or some shit. Some people just had everything fall into place for them; no such luck for me.

"Yeah, man. She's coming tonight."

"Nice one."

"Bringing a friend too, if you're interested. Might

cheer you the fuck up. They're younger than us, and if I remember correctly, her friend was a hot blonde."

It didn't sound too bad. Maybe if I started seeing someone, I'd forget about Ella and start living normally.

"Alright, text me later, and I'll be there. She better be a hot blonde, though," I said with a frown. "I'm not third-wheeling."

"As if you could ever fucking third wheel, man. You're a God with women," Cruz reminded me, picking up the pace on the rower.

"Says Orlando Bloom." I laughed.

"Just leave mine alone; she's off-limits." Cruz shot over his shoulder as I held the punching bag still, catching my breath.

"I don't do sloppy seconds, so you're safe."

"I haven't done that yet."

"Yet being the operative word there, huh?" I glanced at the treadmills, noticing one was available. "I'll catch you later. I'm gonna run."

I jammed my AirPods into my ears, the sound of drum and bass deafening my thoughts as I ran, slowly at first before picking up speed.

I'd had girls, plenty of them.

But none that held my attention like Ella. Part of me had hoped she'd get a boyfriend, and he'd be decent enough for me to back off; see her in the way I should.

But she didn't.

The flirting has gotten heavier lately, too. I'd catch Ella staring at me, biting her fucking lip, and turning away when I met her gaze.

Why was I still thinking about her?!

I ran for another twenty minutes before moving to the weights, still thinking about my fucked up situation.

Maybe the blonde tonight would take my mind off her.

Providing she was willing, I wanted to fuck the ass off her and wake up with a banging headache but empty balls.

Twenty-four and still lusting after your niece. Prick.

The worst part was, it was a lonely fucking existence.

There was no one I could talk to about it because I sounded like a fucking hillbilly freak. It didn't matter that all my friends would jump on Ella given a chance—blood rules out any kind of relationship.

The problem was; I felt more for her than sexual urges.

That shit had to be locked down and repressed; otherwise, I'd end up with kids with serious fucking defects all because I kept it in the family.

I sighed, focusing on my reps.

"One, two, three…."

I guess it had to be shut down in my mind. The girl was almost twenty; she would soon be moving out and fucking around with guys.

There was nothing I could do about it other than look out for her.

I just hoped I had time to get this shit out of my mind before I saw her with someone because if the way I was gripping these weights were anything to go by, the idea of it had me raging.

I had to stop thinking of Ella as an option.

Later that night, I was necking my third beer, scanning the room for this hot blonde I'd been promised. My dick was aching to be sucked, and I needed to clear my mind of Ella before I did something fucking stupid.

Smoke filled the room, and I added to it, inhaling my cigarette as I moved my head in time to the music. Cruz slapped his hand against my chest, nodding over at the door.

"Here they fucking are, my man. Remember, the brunette is with me."

I rolled my eyes, focusing on the crowd to see where this hot chick was. I was intrigued about the brunette, to be fair; Cruz was a friend, but we were hardly best buds.

The legs were the first thing I noticed, encased in thigh-high black boots and tiny shorts that left nothing to the imagination. A silky pink tank top held an impressive rack, the chestnut brown hair falling in waves around her shoulders.

This brunette was fucking hot, and I was yet to get to her face.

"You made it!" Cruz said, pulling the girl into his chest, winking at me. "This is my buddy, Franco."

I was mid inhale when I saw her face, the hazel eyes that widened at the mention of my name. The smoke caught in my throat, but I managed to exhale it out of my nose, my eyes watering.

"Ella?" I growled, jamming my cigarette into the wall beside me, dropping it on the floor.

I couldn't care less; the house could burn down for all I care.

Standing in front of me, looking like she'd been designed for all men, was Ella.

Cruz frowned, holding her to him possessively.

"Ah, come on, how'd you two know each other?" He grumbled, his gaze moving from me to Ella, then back again.

"Hey! Where's your friend? Oh, Franco! What a nice surprise!" A blonde head appeared from beside Ella, and there stood Vanessa, all tits and teeth.

Vanessa was hot and all, but she wasn't Ella.

Right now, all I could focus on was Cruz's hands on her, Ella's eyes pleading with me to behave.

"Yeah, this is Ella's uncle!" Vanessa grinned, giving me a side look. "I know, too young to be her uncle, too hot to be single, but hey...it looks like you're my date for the night." She slid her arm around my waist, my body tensing at her touch.

Ella scowled, shaking her head as she turned away.

"Fucking uncle?" Cruz laughed, pulling Ella closer to him. "If you were my niece, I'd be breaking all kinds of laws."

"Ew! Don't be gross. I need a drink; what about you?"

I couldn't even respond; despite the smile on Vanessa's face, she had none of my attention.

None.

"Yeah, you and Cruz go get one. We'll wait here," I commanded darkly, my eyes pinning Ella to the spot.

Her defiant gaze only made me want her more, but fuck me, my hands were trembling, my blood turning fire hot in my veins.

This cannot be happening.

FIVE

ELLA

"WHY ARE YOU GLARING AT ME?" I snapped, throwing my hands up in the air at Franco. In his ripped fucking black jeans and tight white t-shirt, his brown eyes swirling with fire.

"You're out with Cruz?" Franco moved close to me, his nostrils flaring. "What the *fuck*, Ella?"

He smelled delicious. The cigarettes should be off-putting, but they weren't.

Franco made Cruz look like a boy, yet they were around the same age.

"Hey, you're on a date with Vanessa!" I hissed back, folding my arms as Franco gripped my arm, his mouth close to my ear.

"What the *fuck* are you wearing?"

I turned my head to him, our eyes locking in a passionate blaze of war.

"Don't pull that card on me, Francesco. I'll wear what I want, don't embarrass me."

"Embarrass you, sweetheart?" Franco's eyes drifted

down my face, stopping on my lips. "Why would I do that?"

"Because you're possessive and controlling, it's *weird.*"

"You've got no fucking idea."

"Everything okay?" I heard Cruz ask cautiously, pushing a beer bottle into my hand. Franco took it from me, gulping some down before giving it back gruffly.

"Haven't I told you not to accept drinks from guys at parties?"

He surprised the fuck out of me then, turning to Vanessa with a smile.

"Sorry. You look beautiful, but I'm not feeling it. Excuse me."

Franco pushed past her, leaving her wide-eyed and stunned.

"I think your uncle just blew me off," Vanessa frowned.

"I'll talk to him," I huffed. "I'll be back. Sorry, Cruz."

This is ridiculous.

I caught sight of Franco disappearing outside, and I followed him, cursing when people refused to move out of my way.

"Can you please move?!"

Getting angry with drunk people at parties was like screaming at the sight of a snake in the zoo. They're always going to be there.

Franco was hunched over, lighting another cigarette, when I stomped over to him, pushing in front of a buxom blonde who had him in her sights.

"Listen, you've got an attitude problem." I snapped, glaring at the eyes that burned into mine.

"Is that right?" He growled, sucking on his cigarette, blowing smoke over his shoulder. "If you wanna go and kiss that guy, I'm not sticking around to watch."

"I've already kissed Cruz, Jesus, Franco. You're my uncle, not my dad!"

"I don't care, Ella!"

"Seriously, you've just walked out? Very mature." I folded my arms as I glared at him, my heart slamming into my chest when he shook his head.

"What do you want me to fucking do? Come and hold your hand?"

I didn't know how to answer that.

Why was I standing out here with him?

"You're family. I can't have a good time if you're pissed off out here."

Franco rolled his eyes, turning as he motioned to the house.

"You come dressed like *that*—"

"Like *what?*"

I put my hands on my hips, my foot twitching as I considered kicking him in the balls.

"Like a…" Franco stopped, biting his lip as he looked at me through lowered lashes.

I could barely breathe as he battled with something internally.

"Like what? Slut?" I whispered, praying he didn't use that word to describe me.

Franco winced, then shook his head.

"Nah. Never that. You look good."

"For real?" I arched a brow, wondering if I was imagining the way he licked his lips, his fingertips brushing mine…

"You're fucking gorgeous, Ella. You know this." Franco rasped, moving closer to me. Wood spice filled my nostrils as I looked up at him, the feeling of his fingers on mine enough to send me dizzy.

"Why are you so angry with me?" I asked, his finger

and thumb moving to grip my chin, turning me towards the wall.

I shivered as the cold brick hit my back, but Franco moved in front of me, his mouth inches from mine.

"I can't help it. I'm sorry. You've done nothing wrong."

His voice, God, his voice. I bit my lip, wondering if I could get away with kissing him again.

Fuck, no.

"Okay," I whispered, expecting him to move back. But instead, his eyes scanned mine, his jaw clenching as he swore.

"Fuck Ella, you need to go back to your friend," Franco growled, moving back as I felt disappointment well up inside me. "Now."

"Why?" I challenged him, watching as he scowled at me, dragging his hand over his mouth.

"Just fucking go."

I knew I had to leave because the darkness in his eyes scared me. He looked like a man who was clinging to the last thread of sanity.

I pushed away from him when he tugged me back, slamming me against the wall.

"Just once," he whispered, his lips brushing against mine, my knees trembling as he caught me in his arms. I didn't know whether I was delirious, but I was positive this wasn't the same kiss as you'd give someone in your family.

No tongues, but the way he pressed his lips against mine made me want to devour him, whatever he was to me.

My skin felt alive, my heart pounding in my throat at his touch.

"Ella, go," Franco whispered, moving back. "Go on."

I didn't want to; my feet planted firmly to the ground.

"Go!" Franco hissed, turning away from me, his hands running through his thick hair.

I moved as though under his command, pushing my way through the crowd until I saw Vanessa and Cruz stood side by side, looking glum.

"There you are!" Vanessa hugged me, looking around me. "No, Franco?"

His name hurt my ears.

"No, he's with some girl outside…sorry, V." I lied, still able to taste the cigarettes on my lips.

"God, you look so good, come here, girl," Cruz murmured into my ear, his lips having zero effect on me compared to Franco's.

"Let's dance, hmm?" I suggested, pulling Vanessa close to me, burying my head in her shoulder.

"You okay?" Vanessa hissed, following me to the makeshift dance floor. "Is Franco giving you shit?"

"No, he's alright. Let's find you someone else."

Soon, our bodies were moving in time with the music, and the more crowded the party got, the better I felt. Vanessa was beautiful—why didn't Franco want her? As she danced, even Cruz watched her, but his attention was more on me.

I sent him a small smile, my heart jumping into my throat when I saw Franco join him, leaning against the wall as his eyes locked onto mine.

The flutters in my heart almost took my breath away.

I focused on my dancing, laughing with Vanessa as she slut dropped, indicating that I did the same.

I shook my head, nodding my head towards Franco and Cruz, and she grimaced, rolling her eyes.

"Your uncle may be hot, but man, he's grumpy," Vanessa shouted into my ear, and I nodded, continuing to dance with her, aware of the fact that Franco was watching me, along with Cruz.

"I think he might be coming around." Vanessa scowled as I turned to see Franco making out with some girl, his hands on her ass as he kissed her deeply. Burning rage swept through me as he kissed this random bitch, their mouths curving into smiles as they spoke between kisses.

What the fuck is his problem?!

Seeing red, I strode over to Cruz, whispering in his ear loud enough for Franco to hear.

"Kiss me, Cruz."

SIX

FRANCO

I FUCKING KISSED HER.

My niece.

I'd had to restrain myself and managed to pull away before I'd ripped her fucking clothes off then and there.

Then Nicole had spotted me, and I took the opportunity to get lost in her for a bit.

Ella was dancing, hands in her hair, a broad smile on her face as I kissed Nicole, her eager tongue nothing like the soft kiss I just had with Ella.

Still, I was so sexually frustrated I felt like it was making me sick, in the fucking head, not just the body.

Ella strode over, a steely glare in her eyes as she clocked me with Nicole, wrapping her arms around Cruz beside me, her throaty voice asking him to kiss her.

Fuck, no.

I pushed Nicole away slightly, gripping her wrists as I stared at Ella, my eyes wild.

"Don't."

Cruz gave me an exasperated look, his hands on Ella's

chin as he turned her face to his, his smirk disappearing as he kissed her.

"Baby," Nicole purred, trying to distract me.

Trying unsuccessfully.

"Get the fuck off her," I commanded, shoving Cruz back against the wall, my hand around his throat. "Don't fuck with me, man; I ain't playing."

Ella had her hands on mine, her eyes pleading with me as she spoke to me in a whisper.

"Stop, Francesco, please!"

Cruz shoved me back, and Ella moved between us, her eyes locked on mine, her head shaking as she told me no.

"Francesco!" She glanced around us, her cheeks flushing as she realized we'd drawn attention. "Jesus!"

"I don't wanna see that shit," I growled, grabbing Ella by the hand as I stormed away, ignoring her protests.

We reached a hallway, and I released her.

"Did you do that on purpose?" I demanded, slamming my fist into a wall, the plaster cracking around it.

The pain was nothing compared to what I'd just felt watching Ella kiss Cruz.

"Did you, Ella?!"

Vanessa ran up, but Ella waved her off without removing her eyes from mine, her chest heaving. Vanessa backed away slowly, and I turned to see Ella nodding so slightly I could've imagined it.

"Why? Why would you fucking do that?" I snapped, furious with this fucking girl. "I could've killed him, Ella!"

Ella reached forward, dragging me toward a room to the left. She tugged me in, slamming the door shut behind us.

"No shit, Francesco, tell me what the fuck that was, right now!"

Ella's eyes were wide in the dimly lit room, and the silence was deafening.

We stood glaring at each other, our thoughts ricocheting around like loose cannons.

Ella stepped forward, her frown narrowing her beautiful eyes.

"No shit, Francesco," she repeated, looking up at me.

My stomach twisted, my heart hammering in my chest. How could I tell her?

"It's not that fucking simple, Ella." I hurled back, turning to sit on the edge of the bed. "But maybe we should go. I can't see that again. I'll fucking murder him."

Ella crossed over to me, standing in front of me. The bare skin between her shorts and thigh-high boots made me close my eyes.

"I don't care, Franco!" Ella hissed, leaning down to fix me with the fucking stare that told me she would lose her shit. "Why? Why can't you see me kiss Cruz? Why can't I see you kiss anyone either?" She added in a whisper, resting her forehead against mine.

"You can't?" I dared to ask, wondering how much resistance I had left in the tank and if my brother would slit my throat or shoot me when he found out.

"No."

"This is so fucked up," I muttered, inhaling her sweet scent.

"What's fucked up is the fact you're not saying how you feel."

"I'm your uncle, Ella. What can I fucking say? That I wanna throw you on this bed and fuck you until you scream my name? Huh? How does that make you feel?"

Ella slammed her mouth on mine, a moan leaving her lips that told me she wanted me as much as I wanted her.

I couldn't stop this.

Ella's tongue probed my lips, and I let her in, falling back on the bed with her on top of me, her hands lost in my hair as she kissed me like a fucking professional. I flipped us over without breaking the kiss, my hand resting on her thigh as she dragged me further into her with her hands.

"I want you, Franco," she moaned into my mouth, biting my lips, my tongue, anything she could reach. "Do you want me?"

"I do, but it's so wrong," I admitted, wrapping my arm around her waist as I stared down at her.

"I don't care," Ella breathed, her eyes searching mine. "I mean it."

"That's okay for you to say, but your dad will fucking kill me. But…" I stared into her eyes, my thumb brushing against her lips. "It would be worth it. So fucking worth it."

I tugged her to her feet, glancing around as I tried to compose myself.

"We should stop, right?"

"Do you want to?" Ella asked, biting her lip.

"No," I groaned, turning her around and walking her to the door so she was up against it. "There's no lock on this door, Ella, so body weights gonna have to do."

Lifting her legs around my waist, she gasped, her mouth sinking into my neck as I searched for her lips, capturing them mid-bite.

"Don't fucking bite me, Ella."

She sucked on my tongue, her eyes rolling as I lost control, kissing her with such force she cried out.

Her hands wrapped around my neck, her hips grinding against mine as I screamed at myself to stop.

Social suicide.

But could I stop my mouth from being one with hers?

Fuck no.

"This is wrong," Ella whispered into my mouth. "But I mean it, Franco, I don't care."

"Next, you'll be begging me to fuck you, and I haven't got the restraint to tell you no." I exhaled, her lips on mine again, soft moans leaving her mouth that drove me fucking insane.

"Ella, stop making those fucking noises, please, Jesus…." I pleaded, my mouth moving to the crook of her neck, my tongue flickering against the soft skin there.

Ella gasped out, digging her fingers into my shoulders as she ground against me.

"Right, stop," I muttered, dropping her legs to the ground. "Stop."

Ella looked up at me, her hand cupping my face.

"Don't you want me?"

"Yes, Ella, isn't it obvious?!" I snapped, turning away from her. "We need to go."

"Go? Where?" Ella demanded with her hands on her hips.

"Home, girl. We can't stay here with fucking Cruz and Nicole. She won't leave me alone now."

Ella's eyes darkened.

"Then let's go back to yours."

I stared at her, a chuckle escaping my lips.

"Now you're playing, right?"

Ella lifted her chin in the air, arching a brow at me defiantly.

"Nope."

"I can't have you in my house, not after this."

"Surely you can control yourself, Francesco?" Ella asked innocently, texting on her phone.

"Who are you texting now?" I asked with irritation, wondering how many cold showers I would need with her in my house.

"Uber. Two minutes away. I'll offer Vanessa a lift home, but we're going. Right?"

"What about lover boy out there?" I smirked, folding my arms.

"I've got a possessive uncle. What can I say?" Ella purred.

"That you're not fucking seeing him again," I muttered. "Stop fucking teasing me, Ella. It's not good."

I moved her aside, storming out of the house to have a quick smoke before the car got here.

My fingers were shaking, my adrenaline through the roof.

I'd just signed my death warrant.

SEVEN

ELLA

VANESSA THOUGHT Franco was going to kill me; I was sure of it. Her eyes darted between us as we sat across from each other in the cab.

"Is everything okay?" Vanessa asked as Franco ignored her, leaving me to nod.

"Yeah, sorry we left early."

Vanessa shrugged. "I wasn't feeling it. Didn't wanna sit and watch you and Cruz all night, plus my date kinda bailed."

Franco cut his eyes at Vanessa, who gulped, looking out the window like she'd seen something interesting.

My brain was buzzing with thoughts as we drove through the wet streets until the cab pulled up at Vanessa's.

"Are you staying with me, or…?" Vanessa looked at me, her hand on the door handle.

I swallowed, shaking my head. "No, I'll go home."

Vanessa cringed, shooting me a sympathetic look.

If only she knew.

The door slammed shut behind her, and we waited

until she was safely in her house before the cab pulled away, heading for Franco's.

We didn't say a word to each other until the cab pulled up, and Franco sighed, handing the driver a cash tip.

"This is so fucked up, Ella."

His gruff voice sent shivers down my spine as I watched him putting the key into the lock, my heart smashing against my chest.

What was I thinking?

Franco strode in, running his hands through his hair.

I locked the door after me, turning to see Franco gazing at me, his dark eyes burning with desire.

"Listen," he started, his eyes avoiding mine as I walked up to him slowly, my fingers dancing up his arms as he stiffened. "We shouldn't do this. It's not right, Ella."

"What's not right? The fact we want it?"

"Doing it, Ella. I'm serious. Kissing is one thing, but anything else…." His voice trailed off as I moved closer, pressing my body against his.

Wrapping my arms around his neck, I sighed into his chest. His hands met behind my back, and I prayed for him to take control of the situation before I did.

I didn't care who he was to me. He'd never been an actual uncle to me- he was barely five years older than me, for god's sake.

I dragged my hands over his shoulders as I played with the button on his shirt, his eyes fixing on mine.

"Ella. We *can't* fuck."

"But you'll kiss me?" I whispered, moving his chin with my fingers, my tongue licking the fragranced skin that tasted almost as good as it smelled.

Franco growled, his fingers gripping my wrists as he pushed me back.

"No fucking. Right?" He muttered, slamming me against the wall as I nodded breathlessly.

His hands ran down my body as I groaned, throwing my head back as he gazed at me.

"I'm not supposed to feel this way," Franco admitted, his plump lips brushing against mine.

"I'm not either, but no one will know!" I snapped with irritation, twisting us so that I had him against the wall. "I want you, Franco, so say yes or no, right now."

Franco stared at me, fury in his eyes.

"No."

"*No?*" I repeated, matching his tone.

"Go to bed." Franco bit his lip, shaking his head.

"Come with me." I threw back at him, hands on my hips. "I'm not asking."

"No. Ella, come *on.*"

Franco ran his hand through his hair again, and I knew he was battling internally.

"Fine, I'm calling Cruz."

Franco gripped the chair he was resting on, shaking his head.

"Don't test me, Ella."

"So you keep saying, Franco! This was such a shit idea. Forget anything happened, I'm going."

I stormed toward the door, my veins filling with annoyance and rage. "You can't walk home on your own at this hour," Franco drawled, almost with amusement.

"Watch me." I snapped, my fingers on the lock as he finally moved, slamming his hand on the door.

"What the fuck do you want me to do, Ella?"

I turned to him, pushing him away from me.

"Nothing, because you're too chicken to do what you know we both want! I get it. It's taboo. But you aren't like that to me! You've never felt like my uncle, and you know it!" I yelled at him. "So don't kiss me like a fucking lover at a party and then turn into Uncle fucking Buck when we get home!"

Franco burst out laughing, and I glared at him, dragging my phone out of my pocket.

"Fuck this, I'm calling—"

"Careful," Franco muttered, glaring at me.

"Come to bed with me, or I'm leaving." I challenged him, folding my arms.

"I won't stop you from leaving, beautiful, but fuck it. I'll come to bed with you if it shuts you the fuck up." Franco shrugged, a glint in his eyes.

My stomach flipped with anticipation, but I knew he wouldn't take it further than a kiss, and it infuriated me.

I stomped up the stairs, hearing him sigh as he followed me.

"I sleep naked," I declared as Franco froze in the doorway, his eyes locked on mine.

"Ella…" he warned, his voice hoarse.

"What? I do," I smirked, getting high from the argument we were having. His jaw clenched as he rubbed his forehead with his fingers, exhaling heavily.

I slid my boots off first, wriggling out of my shorts as he stared at the floor, refusing to look at me.

Leaving my panties on, I shrugged my top off, allowing my hair to fall in front of me, covering my nipples.

"Franco."

He cut his eyes at me, dragging his fingers and thumb on his cheeks as he groaned.

"Fuck, Ella, cover-up! Get in bed. Do you do this with other boys?" Franco barked, watching me as I climbed into his bed.

"Hardly! Come on; it's your turn."

My heart skipped a beat when he stripped off, leaving

him only his boxers.

Uncle or not, he was fucking insane looking.

Tattoos that I wanted to trace with my tongue.

"Losing that big girl confidence now, huh?" Franco smirked as I watched him climb into bed beside me, my eyes widening at the bulge in his boxers. "Go on, Ella, keep giving it the big talk."

He hit the lights, and we were plunged into darkness.

I was suddenly aware of my breathing, and Franco shifted, dragging me against him as he kissed my shoulder.

"Stop this now. Get some sleep."

I lifted my hand to caress his cheek, pressing my ass into him as he exhaled heavily. I turned my head to him, his head shaking as I pulled him close.

"You ain't gonna quit this, are you?"

"No," I whispered, twisting so I could hook my leg over his hip, his hand tilting my chin to his.

"Do you want me to make you cum, Ella?" Franco murmured against my lips, moving so he was able to run his hand down my ass cheek, a finger caressing my underwear. "Wet already, hmm?"

I wriggled against him, my lips searching his in the dark.

Something about kissing in the dark was different, and as his tongue swept across my lips, parting them, my tongue dove into his mouth, begging for him to touch me.

His fingers slipped into my underwear, stroking my wetness so gently I almost screamed out.

"You like the fact we shouldn't be doing this, don't you?" He muttered in between our hot kisses.

"I don't care, Franco. You can't help who you want," I gasped as he flicked his finger against my clit, making me throw my head back, which only gave him access to my neck.

Excitement bubbled within me when he moved in between my legs, his fingers now thrusting into me as his mouth attacked mine. I felt his chain on my throat, and I dragged him closer to me, my breath escaping in pants between us.

"Please, Francesco…"

"Ella, don't," Franco warned as I wrapped my legs around him, feeling his hard dick against my wet panties.

"Franco, do it," I said, no longer caring if I was begging. "I need it."

Franco swore as I gripped his cock through his boxers, pumping it as he grabbed me tight.

"Just once," I whispered as he shook his head.

"No."

"Please!" I moaned as he picked up the thrusts of his fingers.

"Fuck, Ella!"

He withdrew his fingers, moving away to lie beside me, his annoyed breaths filling the silence between us.

"Just once," I repeated, dragging my nails down his chest. "Don't you want to?"

Franco gripped me by the throat, tugging me to his lips as I gasped, excited and dizzy with lust,

"You know I fucking do."

"Then do it!" I huffed, knowing I'd won when he threw me off him, throwing open his bedside drawer, tossing the contents onto the bed.

"Choose whichever you like, and I'll fuck you so hard you won't be able to walk for a week." He sighed as condom wrappers covered the bed.

"Promise?"

"Oh, I fucking swear."

Music to my ears.

EIGHT

FRANCO

ELLA SELECTED A CONDOM, holding it up between two fingers as she stared at me. She had been winding me up all fucking night, and incest be damned, I was going to have her.

Her eyes widened when I pushed my boxers down my thighs, letting them slip to the floor.

"You sure?" I asked, enjoying her reaction to my dick.

"I'm sure." She wet her lips, and I wrapped my dick, pushing her onto the bed.

Her thighs trembled when I parted them, rubbing myself against her wetness.

"Is this your first time?" I muttered, positioning myself at her sweet hole.

Ella nodded, and I smirked, easing myself into her.

"Never known a virgin beg like that."

Fuck, she was tighter than I'd imagined. As soon as I had a taste, though, I couldn't control myself when I slammed into her, her cries echoing around the room.

"I didn't think you had the balls," Ella whispered, biting her lip as I glared at her.

I wrapped her hair around my hand, yanking it back as I thrust into her repeatedly, the desire to own her taking over.

"Shut up, Ella," I growled, taking her nipple into my mouth and sucking on it hard. Her skin tasted sweet and clean, her gasps and moans fueling me to nibble on the pert bud.

"No, I wanna see what you've got," Ella gasped, and I shook my head at her stupidity.

Slamming my mouth down on hers, I lifted her legs over my shoulders, her pussy walls gripping my dick so hard I thought my dick was going to snap. I dragged my tongue up her calf, my hips moving at record sped as she screamed beneath me in desire.

"Hard enough?" I muttered, my mouth salivating at the view of her held prisoner by my dick, my arms now folded across her legs as I held them in place.

I shoved her legs down as she trembled beneath me, her eyes rolling back in her head as I flipped her over, pushing her face down into the bed.

"Oh my god, Francesco…." Ella moaned into the bed, her voice muffled. I entered her again, my hand pushing into her mound as I searched for her sweet spot. She was so wet I could barely control myself, but when I massaged her clit and bit into her shoulder, she fell silent, her body stiffening as I manipulated her.

"Don't stop!" Ella begged, and I ripped her head back to see the expression on her face when she came for the first time around my dick.

"Are you coming for me, Ella?" I growled, releasing her clit when she bucked and moaned, shoving my fingers into her mouth as she choked on her juices.

It was too much. I gripped Ella's throat for leverage,

then remembered she couldn't walk around with marks on her, so I slipped my hand beneath her to grip her tits.

As I came, I buried my head into her neck, grunting and groaning as I gripped her tightly.

Ella moved beneath me, milking my dick for all it was worth.

"Yes, Franco, fill me with your cum."

I almost came again when she said that, and I slammed into her one last time.

Our bodies were slick with sweat, and both of us were panting like fucking dogs.

"Just once, yeah?" Ella mumbled as I pulled out of her, biting her ass on my way off the bed.

I threw the condom in the toilet, leaning over the sink as I stared at myself in the mirror.

What the fuck had I just done?

I hit the lights, climbing back into bed beside Ella as she snuggled against me with a contented sigh.

"It doesn't feel wrong." Ella yawned as I kissed her shoulder where my teeth had left indentations.

"Get some sleep," I ordered, forcing my eyes closed.

I wanted to fall asleep with her in my arms just once.

ELLA

HOLY FUCK.

There's no way what Franco just did to me was real—this must be some kind of dream. No man could reduce me to a fucking mess like that, let alone tell me to shut up and go to sleep.

His arms wrapped around me, our legs entwined as we rested, his breathing deepening as he fell to sleep.

His scent drove me insane.

What the hell came over me?

I'd given him no choice; he had to fuck me. I'd felt like a siren luring him to his death or something.

But from the moment he kissed me, my world turned upside down.

There wasn't anyone else I wanted like I wanted Franco.

I couldn't allow my brain to entertain what would happen next, and I pushed away the thoughts when they came.

I inhaled his scent once more, kissing his fingers laced with mine.

No one could ever know.

The worst, though, was that this was just a one-off, just once.

The idea of Franco doing this with anyone else made me feel sick with envy, and I gripped his hand tightly.

"Stop thinking, beautiful. Nothing can be solved by overthinking," Franco mumbled into my ear, his lips on my ear.

"I know, but I can't stop."

"Sleep, baby."

"Just once?" I asked, staring into the darkness.

There was a pause; then, his voice broke the silence.

"Yeah. It will be our secret, so relax."

I couldn't help the tears that sprang into my eyes, but I scrunched them shut, refusing to show how much tonight had meant to me.

How stupid of me to think we could do this on a regular.

Franco wouldn't.

I shouldn't want to.

I needed to lock this shit up in my brain forever.
No one could ever know.

NINE

FRANCO

I WOKE EARLY the next day, my stomach twisting at the sight of a naked Ella in my bed.

Shit.

I rolled onto my back, and she tugged the covers, snuggling into the pillow with her back to me.

What the hell, man.

I swung my legs out of bed, heading for the shower. I stood under the water until my skin began to wrinkle, and I begrudgingly got out. My mind was pretty clear considering that I'd fucked Ella because I knew it was what we'd both wanted. It had been fire, fuck. I dressed in grey joggers and a white t-shirt, heading down to my kitchen as I stuck some bacon on the grill.

Fucking someone you shouldn't was always a turn-on; fucking someone you're related to was even worse, but there were no regrets. Not on my behalf.

Hopefully, now we'd got it out of our system, and we could share the secret for years to come.

I butter the bun, hearing the floorboards creak above me.

She's up.

Moments later, she padded down the stairs wearing one of my shirts, yawning.

I tore my eyes away from her legs, nodding at the coffee machine.

"Coffee?"

"No, thanks," Ella said, wincing when she sat on a stool beside the counter.

"You okay?" I asked, arching a brow at her as I turned the sizzling bacon.

"Mmhmm."

I grabbed a carton of apple juice from the fridge, dropping it in front of her.

"I know you like that."

"Can I have a glass?" She laughed, pinching the carton at the end.

"Ah, come on. I thought you'd suck it from the carton."

"Suck it?" Ella echoed, her eyes on mine.

"Drink it; you know what I mean. Bacon?"

"Yes, please."

Silence fell as I made us breakfast, and I chewed on my roll wordlessly as I gazed out of the window.

"So, are we going to talk about last night?" Ella sucked her finger, polishing off her roll.

"Nope." I shrugged, handing her another roll. "We forget it happened."

Ella frowned, taking the roll from me slowly.

"Seriously?"

"Ella. You're my niece." I snapped with irritation. "Imagine if anyone found out. It would ruin both of us."

"Can't we keep it a secret?" Ella asked, staring at her plate.

"Look at me," I muttered, placing my hands on the counter. She did, but not without a deep sigh. "The world isn't ready for that. Ella. It's classed as weird and fucked up and not in a good way. How did you meet? Oh, she's my brother's daughter."

Ella opened her mouth to argue but stopped, frowning when I continued.

"Think of your Dad and Grandpa. For real, baby." My tone softened then, and she shrugged, lifting her eyes back to meet mine.

"Fine."

I groaned when she pushed the plate away from her, leaving her second roll untouched.

"Where are you going?" I sighed as she pulled on her shorts and boots. Teamed with her panda eyes and my shirt, she looked even more fuckable than she did last night.

"Home, Franco," Ella muttered, rolling her eyes at me.

"Stay for a bit. We can chill together—"

"No, I've got some college work to do."

"Ella." I grabbed her wrist; her cheeks flushed as she whirled around to me.

"No, I'm not that girl, Franco. Do you think I fucked you because you're hot? Do you think that's the only reason I did that?"

"You're acting ridiculous." I snapped, my heart sinking.

Had I missed something?

"I don't just think you're hot, Franco. But even if I did, it wouldn't be worth risking it all."

I frowned at her, refusing to release her as she stared pointedly down at my hand.

"Get your fucking hands off me."

Her words were ice cold.

"Whoa, Ella, don't leave like this—"

Ella glared at me, tugging her hand away from mine.

"No! I thought it was more than sex."

"Ella, you fucking said just once!" I yelled back, dragging my fingers through my hair. "What did you want, fucking marriage? Not gonna happen, sweetheart. Considering we have the same surname and all." I spat, regretting the words when she nodded slowly.

"You're right. What did I expect?" Ella whispered, shaking her head. "At least I'll always remember my first time, huh?"

The door slammed shut behind her, and I groaned, watching her stomping up the street.

It didn't matter that I wished she was my girl because it wouldn't happen.

It couldn't happen.

Ella would get over it, and so would I.

ELLA

Tears blurred my vision, but they weren't tears of sadness, oh no. Tears of anger, the sort that burned your cheeks, your hand shaking them away with frustration.

I'd honestly thought he'd still feel something for me, but he didn't.

What did you want, fucking marriage?

He was right, I realized. Maybe I was acting ridiculous, but I had at least expected him to hug me.

Or kiss me.

Dad was out when I got home, but Maria was sitting at the table, watching TikTok videos on her iPad. Her hair was twisted in rags, and I didn't even bother asking what effect she was trying to achieve.

"Dirty stop out, ha!" Maria grinned, nodding at me. "Jackson?"

I didn't even answer that.

"I'm going to bed. Tell Dad I'm sleeping my hangover off."

Maria rolled her eyes, returning her attention to her phone.

"Whatever."

I forced myself into the shower, my core stinging as the water touched it.

Fuck.

I washed my hair and scrubbed my body, covering myself in moisturizer when I was out. My fingers combed through my hair, and I left it in a loose braid as I dried it with the dryer, all the while my mind was on overdrive.

I don't care that we're related.

Being in his arms felt right, and that's all that mattered to me.

But Franco didn't want the shit that came with it.

He didn't want to be the sicko that banged his niece.

I climbed into bed with irritation, my body still aching from his touch.

Luckily, I didn't have any college work to do, so I forced my eyelids to close, my anxiety owning me like a dog on a leash.

I kept my eyes closed, focusing on my breathing as my phone beeped somewhere below me.

Fuck whoever it was.

I needed to sleep.

TEN

ELLA

"YOU'VE BEEN AVOIDING ME."

I looked up to see Jackson smiling at me over the counter, his hair flopping into his eyes.

"Hey." I forced a smile. "I haven't; I've just been busy, you know what it's like. What can I get you?"

"Coffee? You choose; I don't care. I just wanted to see you."

"Jackson, it's not gonna happen," I said, running his order through the till. "I'm not going to be your next ex-girlfriend, trust me."

"Nah, Ella, you'd always be my girl, no ex about it," Jackson smirked, scanning his card as payment. "Come out with me."

I glanced at the line behind him, rolling my eyes.

"Can't you text like normal people?"

"I'll buy you flowers, sing you a song..." Jackson continued, moving down towards where Ria was making the drinks.

"I can't. I'm seeing someone."

The words were out before I could consider what I'd said, and Jackson looked like I'd punched him.

"For real?"

"Jackson, I've got to work…" I turned away, my cheeks flushed with the thought of him asking who I was seeing.

There was Cruz, but considering I'd walked out and left him at the party, he'd not called me since.

I knew who I wanted to say, but I couldn't.

Franco.

My heart ached, and tears blurred my vision as I took the next order, trying to busy myself so the customers didn't notice. Ria kept checking on me, but there was nothing I could say.

Imagine the truth.

When the line had died down, I wiped down the tables, filling the mop bucket to give the floor a clean.

Anything to take my mind off Franco.

It's been a week.

Seven long-ass days.

I'd not heard from Franco, and he's not been over to our house either, which wasn't like him.

I was furious with myself for begging him to fuck me, but I know given a chance, I'd do it all over again.

When my shift ended, I trudged to the bus stop, inwardly groaning when I saw I'd missed the bus.

I leaned against the bus shelter, preparing to become victim to my thoughts for another half an hour until the next bus showed.

I couldn't believe I'd slept with my uncle.

Memories of his fingers on my body made me weak, my core clenching at the recollection of the one night we'd spent together.

I couldn't fall out with him; it had been me that had

orchestrated everything between us—fuck. I begged him, telling him it would be just once.

Then he kicked off when he'd said we would keep it a secret and not repeat it.

I closed my eyes, exhaling with irritation.

Why wasn't I normal?

Cruz.

Jackson.

Two completely normal guys, both gorgeous and into me...and who did I want?

Francesco Russo, the one man *everyone* wanted and the one I *couldn't* have.

I swallowed down the pain in my chest, tears spilling down my cheeks as I realized it wasn't ever going to happen.

Franco would meet someone else and get married—no. I couldn't imagine that.

The pain that ripped through my chest took my breath away, and it scared the hell out of me.

Why was my heart doing this to me? Why did it only skip in his presence?

Was it the fact he was forbidden?

No.

But whatever it was, Franco and I could never be.

I needed to realize that, and the sooner, the better.

FRANCO

"You need to come over. You've not been here all week; you got a woman or something?" My brother huffed, guilt weighing on my chest like a dead body.

"No, man. Just working."

"All work and no play makes Franco a very dull boy."

Oh, if you fucking knew.

"Yeah, I know. How's Pops?" I attempted to move the conversation away from women, but my brother was having none of it.

"He's old. But he still thinks he's twenty-one. Whatcha gonna do?" He laughed before coughing. "Listen, something's up with Ella. I need you to talk to her."

Nah, fuck that.

"Why? What's up with her?" I closed my eyes and held my head in my hands.

"I think it's a boy, bro. She's all weird, staring into space and shit."

"I'm sure she's fine—"

"What's with you?" Christopher snapped. "Just bring your ass around here for some family time."

"Alright, Chris."

I hung up, leaning back in my chair to stare at the ceiling.

What the fuck am I going to do when I see her?

I finished my shift a little after six, making my way to my brothers as slowly as my car would go. It didn't matter that I wanted Ella, nor that I wanted her in my bed every fucking day—she was my niece.

When I turned up, I braced myself for her glares and snide remarks—what I wasn't prepared for was her *absence*.

"Where's Ella?" I demanded, knowing if she were in, she would be serving me my ass by now.

Christopher popped the lid off a beer, giving me a look that told me I wasn't going to like what he had to say.

"What did I tell you it was? Boy trouble," he said with a chuckle. "So he took her out tonight. Good looking little bastard."

I gripped the bottle in my hand, the jagged edge of the lid digging into my skin.

"What do you mean she's gone out with some boy?" I snapped, earning myself an amused look.

"She's nineteen, little bro. It was bound to happen at some point; she's beautiful."

"So? Who the fuck is he?"

Christopher stared at my hand, pointing at it with concern.

"What the fuck have you done to your hand, man?"

I glanced down to see a pool of blood on my jeans, dripping from my hand.

"Fucking hell," I muttered, getting to my feet. "I cut it earlier; it must still be bleeding."

More fucking lies.

I wrapped a kitchen towel around my wound, gritting my teeth as it stung.

"So, where have you been? I've got my money on some broad." Christopher called.

"Yeah, just some girl." I lied, hating myself.

"Yeah? Come and tell me about her."

I'm going to hell. Might as well make it worth it.

"Nothing to tell; we just hooked up." I shrugged, slumping back into the chair as I stared at the television.

Where the fuck is Ella?

More importantly, who is she with?

"Hey, in your entire life, you've never once missed lasagne night. Not for a girl, a game, nothing. She must be special."

"It doesn't matter; it won't work out between us." I drank my beer, hoping he would lay off now.

No such fucking luck.

"She married?"

"What?" I frowned, shaking my head. "No—"

"She in prison?"

I laughed, rolling my eyes. "You're so dramatic, man."

"Hey, you said it wouldn't work out. So that means you like her, but you can't go there. So I figured it must be marriage or a felon, you know?" Christopher shrugged, turning his attention back to the television. "You need a woman, Franco. You're a good-looking man; women fall over themselves to even talk to you. So what are you waiting for, Megan Fox?"

"I mean… I wouldn't say no," I joked, praying I didn't have to give him eye contact. "So, who's Ella with?"

"You're so protective. Like the older brother she never had." Christopher grinned as my mouth went dry.

"Huh. Who is he?" I pressed, feeling irritated.

"Oh, some jock. Eyes nearly fell out of his goddamn head when she kissed him on the cheek. Imagine that, the cheek! Poor bastard might have a heart attack if she lets him kiss her properly—"

"She won't," I growled, gulping at my beer.

"Franco, she's almost twenty. You have to accept that she's going to settle down, meet someone. Shit, maybe you will."

"No one is good enough." I snapped.

"Yeah? For you, or her?" Christopher asked, watching me with interest.

"For either of us."

ELEVEN

ELLA

I BARELY FOCUSED on the movie.

Jackson didn't either, but that's because he had his tongue halfway down my throat for most of it.

"Come back to mine," Jackson muttered against my lips as we leaned against his car. "No one's home."

"Is that what you think of me?" I snapped, moving my head, so his lips landed on my neck.

Bad move.

"No, Ella, it's what I think we both *want.*" Jackson sighed, gazing at me. "Isn't it?"

I shuffled, staring at my house behind him.

"Jackson, if my father sees us like this, he will shoot you."

Jackson grinned, shrugging his shoulders.

"I like breaking the rules, Ella."

Try being me.

I needed to move on from Franco; it wasn't able to happen. It wasn't *right.*

This was what I should be doing—dating guys my age. *But, guys I'm not related to.*

I lifted onto my tiptoes, grazing my lips against his. Immediately Jackson crushes me to the car, his hands dropping to my ass when a voice interrupts us.

"Bit hot and heavy for a goodnight kiss, isn't it?"

Fuck, no.

I'd purposely gone out the minute Dad told me Franco was coming around. It was late too—why was he still here?

I glared at him over Jackson's shoulder, whispering into his ear as I did.

"I've got to go. Thank you for tonight."

Jackson reluctantly released me, spinning around to face my uncle.

"I'll call you beautiful."

Franco stiffened, and as I nodded at Jackson, I stormed past Franco.

Wood spice filled my nostrils, and his hand gripped my wrist, making me stumble back. Jackson's car gunned down the street, tires screeching as it peeled around the corner.

The street was silent.

"What the fuck was that?" Franco growled, his gaze burning into mine.

"That? That was me *moving on,*" I hissed, tugging my arm back. "What are you even doing here? Go home."

My chest tightened when he cocked an eyebrow, shaking his head in disbelief.

"I asked you a question, and you're giving me shit? Who the fuck was that?"

My eyes narrowed as I tossed my hair over my shoulder.

"It's irrelevant. Go—"

Franco walked up to me, pressing me against the wall of my home. I could barely breathe when he tilted my chin back, his eyes boring into mine.

"Who. Was. That."

"He's not my uncle," I whispered, glancing around us nervously. "If Dad—"

Franco silenced me with his lips on mine, a groan leaving my mouth as his tongue dove into my mouth, my fingers lost in his hair.

I pressed my palms against his chest, pushing him back as he stared at me.

"We *can't.*"

Franco smirked, and it took everything in my power not to reach into his trousers and grip his dick.

I wanted him so much.

"Let's go inside," Franco suggested, his tongue wetting his lips.

"You should go home," I argued, but then he looked at me, rolling his eyes.

"Inside. Now."

I *hated* the way my body reacted to him. Everything about him drove me insane.

I dropped my bag onto the side, sighing.

"I'm tired. I'm going to bed."

"Come and watch a movie with me."

"Franco, I've been at the movies all night. I didn't see *any* of it; you think I can't see what you're trying to do?" I snapped, tugging my heels off.

Franco glared at me, his eyes narrowing.

"Why didn't you see any of it?" He asked in a cool tone.

Fuck.

"Why'd you think?"

"You let him touch you?" Franco folded his arms. "Where?"

I shook my head, mirroring his arms.

"Nowhere."

"Ella, look at me," Franco said softly.

I did, and my heart reacted by smacking against my chest so hard I felt nauseous.

"What are we doing?"

I blinked with surprise when he held his hand out to me, nodding to the family room.

"A movie. We can talk if you want, but don't say no. Don't fuck off to bed in a mood."

I hesitated an argument on the top of my tongue.

But the thought of sitting with Franco and watching a movie made me feel warm and giddy inside.

Plus, if Dad or Maria came down, there wouldn't be anything to worry about.

Watching films late at night wasn't unusual for us.

"Only if it's a horror."

FRANCO

I'm going insane.

Some fucked up movie was on, and Ella was sitting rigidly beside me on the sofa, a blanket draped over her legs. She stared at the screen, chewing on her fingernails like she always did when she was scared.

Seeing her kiss that fucking *cunt* had cut me deep. I'd never seen Ella kiss someone like that—not even Cruz. I knew then that Jackson was the douche she'd been kissing since way back.

The way he looked at her too. Like she was *going* to be his.

I was too busy gazing at Ella to fall victim to the jump scare on the screen, but Ella shot up, grabbing my leg as she yelped.

"Such a fucking pansy," I drawled, tugging her closer to me. "Come here."

"I'm *not* a pansy. The only reason you didn't jump was that you were too busy staring at me." Ella shot back, crawling into my open arms.

"Can you blame me?" I murmured, stroking the side of her cheek.

"Stop confusing me, Francesco," she whispered, her eyes filling with uncertainty. "One minute it's just once, then you avoided me for a week, now you're kissing me and staring at me. What gives?"

I swallowed, knowing I was absolutely fucked.

"You're fucking perfect, despite your attitude and desire to get innocent men killed." I sighed. "I can't control myself around you. Look at us now."

She glanced down, and a small smile played at her lips.

Our hands entwined, yet I couldn't remember that happening. Ella's body pressed against mine; her lips were inches away from me.

"I know. But you said—"

I groaned, throwing my head back. "I know what I fucking said, Ella; I said it!"

Ella frowned at me, moving back until I stopped her, cupping her face in mine.

"I don't know what to say or do, sweetheart. I just know when I'm around you...I feel things I shouldn't."

"Here we go again!" Ella cried out. "Just admit how you feel about me!"

"I love you, Ella, you know that!" I argued, sitting up.

"Yeah? In what way?" Ella whispered, tears forming in her eyes. "In the way I love you?"

"Ella," I warned, my heart sinking. "I don't know what to say here."

"You know we can do this, Franco. I said we could keep it a secret." Ella reminded me, hopefully.

"Do you realize what you're saying?" I whispered, closing my eyes as I rested my head back on the cushion.

Soft lips grazed mine, her hair falling onto my shoulders as she sat astride me.

"Yes."

My hand cupped her face, bringing her deeper into me as I felt the wetness of her tears on my cheeks.

"Franco, I love you. Not like you love me. Not like I *should* love you." Ella sobbed quietly, her forehead resting on mine.

"Oh, Ella…" I muttered, wiping her tears with my thumbs. "Shit, baby…"

"I can't help it, Franco."

Her lips met mine, and I allowed her to kiss me softly, her tongue probing mine as I finally lost control, forgetting who I was, who she was, and where we were. Instead of tearing each other's clothes off, we kissed slowly, her hands wrapped around my neck as we became one with the darkness, the blanket covering our sins.

I shouldn't be doing this, but there was no fucking way I could stop.

I was going to have a forbidden relationship with my niece.

Consequences be damned.

TWELVE

ELLA
———

FRANCO SLEPT ON THE COUCH.

I woke up the following day to hear him groaning, begging for more sleep as Maria blasted music from the kitchen stereo. I smiled, pushing my head into the pillow. I couldn't stop thinking about the way we'd fallen asleep in each other's arms and how he'd walked me to my bedroom, kissing my forehead before making his way back downstairs.

Today was a Saturday, and that meant Dad and Grandpa would be at golf. Maria was getting ready for her dance practice, so I knew the house would be ours within the hour.

I just hoped Franco hadn't changed his mind again.

I must've dozed off because the next thing I knew, the duvet was lifting, and a warm body climbed beside mine, the heavenly scent enveloping me as I blinked the sleep away.

Lips grazed my shoulder, fingers slipping beneath my camisole as my body stretched in response.

"Mmm. Morning," I mumbled, arching my hips to allow Franco to slide beneath me.

His eyes shimmered with bronze beneath the thick lashes, his teeth sinking into his lip as he studied me.

"You'll be the death of me, Ella Russo."

Wrapping my legs around him, I grinned, lifting him to a sitting position. His muscular forearms slipped around my waist, his kisses soft and teasing on my lips.

"Shut up and kiss me," I commanded, losing my fingers in his curls.

My cami pushed up to reveal my breasts, his mouth covering the soft bud as it hardened beneath his skilled tongue.

"Yes. I love that."

My hand slipped to his waistband, pushing beneath the elasticated fabric. My fingers brushed the tip of his dick, a warm sticky substance greeting me.

"What can I say? You excite me." Franco gripped my ass, his mouth back on mine as we fell back on the bed.

"I thought you'd change your mind," I breathed, pushing his joggers down with excitement.

He was big. I knew that much, but I still wanted him.

I wanted him inside of me.

"You're gonna tell me you haven't got any condoms, aren't you?" Franco groaned, his dick pressing against my damp knickers.

"Argh," I wailed, covering my eyes with my hands. "I'm sorry…."

My shorts were off, my legs parted.

"There's other ways, Goddess."

I bolted upright, panicking that I wasn't exactly *trimmed* down there.

"Oh, no, I haven't…I mean, I'm not—"

"Lie down, Ella," Franco commanded, slipping from the bed to his knees.

Oh. My. God.

Wrapping his fingers around my knees, he tugged me to the edge of the bed in one swift movement, the mop of black hair hovering precariously between my legs.

"Let me, Ella."

Before I could protest, his warm mouth covered my intimate place, his tongue stroking and flickering against me as I arched, unfamiliar moans leaving my mouth.

"Mmm," he rumbled against me, sending a fresh wave of delight through my core.

I shuddered, aware my eyes were rolling in my head when he teased the entrance to my core with his finger, using my juices to lubricate it thoroughly before going any further.

"Franco!" I hissed when his tongue flickered against my clit, the nerve ending me in my body, climaxing simultaneously with each stroke.

Wordlessly Franco continued, keeping the beautiful rhythm going as I became undone. My moans seemed to urge him to go deeper, a second finger joining the first as I rode his fingers, his murmurs of delight vibrating through me.

My orgasm forced my eyes shut, and Franco stilled, my thighs clamped around his head as he lapped at my juices.

"Stop, please stop," I begged, unable to take the feeling of anything touching me; my entire core felt like it was on fire.

Franco released me, and without thinking, I sat up, slamming my lips into his.

I gasped at the powdery taste that greeted me, the taste of *myself* on his tongue.

"You taste good, girl. Enjoy it," Franco muttered, lifting me back into the bed, my legs still trembling.

"So you didn't change your mind." I pushed my hair back, aware I probably looked like a hobo.

Franco's gaze held mine, and he climbed over me on the bed, his silver chain tickling my throat as he paused.

"About us? No."

Wild butterflies filled my tummy as I nodded, smiling both in fear yet happiness.

"No one can ever know," I whispered, my fingers stroking his firm jawline.

I'd waited so long to touch him this way, to taste him. Feel him.

"I know, girl. I know." Franco sighed, pushing himself away from me. "Wanna have a movie night at mine tonight?"

He gave me a boyish grin, his eyes dancing with excitement.

"Only if I can wear your shirt again."

He groaned, shaking his head.

"Deal."

THIRTEEN

FRANCO

I HIT the gym hard later that afternoon. I was midway through my run when I saw Cruz scowling at me from the weights, throwing his towel to the ground as he did.

Fucker.

Let's see if he has anything to say.

I finished my run, mopping my brow with my towel. I headed to the showers, passing Cruz, who dropped his gaze.

Just as I thought, pussy.

In the shower, I thought of Ella about how she tasted this morning and how I felt when I was around her. I was falling for her, and I was powerless to stop it.

"It's not normal how you are with Ella." A voice drawled as the shower to my left came to life. "You're her uncle, man. It's fucking weird."

I flicked the shower off, wrapping a towel around my waist as I glared at Cruz, soaping himself in the shower.

"What did you say?" I asked, my fists clenched.

Cruz didn't bat an eyelid. "I said it's fucking weird. So

you've got a hot niece. Do you want some of that? Huh? Off-limits, bud. So step back in line. Let me handle it."

I saw red, my hand gripping his throat with one hand as I slammed my fist into his cunt face; the sound of bone cracking beneath my knuckles made me grin like a madman. I drew my fist back, this time aiming for his nose. Blood streamed from his face as he fell to the floor, his leg sweeping under mine, but I was too quick. I hopped over him, my foot connecting with his ribs as I kicked him repeatedly.

"If—you—go—near—my—girl—again—" I growled out, the space between my words being my foot pounding into him. "I'll fucking kill you."

Cruz wheezed and coughed beneath me, his body curling into the fetal position as I backed away, knowing if I carried on, I would kill him anyway.

I backed out of the showers, taking my time to get dressed as Cruz moaned in the background.

"Alright, man?" One of the gym heads asked, poking his head through the door with concern. "I thought I heard something."

I shrugged, picking up my bag. "I dunno, man. Maybe you better ask Cruz."

I jutted my thumb towards the shower and headed to my car.

What did Cruz expect? Fucking prick.

I smacked the steering wheel with frustration, dragging my hands through my hair.

What the fuck was going to happen now? People wouldn't ever accept us, and if I valued my life, my pops and brother could never find out.

But I couldn't keep away from her.

I drove home, stopping off to pick up some flowers on

the way. I wanted to see Ella's eyes light up, and I wanted her to know how much I'd thought about her today. Pulling into my drive, I grabbed the flowers from my passenger seat, humming to myself as I walked up the steps. There, with her legs crossed, and her head buried in a book, was my Ella.

My heart soared, my cheeks aching from the width of the smile she commanded from me.

"Ella," I breathed, crouching down in front of her. "What're you reading?"

I peeked at the book, widening my eyes.

"Linzvonc? Who's that?"

"She writes forbidden romance." Ella shrugged, closing the book. "This one is about a teacher and his student."

I arched a brow. "Yeah? Do they fuck on his desk?"

Ella bit her lip, her eyes narrowing as she wiped my cheek. "I've just started it. Are you cut? You're bleeding."

Her touch made me close my eyes, resting my forehead against hers. "Something like that."

"You've been fighting, Francesco?" Ella asked, her voice panicked.

"Let's go inside," I said, helping her to her feet.

Her eyes fell to the flowers in my hand, her cheeks flushing. I opened the door, allowing her to walk through first. Only then did I see she was wearing the fucking thigh-high boots over leggings, an oversized tee reaching her upper thigh.

"You're wearing those boots," I stated, allowing the door to close softly behind me. "You trying to kill me?"

"These old things?" Ella lifted her tee, allowing me to see her toned stomach. "Have you bought me flowers, Franco?"

I held them out, coaxing her to reach for them. When

she did, I pulled her close to me, inhaling her sweet vanilla fragrance.

"I wanna buy you flowers every day if it makes you blush like that," I murmured into her ear, kissing her cheek softly.

Ella colored further, her fingers curling around the stem of the roses.

"I love them."

Her whisper escaped her lips before they brushed against my stubble, her hand gripping the back of my neck as our eyes met.

"They're beautiful, like you."

"I want you so much, Franco," Ella choked out, the emotions in her eyes like a knife through my heart. "I don't mean just sex—"

"Hey," I stilled, my finger pressing against her plump lips. "I know."

"But it won't ever happen, and you'll get bored—" Ella whispered, her eyes shimmering with tears.

"Hey, no. *No*. Stop this, baby." I kissed her lips, pressing them against hers as we inhaled one another. "We'll figure something out."

"But…" Ella protested, but my tongue entered her mouth, silencing her. She groaned, and I held her, not taking it further.

"Listen." I sighed, holding her in my arms. "Tell the world you're busy. Let's order takeout, watch a film and just be together, hmm? I want you in my arms all fucking night."

Ella nodded, sighing heavily.

"Yeah, okay."

I kissed her again; this time, her hands slipped under my shirt, her nails dragging down my back.

"Can we go upstairs first?" Ella smirked, stroking me through my joggers. "You've got plenty of condoms, right?"

I laughed, waving a hand toward the stairs.

"Fuck yes."

FOURTEEN

ELLA

"WHO WERE YOU FIGHTING?" I asked him, falling to the bed with a giggle.

"Cruz," Franco muttered, tugging his shirt over his head. "Fucking dick."

My heart flew into my mouth as I bolted upright. "Cruz?! What? Why?"

Franco sighed, folding his arms across his chest as he glared at me. "Why? Because the way I am with you is *weird*. You need someone like *him*."

I froze, staring at Franco with wide eyes. "Wait, you fought over *me?* But...why? I haven't even spoken to him since that stupid party!"

"Can we forget about fucking Cruz, Ella?" Franco groaned at my expression.

"What did you do?" I watched as he sat beside me on the bed, his shoulders slumping slightly.

"I just gave him what he deserved." Franco shrugged, and I grimaced. "Baby, he was out of order."

"What did you say?" I asked, my stomach in knots. I knew Franco wouldn't be calm when it came to me.

"Fuck knows. I was pissed."

"Franco…" I warned, hating the way he narrowed his eyes at me. "You did the whole possessive uncle thing, *right?*"

Franco frowned, groaning slightly.

"I may have said you were my girl."

The blood drained from my face, dizziness overwhelming me.

"The *fuck?!*" I whispered, my hand slapping the back of his head without thinking. "*Franco!*"

"He won't remember! Don't fucking hit me!"

"You can't go around saying shit like that! Imagine if Dad found out! Or worse, Grandpa…." I felt like I was going to be sick.

"Calm down, Ella, Cruz won't say shit, or I'll bury him," Franco muttered, turning to fix me with his gaze. "You said you wanted this, and now you're panicking? Fucking hell, Ella, you don't get much more forbidden than this."

"I know, but calling me your girl…."

My breath hitched in my throat as Franco glared at me. "I didn't mean to say that. I just reacted."

"I wish I could be," I admitted, reaching for his hand. "Fuck!"

"Cruz won't say shit. He said you needed someone like him, Ella, while I could still fucking taste you."

My cheeks flamed at his words, but more than anything, my body screamed for his touch.

"I want you too, Ella, and to me, you've always been my girl," Franco said gruffly, lifting my hand to his lips. "I'm sorry. I didn't think so."

"You did what felt natural, right?" I cocked my head to the side, and his hand cupped it instantly.

His eyes softened, and he nodded.

"Yeah, baby. I did. I said you were my girl because I want you to be, more than anything in the fucking world."

"I don't suppose you were adopted?" I said hopefully, and he gave me a sad smile.

"Nah. I wish."

"Maybe I am," I joked, wishing it were true. "Why you? Why'd I fall for you?"

"Because," Franco muttered, leaning forward to graze my lips with his. "You know we'll never get this with anyone else."

I allowed my eyes to close, his body pressing against mine as we fell back on the bed, our tongues dancing in a rhythm that needed no effort whatsoever.

"All my friends like you, you know," I confessed, as his mouth moved to my neck, his fingers stroking my lips, my mouth sucking on them as he groaned.

"All my friends like you, too. Never gonna happen, sweetheart."

I don't know if it was the fact that we mentioned other people, but we tore each other's clothes off, our mouths locked together the entire time. The amount of time it took for him to slide the condom on nearly killed me off, but then he was inside me again, and everything felt right.

Every movement was primitive, his thrusts slamming me into the headboard as I begged for more, his tattooed body commanding my attention as I tried to trace my tongue over the fine lines of art.

Franco captured my chin, twisting it toward him as he kissed me roughly, the familiar feeling overtaking my body as Franco slowed, allowing my senses to slow.

"What are you doing?!" I whimpered, looking up at him as he paused.

"I'm sorry, I just can't believe how beautiful you are."

Franco rocked his hips against me, his eyes boring into mine.

"Mmm," I moaned, the excitement and euphoria building up once more.

"I need you to be mine, Ella."

"Only if you make me cum," I purred, enjoying the devilish smirk that filled his face.

"Deal."

FRANCO

Ella is something else entirely.

After the intense session upstairs, we were snuggled on the sofa together, watching some bullshit horror movie.

As usual, some ditzy broad was running around a house, ignoring every possible exit as she stomped around, only for her to get killed seconds later.

"Stop sighing," Ella instructed, looking up at me. "It's not real life, and there has to be drama."

"Yeah, but it's hardly believable, is it?" I snorted, holding her tight. "No one would do that."

"Huh, I probably would." Ella laughed, gathering her hair over her shoulder.

"With balls like yours? The killer would end up running."

"He'd better because I'd whip his ass."

"Sounds hot," I muttered against her mouth as the doorbell rang. "Chinese food. I'll go."

I grinned at her as she watched me with a heated expression—fuck knows who I had been in a previous life to deserve Ella.

But then, I only had her in secret.

I paid for the food, grabbing some forks for us to eat straight out the boxes—we'd done this since we were young.

"Yes, I need this so bad." Ella reached out for her noodle box, licking her lips with anticipation.

"I swear I'll throw the contents over me if you lick me like that," I teased, digging into my box.

"I'll lick you better than that," Ella said with a wink.

We were in silence, watching the killer finally get caught by someone with half a brain cell. I glanced over at Ella, and I felt a shooting pain in my chest. It took my breath away, and I had to turn so she couldn't see the expression I knew I was wearing.

Fear.

This couldn't last.

I forced the thought away, jabbing my fork into the noodles to distract my mind.

"You okay?" Ella asked quietly. As always, she sensed my mood.

"Yeah. No." I laughed bitterly. "This feels almost normal, you know? Nice."

I shook my head as I pushed my box to the floor, my appetite gone.

Ella looked like I had slapped her, and I regretted my words. After that, I never wanted to upset her.

"I know."

She didn't say anything else, but I knew she understood.

"I can't ever let you go, though." I met her eyes, watching as she pursed her lips. "So, what the fuck does this mean for us?"

Ella dropped her gaze, her fingers moving the fork around the noodle box as she exhaled.

"It's going to be obvious if neither of us gets with anyone else."

"Well, that's not an option." I snapped.

"No, it's not." Ella agreed, barely flinching when I raised my voice.

God, she was amazing.

"But our family isn't stupid. They don't deserve to be lied to."

I nodded, my throat going dry.

"You want to tell them?" I whispered, bracing myself for her answer.

In truth, I didn't care. I'd tell the world, and the world could suck my balls, but my brother and father knowing?

I hated the pain it would cause them.

"No, but I don't have an answer." Ella lowered the box to the floor, her lower lip trembling. "I just feel like you're who I'm destined to be with, and it will never be accepted."

I reached for her hand, pulling her close to me as I kissed her head.

"So it will come to an end, won't it? It'll have to." Ella's voice told me that tears were threatening to spill down her beautiful face, and I was powerless to stop them.

"I don't want to think about that, El," I muttered into her hair, holding her close.

"Me neither."

FIFTEEN

ELLA

"EXPLAIN SOMETHING TO ME, HOT STUFF." Vanessa peered at me from across the table in my backyard. "How the fuck do you do it?"

I tore my eyes away from Franco, who was operating the grill. Now and then, he'd catch my eye, a small smile on his lips.

"Do what?"

"You've got Jackson begging for you to be his girl, and Cruz—wow, he's just sexy as fuck. Yet you don't seem interested at all."

Vanessa sighed, swiping at her phone before turning it toward me. "Look at Cruz there. Seriously, why don't you like him?"

I didn't bother looking at the image, but I wondered why Vanessa was all over his Instagram.

If Franco had one, I would be too.

"I'm just not interested in anything serious," I lied, watching Franco from behind my sunglasses.

"Huh. I'd marry Cruz tomorrow," Vanessa drawled,

zooming in on the photo. "Do you mind if I message him?"

I shook my head; no. She could marry him for all I cared. All I wanted was the man standing in front of me, his tanned shoulders deepening beneath the afternoon sun.

"I love you!" Vanessa squealed, firing off a message to Cruz.

Franco looked over, lifting his brows quizzically at me as I waved my hand away.

"Ella, come help me with the food," Franco instructed, pointing at the grill.

"Burger?" I asked Vanessa, who nodded.

"With ketchup, please."

Grandpa was napping in his chair when I passed him, his mouth slightly open as he snored.

"Where's Dad?" I mumbled, reaching for a bread roll.

"He's gone to fetch Maria. Why?" Franco let his fingers brush over mine, and I shivered.

"I just want to kiss you, that's all," I admitted, as Franco wedged a burger in the bread roll. I turned back to Vanessa with a sigh.

"Ella, can you give me a hand?" Franco grinned, nodding towards the house.

My heart thudded in my chest when he disappeared into the back door, and I thrust the burger into Vanessa's hands.

"Mmm, thanks, babe. Cruz is typing!"

I nodded, glancing back to the house.

"I just need to help Franco…."

Vanessa nodded, barely looking up.

"Sure thing. Unless Cruz wants *me* to help him?"

I rolled my eyes, trying to steady my breathing as I made my way into the house.

"We need wine," a voice muttered in my ear, tugging

me into the pantry. The door slammed behind me, and before I knew it, Franco's lips were on mine.

I let out a soft moan. My fingers lost in his hair as he moved against me, pressing my back against the shelves of pickles and fucking tins.

"God… you're fucking beautiful."

My fingers ran over his biceps, squeezing softly.

"I want you so much," I whispered, our lips smashing against one another.

"I know, baby, me too."

We were so into one another that we didn't hear the footsteps that strode over to the pantry, filling it with light as they tugged the door open.

"Oh my god!" Vanessa yelped, falling back against the kitchen table as Franco stepped back, his eyes narrowing.

"What do you want?" Franco snapped as I tried to catch my breath.

My best friend stared at me, a mixture of shock and disgust on her features.

"Ketchup," she whispered, and Franco reached behind me, almost throwing it into her hands.

"Anything else?" Franco asked, reaching for the door.

"N-no."

Vanessa stumbled back, making her way outside as I hissed with annoyance.

"Fuck!"

Franco exhaled, stroking my face as I slapped his hand away.

"Franco! Vanessa *knows*!"

Franco's gaze hardened.

"She's your best friend. She won't tell anyone."

"How do you know that?!" I groaned, pushing past him into the kitchen.

I felt sick and dirty for the first time. The way Vanessa

had looked at me...like I was *disgusting.* I didn't know how to face her or what to do next.

The secret is out.

FRANCO

Fucking Vanessa and her *fucking ketchup*.

Ella wouldn't let me touch her, so I stomped out into the yard, determined to have it out with Vanessa.

To my surprise, she gave me a wide smile.

"Hey."

"Look, I know what that looked like—"

Vanessa held her hand up, walking over to me with a strange expression on her face.

"Oh, I know what that *was.* You and Ella, huh?" She whispered, glancing at Dad with a low whistle. "I guess that explains *a lot.*"

"You need to keep your pretty mouth shut, Vanessa," I warned as she widened her eyes.

"I won't tell anyone! But you can't do this, either of you! It's *wrong!*"

Ella walked out, folding her arms as she glared at us both.

"Vanessa, can we talk?"

I tried to meet her eyes, but she refused to look at me. Instead, she focused on Vanessa.

"Why do I get the feeling I'm the bad guy?" I muttered as Ella shook her head.

"You're not...I just want to talk to Vanessa."

Vanessa hesitated, looking over at my sleeping Pa.

"Sure. Your room?"

I internally groaned as Vanessa sent me a dirty look,

following my goddess into the house.

So someone knew; finally.

I slumped into a chair opposite Dad, groaning as I dragged my fingers through my hair.

"What's up, son?" Dad yawned, rubbing his eyes sleepily. "Did you think I was dead?"

"No." I smiled, shaking my head. "Just complicated shit, that's all."

"Yeah? What kind of complicated shit? You in trouble with the law?" Dad reached over for a cigarette, coughing his lungs up in the process. He offered one to me, and I took it, allowing him to lean forward and light it.

"No."

"Is it this broad Christopher told me about? Someone you can't be with?"

I nodded glumly. My stomach twisted with the agony of hiding this from Dad, but it would tear the poor guy apart.

Not to mention my brother.

"You know, there's no such word as can't. Been telling you this for years." Dad exhaled before falling into a coughing fit.

"Quit the smoking, Dad." I winced, handing him his whiskey.

"I'm old, kid. Old and tired. I miss my wife."

"Don't start this again." I sighed, wondering if it was possible that my dad simply didn't want to live without my mother anymore.

"Your mother blew me away the first time I saw her. I knew straight away she was mine. I wouldn't have cared who she was with or who she was. I loved that woman before I even knew her name."

I smiled, wishing I could remember her. She'd died from complications of having me, and I'd only ever known my dad. My brother was an adult when I was born, so Ella, his daughter, was the only kid my age.

The woman I loved.

"If you love this woman, you need to tell her; the rest of the world be damned." Dad coughed, still trying to inhale his cigarette. His eyes watered, but he waved the glass I offered him away impatiently.

"What if it would tear a family apart?" I asked quietly, staring at the floor.

I couldn't look at him; I knew it would be written all over my face if I did.

"You can't help who you fall in love with, Francesco. Believe me. I was lucky enough that it was set up for me to marry your mother because if not, I'd have left anyone for her."

"You had an arranged marriage, right?"

Dad nodded, leaning back in his chair.

"Best damn arrangement I'd ever come across."

"Tell me about it."

"One day, son, you'll know all about it. But for now, I have to sleep. So fucking tired."

He rested his eyes, taking a long drag of his cigarette before jabbing it into the ashtray beside him.

"Always so fucking tired."

SIXTEEN

ELLA

VANESSA SANK ONTO MY BED, her eyes wide. I wish I'd taken up drama—anything to help me pretend that what my best friend had seen wasn't true.

My mouth felt like it was filled with cotton wool balls, and every time I opened my mouth to say something, nothing happened.

"Look, Ness, whatever you think you saw—"

Vanessa dropped her eyes, shaking her head. "What I *think* I saw?! For real? I *saw* you and your uncle...kissing! In the pantry!"

"Bullshit, we weren't." I lied, trying to keep my expression neutral. "You can't prove *anything.*"

Vanessa frowned, throwing her head back with a groan.

"I'm not going to say shit to anyone, Ella. Shit, you and him? Wow."

I couldn't deny it now. Vanessa had seen enough to make up her mind.

"Vanessa, listen. If this ever gets out, it will destroy my family."

"I won't say anything," Vanessa repeated. "Shit, how did you not tell me? Well, I think I can answer that, but jeez, that's a fucking secret."

I exhaled, pinching the bridge of my nose. Vanessa's legs swung back and forth as she watched me, her face still frozen in shock.

"How the hell did this happen?"

"I don't know," I admitted, dropping my head into my hands. "But I know it's wrong."

"Fuck yeah, it is, but you two didn't seem too subtle about it earlier! Imagine if your dad—fucking *hell*, Ella! What are you doing?!"

"Just making sure I've got a first-class ticket to hell," I mumbled. "I know it's wrong. He knows it's wrong. But we can't help it…."

"You can help it. You have to stop this, El! What if it goes further? You're *related*. I can't even imagine that." Vanessa shuddered, and shame washed over me in waves. "I mean, I get it. He's the hottest guy like, ever…but Ella, this is wrong."

"I know that!" I snapped, annoyed with her. "But I'm the one that pursued it, Ness. I practically seduced him. I just can't explain how he makes me feel."

Vanessa's eyes bulged.

"Look, if you have to fuck him and get over it, that's your call. But you can't have a *relationship* with the guy!"

"Why not?" I replied hotly. "We can keep it a secret—"

"Oh *yeah*," Vanessa scoffed, folding her arms over her chest. "How's he going to be about spring break? You can't even fucking *date*, Ella!"

"I don't have a choice!" I hissed back, tears filling my eyes. "I'm in love with him!"

Vanessa paled, her fingers pressing into her cheeks as she gaped at me.

"I need a fucking drink."

"Please, Vanessa. Try to understand…."

"Has he groomed you?" Vanessa whispered, reaching for my hands. "Has this been going on since you were younger? Please, talk to me—"

"*Groomed me?*" I pushed her hands away, shaking my head in disbelief. "He's barely five years older than me, Vanessa! No, he's not a sexual predator! I begged *him* to sleep with me!"

I realized what I'd said, forcing my lips together as I paced my bedroom floor.

Vanessa was as still as a statue, her features fixed with astonishment.

"You've…"

"Yes. We have." I sighed, knowing she was probably going to walk out right now.

"You're serious," she breathed.

"I don't know what to do. I have to be with Franco."

"No, Ella, everyone would go mad!" Vanessa hissed as a soft knock on the door interrupted us.

"Who is it?" I asked with irritation.

"It's me."

Franco.

FRANCO

I closed the door behind me, sighing heavily. Ella's eyes softened upon seeing me, but more so the bottle of wine in my hand.

"I was gonna bring glasses, but then I thought fuck it." I shrugged, removing the cork. "Swig from the bottle, girls."

Vanessa snatched the bottle out of my hand, gulping it down so fast I thought she was going to choke.

I paused, watching Ella.

She seemed okay, but the worry in her eyes commanded my attention more than anything else.

She was gazing at Vanessa.

I sat beside Vanessa, who gave me a sidelong glance, handing the bottle over to Ella.

"Well, at least I know it wasn't personal. You just prefer brunettes." Vanessa forced a smile, but I knew she felt awkward as fuck.

"It's a shit situation, and I'm sorry you saw us. It's a big thing to ask of someone, to keep a secret like this."

Vanessa pursed her lips together.

"I'm worried, Franco. If this ever got out, Ella would be torn apart by everyone."

I nodded, thinking of the right words to say.

How can I ease this situation?

"I guess you just have to carry on as normal for as long as you can," Vanessa added, her eyes darting from me to Ella.

"Wait, you're not gonna tell anyone?" I frowned as Ella laced her fingers through mine.

Without thinking, I lifted her hand to my lips, dropping a chaste kiss there.

"Is this serious, Franco?" Vanessa asked, her eyes searching mine. "Because she is my *best* friend, and I'm not having you ruining her life."

I went to answer when Ella beat me to it.

"I want him more than I've ever wanted anyone in my life. If I didn't have him…" her words trailed off, and our eyes met.

She didn't need to finish the sentence; the pain etched over her face did that.

"First things first, you've gotta stop with the possessive shit." Vanessa nudged me. "It gives it away."

"What are you suggesting exactly?" Ella asked, clutching my hand to hers.

"Ah fuck, like I know!" Vanessa groaned, lifting the wine to her lips. "But he doesn't look or act like an uncle, El. Instead, he acts like he's your man."

"He is." Ella shrugged, making my heart soar.

"It's some Romeo and Juliet shit. Are you adopted by any chance?" Vanessa mumbled, swigging more of the bottle.

"No," I muttered. "Otherwise, I wouldn't be asking you to keep a secret."

"Full blood? No problem." Vanessa whispered, draining the rest of the bottle in a succession of gulps. "I'm sure we can...think of something…."

"I know it's strange." Ella's voice wobbled, and instantly I pulled her close. "But I don't know what else to do."

Vanessa closed her eyes.

"If I don't see it, it's not happening."

Ella smiled, and I stroked her back with my fingers.

"It's a shock; I get it. I just wanted to make sure you guys were okay." I rose to my feet, kissing Ella's fingers as I dragged them to my lips. "I'll leave you to it. If you need me... I'm outside with everyone."

"The rest of your *family*. Jesus Christ." Vanessa mumbled from the bed, shaking the bottle. "Another one of these might be a good place to start, huh, bestie?"

Locking eyes with Ella, I pushed her hair behind her ear, tilting her chin up to look at me.

"Whatever you want. Whatever you need. Just tell me."

Ella nodded, lifting on tiptoes to brush her lips against mine.

I held her tight, my heart aching with adoration for this girl.

"Don't leave," Ella whispered, stroking my cheek.

"I won't."

SEVENTEEN

FRANCO

I COULDN'T CONCENTRATE at work.

Ella and I had cooled off somewhat since Vanessa had found out about us, and it was pissing me off.

FRANCO:
I miss you :(
ELLA:
I miss you too. How's work? 🖤
FRANCO:
Boring 😑 what are you doing?
ELLA:
Well…Vanessa, Avery, and I just booked our spring break ☺

What the fuck? We hadn't even spoken about this.

I dialed Ella's number, hearing her answer breathlessly.

"Hey, baby."

"Hey yourself," Ella said with a giggle. "Are you on your lunch break?"

I glanced around my office, well aware of the ever-growing pile of paperwork on my desk.

"Kind of. So, spring break."

Ella sighed, and I heard her thanking someone quietly before clearing her throat.

"Yup. Why, have you got a problem with that?"

Feisty.

"Yeah, I fucking have. Where?"

"Mexico. I can't wait, Franco!"

"Great. So what am I supposed to do while you're flaunting yourself around the hot beaches, no doubt drunk and—"

"You can't be like that. It's not fair."

"Like what?" I huffed, forcing images of Ella sitting on a beach towel, surrounded by hungry fucking vultures.

Ella sighed. "Look, you have to trust me, babe."

"I trust you; it's the men I don't trust," I muttered darkly, annoyance seeping through me. "Can I see you?"

"Now?" Ella asked with surprise. "I've just finished class..."

"Let me take you out for dinner."

"Franco." Ella sighed. "You know we can't."

"Not local. I know a place."

"Okay, sure. What time do you finish?"

I logged off my laptop, slamming down the lid.

"Now."

Twenty minutes later, I was at her college. Ella stood out like a fucking angel, her cut-off white shorts showcasing endless legs, a soft blue shirt tied at the waist enhancing her hourglass figure.

She smiled at me as she walked towards me, turning to roll her eyes when some guy yelled something at her.

"You wish." Ella shot back, climbing into my car.

"Fuck *me,*" I muttered, groaning as she leaned over to kiss me. "You smell good enough to eat."

"Nah, you taste like strawberries and cream." I winked, revving the engine. "Who was that prick?"

Ella frowned. "Who?"

"The dude you said 'you wish' to."

"Oh, he's just one of Jackson's friends," she said airily. "He doesn't mean it."

"What did he say?" I asked, dropping my hand onto her thigh.

"It doesn't matter!" Ella laughed, squeezing my hand.

"Ella, baby, I've been a college guy. I'm just curious what he said to my girl."

Ella stared out of the window, pretending not to hear me.

"Ella…"

"He said I'd look good in his bed. It's a joke." Ella shrugged.

My stomach twisted at the thought of Ella being in any man's bed, but more so, I hated how guys called shit like that out to her.

I'd end up knocking every cunt out at this rate.

"So talk to me about Mexico," I said, keeping my attention on the road. I had to keep my jealousy in check because Ella wouldn't stand for it.

"Avery's parents have a villa out there. In Cancun. So it's just the flights we've paid for."

I grunted, gripping the steering wheel. "For how long?"

"Two weeks."

I narrowed my eyes at her, finding her looking up at me through her lashes.

"Are you kidding me?"

"I know, baby, but I need the break. I do." Ella said,

stroking my hand. "Are you seriously worried about me with other guys?"

"No, I know you won't find anyone else. No one compares to you, and I know you feel the same about me. I just worry about you. If anyone touched you...I don't know what I'd do."

"No one will touch me, Franco. I'd cut their balls off; you know this."

"Has this Avery got a man?" I asked, allowing my eyes to drink her in before joining the freeway.

"She likes Nate, and he's going to be around. Why?"

"Great. Boyfriend and his buddies. This just gets better and better," I grumbled, picking up speed.

"Franco...we need to talk."

I glanced at her, anxiety pooling in my stomach.

"Talk then."

"I can't go public about us...right?" Ella licked her lips.

"So?" I barked.

Where was she going with this?

"But I'm going to say I'm seeing someone. I just don't know what to say to Dad." Ella stared down at her hands. "He'll kill us, Francesco."

"Just tell him you're seeing someone, and it's new. He doesn't have to know shit," I suggested.

"What about you? Are you going to say you're seeing someone?"

Ella watched me as I shook my head.

"Nah. He'd wanna know everything."

"But we are together, aren't we?" Ella whispered. "Or are we?"

I drove in silence for a few moments before glancing at her.

"Do you think we have a choice? Look at us, baby."

Our hands were laced together, and her body pressed close to mine.

"If I didn't have to drive, I'd have you on my lap right now."

"Sounds like a plan." Ella laughed wickedly.

"Don't tempt me, goddess," I warned, adjusting my pants.

"I've missed you, though," Ella purred, reaching over to stroke me through my pants.

Instantly my dick responded, and I thanked myself for packing condoms in my wallet.

"You want me to pull over?" I smirked, enjoying how her eyes widened.

"Where, though?"

"I know a place."

ELLA

I'd missed him.

I'd tried to stay away from him, but the minute he texted me, I was like a lost puppy, running back for more.

His gorgeous eyes dragged over me as he pulled into an empty parking lot overlooking a small lake. He slid his car seat back, patting his lap with a smile.

"Come here, Ella."

I shook my legs out of my shorts, climbing upon him in just my g string. When our lips met, it felt like coming home. My body relaxed beneath his hands, which stroked my back softly. I ground my hips against him as I kissed him so forcefully he groaned.

"You horny baby?" Franco muttered, softly stroking me through my panties.

"Mmm," I mumbled, rocking against his fingers. "That feels so good."

"Kiss me," Franco commanded, sliding my underwear to the side roughly. His fingers massaged my clit as I gulped, knowing he was going to destroy me in a matter of minutes. Kissing him was my favorite thing in the world to do, and he knew it.

The rhythm of his tongue against mine matched his fingers, and I closed my lips around it, sucking it as he groaned.

"One minute," Franco muttered, reaching down for his wallet from the side door.

My heart leaped with excitement when he tugged out a condom, and I lifted myself so he could slide it on quickly. The cool material soothed my wet walls as he positioned himself perfectly, but as I sank onto him, our mouths met again, and I was drunk on our lust.

My hips rocked in time with his, but he refused to let my mouth go. His fingers held my g-string to the side, his other hand guiding my hips to keep up with him. Every time he thrust, I slammed down, and the two of us were groaning and trembling with the force of our attraction.

As I came, his fingers stroked my clit, and I gasped out, my eyes rolling back in my head as he sucked on my neck.

"That's it, baby, don't stop; I'm gonna cum."

Despite my body being held prisoner by my orgasm, somehow, I managed to rock my hips, the swell of his dick telling me he was close. Then, when he came, he called my name, the sound so guttural and urgent; I knew we were meant for each other in every single way a couple could be.

"I love you," Franco muttered, shaking his head as he kissed me. "Like, fucking real shit."

I blinked, my mouth feeling like it had been sewn shut.

"You hear me?" He laughed, cupping my face. "I mean it."

"Seriously?"

"Yeah. Can't you feel it? That..." his finger moved between us. "That's not just sex, Ella."

"No. I didn't think it was. I love you, too," I admitted, lifting back onto the passenger seat. Once we'd adjusted ourselves, Franco turned to gaze at me.

"You know, we could leave this place. Fuck off somewhere and be together where no one knows us."

The thought of leaving my family, my sister, and my Dad especially broke my heart. But the need to be with Franco was so intense; I couldn't deny it was probably the only solution.

"When do you finish college?" Franco asked gruffly, starting the car.

"Why?"

"Once you graduate, we could leave. Where'd you want to go? Europe?"

"Europe?" I laughed, shaking my head. "I don't have that kind of money."

"I do," Franco answered, stroking my thigh. "Think about it, Ella. I know it would be hard, but I don't think we can be together here."

He's right.

The alternative was telling our family and friends what we were, which caused more heartbreak and agony than I could bear.

"I can't leave them," I whispered, and he squeezed my hand. "But I can't be without you."

"Tough decisions, beautiful. But one we have to make."

I studied him as he drove, the man I was irrevocably in love with.

I'd tried cooling things off with him, but that only

worked, providing Franco left me alone. The minute he texted me, we were fucking like rabbits in a desolate parking lot. But it wasn't just the sex.

It was the way we were when we were together.

We breathed in sync; our hearts beat only for each other.

They always had, but now we'd embraced the physical side; there was no going back.

We were risking it all.

EIGHTEEN

ELLA

I LEANED back on my towel, elbows digging into the sand. The sun warmed my face, and I inhaled the salty, humid air that drifted over from the waves, gently caressing the shore. Some distance away, music played, a faint beat of Latin that made me wiggle my body.

"Aves, I'd live here if I were you." I exhaled, letting my head fall, my hair tickling my back.

Beside me, Avery chuckled.

"It's beautiful, isn't it?"

"It sure is. Where's Vanessa?" I shielded my eyes from the sun despite having sunglasses on—it was scorching today, and there wasn't a cloud in the sky. We'd already been here three days, and my skin, supposedly Italian, was turning a deep shade of pinky brown... Not like my sister, Maria, who only had to look at the sun to tan.

Urgh.

My eyes found Vanessa in the surf, chatting away to one of Nate's friends.

"She's breathing in again," Avery groaned. "Why does she do that? She's gorgeous."

"I think she's insecure," I said with a frown. "Even though she can have anyone she wants—"

"Not anyone, but that's beside the point. Vanessa shouldn't let men define her." Avery shifted, so she was sitting up.

I had a feeling of dread in my stomach as I watched Vanessa.

"What do you mean, not anyone?" I asked cautiously, chewing on my lip.

"Franco. Cruz." Avery waved her hand. "I'm not sure why they're not into her, though."

This had to be the worst part; lying to your friends. I didn't answer; instead, I relaxed when Nate jogged up to us.

"Avery." Nate grinned, crouching at the bottom of her towel. "You look hot."

Avery flushed, biting her lip as Nate laughed.

"Come and cool off in the sea." Nate turned to the ocean, and Avery stared at me with mortification.

I couldn't help but snort with laughter, the thought of poor Avery thinking Nate had finally called her hot, only to realize he meant the temperature.

Jesus.

"I'm fine," Avery huffed, crossing her arms. "Where's Miss Amazon?"

Nate rolled his eyes, leaning down to scoop her into his arms as she squealed.

"You know, I don't need a girlfriend with a friend like you," Nate grumbled, stomping off to the sea as Avery gripped him with secret delight.

I smiled as he threw her into the sea, watching her gasp for breath when she stood up. It's like watching two kids in school with those two.

I couldn't decide if Nate liked Avery more than a

friend, as he always seemed to turn her advances down. But maybe I could try and get them closer together during this vacation.

I watched as a couple kissed by the shore, not a care in the world. What I would give to have Franco be able to hold me like that, without caring who saw us. I dipped my head, furious that he had to be who he was to me. Then, to my utter disbelief, the man dropped to one knee, opening a box that screamed diamond ring.

"Fuck," I whispered, watching as the girl clamped her hand to her mouth, nodding through her sobs.

That will never be us.

Marriage was important to me, and it was to Franco too. We valued family more than anything, which was why this was as hard as it was. We would never be able to be together, get married, or have kids.

I felt numb.

This wasn't news to me, but when you're wrapped in your own bubble of love and adoration, you seem to forget reality. But here I was, thrown into it with such force that it hurt my heart, body, and mind. But my soul was Franco's. It always has been.

Smack!

A ball hit the side of my head so hard it knocked my glasses off, the ringing in my ear causing me to clutch the side of my face.

"What the fuck!" I yelled, turning to see Vanessa grinning at me.

"Stop thinking about you-know-who and get your ass over here."

"You're a fucking dick; you know that? Fuck!" I cursed, grabbing my glasses and checking them over.

"Come on, pretty girl." Vanessa sang, pointing at the volleyball net. "You know you want to."

"I don't. Especially not now that my head is ringing!" I snapped back, tugging my phone out of my bag.

I couldn't help it. I missed him so much.

ELLA: The weather is shit.

FRANCO: You're a shit liar. I'm not missing you at all.

I grinned, typing back.

ELLA: 😔

FRANCO: You know I am, baby. Are you okay?

ELLA: I wish you were here.

FRANCO: Why? What's wrong?

ELLA: Other than the fact you're not here? Nothing. It's paradise. Just watched a proposal on the beach. 💍

FRANCO: It's full of honeymooners there too. You shouldn't have gone without your man. You probably look like you've been jilted.

ELLA: I do have Avery and Vanessa, you know. I hate not being able to see you.

ELLA: I know. I love you 🖤 you better not be partying every night. You're mine.

FRANCO: Says you?! 😂 living it up in Mexico while I carry my drunk dad home from yours every night 👍

ELLA: Aww, 😊 so cute. Eleven days 🖤

He didn't reply, but he was at work, so it was hardly a surprise. Then again, Franco couldn't give a fuck about work when it came to me. So he blew it off to spend the entire day with me before I flew here.

Mmm. Happy memories.

Avery joined Vanessa and the others, and Nate headed over to me, collapsing on Avery's towel. Droplets of water fell on my leg as he groaned.

"I'm so fucking tired."

"Soooo." I crossed my legs, grinning at Nate. "I've gotta ask you something."

Nate looked up at me, yawning. "I don't do questions

unless it's what I would like to drink. In which case, I would like a JD and Coke."

"You and Avery." I watched as he frowned, lowering his aviators.

"Are good friends…" he laughed, tilting his head to me.

"Yeah, but…" I turned to look at her, and she whipped her head away, pretending she hadn't been watching us intently. "Do you like her?"

"Listen, I'm not sure what you've been drinking, but I'd love some."

I frowned, leaning towards him.

"You do like her!"

Nate hesitated, his gaze flickering over to where Avery was. Finally, his expression softened, and my heart did a little dance.

"Look, she's my friend, that's all. Right, I'm going to get a drink. Want one?"

"No, thanks. But what—"

Nate held his hand up, a finger on his lips.

"No more silly talk. I'm going to start getting drunk. Join me and be quiet, or stay there and be quiet. Either way—"

"Be quiet; I got it. I think I'll come and get drunk, but I can't guarantee I'll be quiet." I hoisted myself up, waving at the others so they could watch our stuff.

I wasn't sure, but Avery looked devastated for a moment, and when I beckoned her to join us, her face lit up.

"Coming to get drunk?" I grinned, nodding to where Nate was positioned at the little beach shack bar.

Avery nodded, clearly extending the invite soon to the others who followed suit.

So much for getting it out of Nate. Maybe I'll have to corner him later.

I love matchmaking.

NINETEEN

ELLA

"TEQUILA!" Someone roared, and I downed the shot, wincing when it burned the back of my throat. I felt bile rise in my throat, but I managed to swallow it down, holding up a hand for a high five.

"I thought you were gonna vom then." A voice chuckled, and I turned to see Julian, one of Nate's friends, grinning at me. He was ridiculously handsome, with all dark hair and tanned skin.

"I'm tougher than I look," I said with a smile, wobbling as I shifted the weight from my left foot to my right.

"Clearly." Julian arched a brow, his mouth lifting in the corners. I fell again, this time leaning against him. "You okay there?"

I looked up, noticing he made no move to back away from me.

"I think I'm just a little tipsy." I shrugged, pulling myself up. "Nate! Avery! Come here," I commanded, leaning past Julian, who watched me with amusement.

Nate's eyes shone with intoxication, and we grinned at

each other like drunk people do when they see someone on their level.

Avery joined us, holding hands with Vanessa, who was still talking to one of the other dudes. I tried to remember his name, but it was pointless. I could barely remember my own name.

"Truth or dare?" I smirked as Julian's hand brushed my elbow, steadying me somewhat.

The air had cooled, but it didn't matter. I was drunk in a bikini and bare feet on a beach in Mexico, the sun setting behind me, surrounded by friends and like-minded souls.

Avery rolled her eyes and opted for Dare.

"I dare you to kiss Nate." I crowed, giggling, when Nate looked up, clearly recognizing his name.

"What? Who's doing what?"

Avery glared at me, shaking her head as she moved towards Nate.

"This is just a dare," Avery mumbled, lifting on her tiptoes to brush her lips against Nate's as he remained utterly still, his eyes open and everything.

Ouch.

"Truth or dare?" Avery turned to me, her eyes filled with sadness.

I swallowed down my regret as I whispered, "Dare."

"I dare you to kiss Julian."

My smile froze on my face, and Vanessa stopped laughing, her eyes meeting mine with alarm.

"Oh, come on, Ella. What happens in Mexico stays in Mexico," Avery said with a grin. "We won't tell Jackson."

Jackson?

"Or you can do truth?" Vanessa added, clearly trying to help me out.

Avery frowned, looking back at Vanessa.

"Is there something I don't know? Why can't she do the dare?"

Vanessa looked like she was going to pass out, so I did what I thought was right.

I turned to Avery, forcing a smile.

"It's okay. I'll do it."

It was just a kiss; it wasn't emotions...it was a dare...

I cupped Julian's face in my hands, and he tilted his head to the right, leaning in as I closed my eyes. His lips met mine, and he moaned against me softly, his kiss deepening as I moved back, suddenly aware that this was wrong.

"You're so fucking hot," Julian said, and I laughed, wagging my finger.

"Just a dare, Julian, I've got a man."

"Yeah." Julian reached out to touch my hip, trying to pull me closer. "Where is he?"

"Live streaming from Mexico!" Avery crooned, making faces at the camera.

"He's back home," I said, narrowing my eyes. "Urgh, no more games for me."

I headed back to the bar where Nate was cradling a beer, staring at the ocean.

"Hey."

"Hey. You and Julian, huh?" Nate grinned.

"No! It was a dare! It's like me saying you and Avery." I pointed out, ordering a beer for myself. "Nice kiss, by the way."

"It was weird. Why'd you dare her to kiss me, Ella?"

Nate turned to me, his eyes burning with curiosity.

"Erm, well..." I tried to think of an excuse, failing miserably. "I think you'd be adorable together."

"Me and Avery?" Nate shook his head, gazing into the waves. "It can't happen."

"But-"

"I'm seeing someone, Ella." Nate blurted out, and I froze, sucking on my beer, so I didn't say anything stupid. "and I really like her."

Oh no.

"But... you were flirting with that girl today on the beach!" I spluttered, my eyes wide.

"So? I wouldn't *do* anything, Ella. That's why I didn't kiss her back."

Guilt consumed me, and the taste of beer in my mouth suddenly felt sour.

I'd kissed Julian back.

"Right. But it was just a dare..."

"If I saw Lauren kissing someone else, I'd flip my shit, whatever the reason." Nate shrugged. "Wouldn't you?"

I couldn't imagine Franco kissing someone else, not for one second.

I couldn't ever tell him.

"No, I guess not."

"Hey, guys, room for a little one?" Vanessa smiled from beside me, ordering herself a beer. "Are you okay?"

I nodded, the alcohol dulling my senses.

"Yeah. I think so, but ask me again in the morning."

The following day I woke to the sunlight streaming through the window, my head throbbing with the after-effects of alcohol. It took me a good ten minutes to open my eyes, and when I did, I found Vanessa curled up beside me on the bed, her mouth open as she snored.

"Oh, god," I groaned, holding my head like it was a fragile egg. "Ow, fuck."

My head pounded when gravity took hold, and I steadied myself on the wall, my hair spilling forward as waves of nausea took over me.

I used the bathroom, splashing some water on my face before I left in an attempt to feel better.

Where was my phone?

I frowned, my eyes scanning the room.

It isn't here!

This couldn't be happening. I tore through the bags on the sofa, emptying sandy towels onto the floor with panic. My purse was on the side, tossed there carelessly by drunk hands.

"Fuck!" I hissed, tears pricking my eyes. "Vanessa! I can't find my phone!"

I strode into the hallway, my heart in my throat.

"Are you insured?" Vanessa yawned, her voice thick with sleep.

"Vee, it's got all my texts from you know who!" I hissed back, tossing cushions from the sofa onto the floor.

"Calm down, go and ask Avery."

"Yeah, good idea," I mumbled, hurrying across the hallway to the large bedroom that overlooked the ocean. "Avery? I've lost my phone-"

Avery was sprawled across the bed, as naked as the day she was born, a thin sheet draped over her intimate parts.

What the hell?

"Good morning," called a voice from the balcony.

I whipped around, my eyes falling onto the table where my phone and a pack of cigarettes sat.

Beside Nate.

"Nate?" Did you..." I wave a hand at my friend, passed out on the bed.

Nate frowned, shaking his head.

"No, she stripped off. She got upset...she was too drunk."

"Is that my phone?"

"Yeah, sorry. I don't know why it's in here, but it's been ringing."

"Sorry, why are you here if you and Avery didn't...sleep together?"

I sank into the chair opposite him as he inhaled his cigarette, squinting in the morning sun.

"Because last night, Avery told me she was in love with me."

"Oh no," I whispered, picking up my phone with relief.

Three missed calls. Franco.

"Yup. I had to tell her about Lauren, and well...she didn't take it well. So I laid with her until she went to sleep, and, well, here I am."

"Shit, sorry, Nate. I need to make a call."

"No sweat." Nate waved me off, sipping on his water.

I dialed Franco's number, eager to hear his voice.

"Hello?"

"Hey, baby." I sighed with a smile.

"The *fuck*, Ella? You think I'm going to be alright with you after what you did last night?" Franco snapped, making me still.

"What do you mean?" I whispered, memories of last night flooding my brain.

He couldn't know.

"You and fucking *Julian*, Ella! It's all over fucking Facebook!"

Dizziness filled my vision as a sob caught in my throat.

"What? It was a dare, Franco; it didn't mean anything!"

"Yeah, well, it shows we were just a fucking joke to you. I risked *everything* to be with you, Ella. Turns out you're just another dumb bitch."

"Franco, I didn't-"

"Save it, Ella. I'm going to find you some medicine to swallow. See how you like that, huh?"

The phone call ended, and I stared at the phone, my heart breaking into millions of pieces.

Had Franco just ended everything with me?

TWENTY

ELLA

I'D TRIED CALLING Franco back repeatedly, but he declined my calls before turning his phone off.

It hurt so bad.

What I couldn't understand was how he knew. He said it was all over Facebook, so I logged on, my heart in my mouth. Then, scrolling through my feed, I frowned, wondering what the hell he was talking about.

I couldn't see anything.

I took a deep breath, dragging my fingers through my hair to the point of pain.

Think, Ella.

Vanessa walked out of the bathroom, giving me a sad smile before wrapping a towel around her damp hair. It would probably dry better out of it considering the intense heat outside, but it looked like she was staying indoors for now.

"You okay?" Vanessa asked in a small voice.

"No. Franco won't take my calls." I bit back tears of frustration.

"Ring him from my phone?" Vanessa offered, searching around her.

"No, it's okay. If Franco wanted to talk to me, he'd answer my calls. But, unfortunately, Franco's stubborn, and clearly, he's fuming."

Knowing Franco the way I did, I knew how he would react to something like this. He meant what he said about me tasting my medicine—and it made me feel violently sick. Of course, I couldn't excuse what I'd done, and my cheeks flushed with guilt and shame at the thought of it, but it hadn't meant anything.

It was just a game—a stupid dare.

"Do we know how he knows?" Vanessa asked, chewing on her lip. She was gutted for me.

"Well, I haven't been tagged in anything," I said with a sigh. "It has to be someone we know."

Vanessa nodded, staring into space thoughtfully.

"Go through everyone's profile, just to be sure. Mine, Avery's, Nate's— anyone. Unless someone filmed it and it's gone viral—"

I stared at her in horror, nausea hitting the back of my throat.

"I highly doubt it has, though," Vanessa said quickly, almost stumbling over her words. "I just mean, shit, I dunno. Let's search together."

Vanessa dressed while I checked out her profile first, once she'd been tagged in something.

"Nothing on yours."

We sat side by side, scrolling through Facebook until Avery strolled into the room. Huge black sunglasses covered her eyes, and she looked killer hot in a red bikini that clings to her curves, a loose sarong hanging around her waist.

"Are you guys ready to hit the beach? Hey, who died?"

"We think someone took a video of Ella kissing Julian," Vanessa said, darting a look in my direction. "Or something. Franco just told her it's all over Facebook."

Avery frowned, then yawned.

"So? What's the problem if it is? Why are you speaking to your uncle when you're on vacation?" Avery wrinkled her nose up, tilting her head to study me.

Good point.

"I called home to speak to Dad... anyway—" I shook my head dismissively. "I want to see it."

Avery slumped down on Vanessa's bed, yawning again as she stared at her phone.

"Oh, it's here." Avery shrugged, leaning over to hand us the phone.

I grabbed it, holding my breath when I stared at the image on the screen. There I was, kissing Julian.

"What is this?" I whispered, sliding the video bar back to the beginning to watch.

"I did a live. Thank God it was the only one I did because I can't remember much after that." Avery grimaced.

"Why did you film *me?*" I wailed, handing the phone to Vanessa. "I'm a private person. I don't want that shit online."

Avery looked puzzled.

"Erm, are you? Since when?"

"Since now!" I snapped, and Avery widened her eyes. "I'm sorry, it's just got me into shit with Franco, that's all."

Avery nodded, still looking skeptical.

"I'll delete it."

I didn't say anything, but Vanessa swept in, filling the awkward silence.

"So, what happened with Nate last night?"

I tuned out. The images of me kissing Julian burned in my mind's eye.

What would I do if I saw Franco doing that?

Urgh, I couldn't bear to think of that.

Now I've seen the video. I didn't know if I even wanted to speak to Franco. I cringed when I imagined his face while he watched that video, his beautiful features contorting into anger.

Oh, God.

"Can we go to the beach?" Avery asked, looking at me with a warm smile. "I'm sorry about the video, Ella. I didn't think it would cause you any problems."

"No, I know. I'll just get ready and meet you guys down there." I forced a smile, avoiding Vanessa's curious gaze.

I tried Franco again, but his phone was still off. I could call my dad, but then I wasn't sure if that was wise either. If Franco were there, he wouldn't be able to hide his emotions.

There was nothing I could do but suck it up and wait until he wanted to speak to me.

FRANCO

I smashed my fists into the punchbag, the aching in my knuckles telling me I had to stop soon.

But I couldn't.

I wish I'd never gone on her friend's page. But, stupid fucking sap that I was, I'd wondered if there have been any photos uploaded. I missed her.

Again, the pain tore through me as the video replayed in my mind in ultra-clear HD with full sound.

His hands on her. Her hands on him. The catcalls and

whistles as they kiss. Sure, it wasn't for long, but it didn't matter.

She's still kissed someone else.

If she could do that, what else could she do?

I knew there was a reason I didn't want her to go to Mexico with her friends—but I didn't think it was because I couldn't trust her.

Turns out I was wrong.

I showered, my hands aching under the hot stream of water.

Fucking Ella.

Did she fuck him? All I could see was his dark hair and his dirty hands on *my* woman.

My thoughts tortured me throughout the next few days, and try as I did, I couldn't calm down. The only way out of this was by rewinding time and stopping the whole stupid fucking charade between us. Ella was due back in a few days, and I had just the plan to give her a taste of her own medicine.

On the night she flew back, I had a party. I let nature take its course and drank until I couldn't see. I wanted to kiss someone, hell, fuck someone, but I couldn't do it.

I loved Ella.

She'd ruined me for everyone else.

Which was why, when I woke up the following morning to the rapping of her knuckles on my door, I devised a plan, it took seconds to conjure up, but it was enough.

Laying on the sofa was a scantily clad girl that I'd never seen before in my life.

"Morning, love. Up you get." I helped the girl to her feet as she frowned, staring at me through panda eyes.

"Where's John?"

"I dunno, babe, but you're gonna have to go." I walked her to the door, avoiding the dark gaze that awaited me.

"Franco—"

"Do you need me to call you a cab?" I addressed the girl as she left, blinking in the sunlight.

"Huh? No, I'm good." Then the woman turned back to me, grinning. "Great party."

I winked, finally turning my attention to the vision on my doorstep.

Her skin was golden brown from the sun, her hair naturally lighter and curly. She wore tight shorts and a cross-over shirt that clung to her curves. Her vanilla perfume made me almost groan with longing, my dick twitching in my pants. My hands moved towards her, but I steadied them, fixing her with a cold stare.

"What do you want?"

The hurt in her eyes made me hate myself, but I was fucked if I took her back so easily.

"Who the fuck was that?" Ella snapped, jutting a finger behind her.

"I don't know her name."

Ella stared at me, folding her arms across her chest.

God, she was a knockout. I couldn't stop staring at her, but she soon flipped from beautiful to fiery angry, her eyes glittering as she hissed through gritted teeth.

"I kissed a guy for a dare, yes, it was wrong, and I'm so sorry." Ella glared at me. "But I told him I had a man, and nothing else happened. Yet you have some skank leaving your house at eight-thirty in the morning? So what the *fuck*, Franco?"

"Nothing happened." I shrugged, leaning against the doorframe.

"You expect me to believe that?!" Ella cried, shoving me in the chest.

"Well, you expect me to believe you, so yeah, I do." I

snapped, moving away from her. "I don't care, either way, Ella. I'm done with you."

"You're *done with me*?" Ella reiterated, her eyes bulging. "That's it? After *everything?*"

"Yes, Ella, after everything." I stepped closer to her, my eyes scanning hers. "I'm not risking everything to be with someone who will cheat on me with the first guy that shows them attention. You *said* you loved me. I believed you, but now I know better. Go home, Ella. *Don't* call me again."

I closed the door, leaning my head against it as I heard her sob.

Part of me expected her to bang on the door and demand I listen to her; part of me hoped she did. But the other part of me knew this was the perfect excuse to stop the debauchery between us, to realize that doing something so wrong was only worth it if it's *so right*.

I thought it was, but Ella thought otherwise.

I had to forget about her.

TWENTY-ONE

ELLA

"WHAT DO you mean he hasn't spoken to you?" Vanessa demanded, licking the milk off her upper lip. "But it was a dare, and how could you not? You'd have had to tell Avery you were seeing someone, and that opens a whole new can of worms! He didn't have to go and fuck someone else."

I held my hands up, agreeing with her. I wiped down the counter, going to fill a mop bucket out back to scrub the cafe floor. I filled the bucket with hot, soapy water and heaved it back into the cafe.

We'd closed half an hour ago, but as I was closing the store, Vanessa had come to keep me company.

I dropped the mop onto the floor with a slosh, pushing the water all over the dried coffee drips.

"He's a stubborn ass fucker. First, he wouldn't even hear me out, and then that skank left his house." I grind my teeth together, taking my anger out of the mop.

"Does he realize *you're* risking it all too?" Vanessa continued as I rinsed the mop. "He makes me so mad."

"Maybe it's for the best." I shrugged, pushing away the

ache in my chest. "It wouldn't have ever been accepted...now it's over."

I still couldn't believe I was saying that.

After everything—every whispered promise, every plan we made, every fucking I love you.

Gone.

"You know, I've been thinking." Vanessa hesitated, sipping on her iced mocha. "It's just a suggestion, but I know I'd want to hear it if I were you."

I continued mopping the floor, feeling a little satisfied when it gleamed back at me. I glanced up at Vanessa, shrugging my shoulders.

"Go on."

"Well," Vanessa drawled. "Why don't you transfer schools? Far away, you know. I know you love your family, but this kinda shit needs to stay buried."

I stopped, staring at my best friend with wide eyes.

"Transfer?"

"Uh-huh." Vanessa nodded. "Get away from everything. You've got another year, babe. You could start a new life after you finish."

I chewed on the inside of my lip, weighing her words upon my mind.

The reason I'd not left was because of my love for my family, and because I was a homebody. I loved my town and knew everyone in it. I considered moving further away, but I went for the safe option when push came to shove.

Not like I did in my love life, ha.

"You know," I said slowly, dragging the bucket into the back room as Vanessa followed me idly. "You could be onto something."

"But I'd miss you!" Vanessa said, staring at me in horror. "It was just a suggestion. So why are you jumping at it?"

"Why not?" I shrugged. "Franco practically lives in my house, Vee. He's there all of the time, and what am I going to do when he starts seeing someone else?"

"Is there no way you might get back together?"

I laughed harshly, letting the sound of sloshing water fill the room.

"After seeing him and that skank? He was in his boxers, and let me tell you; he hadn't fucking slept. He's a dick." I snapped, tears stinging my eyes.

"I'm sorry, El.",

"I just need to put the chairs on the tables, and we can go," I muttered, flicking the lights off. "I'm gonna talk to Dad, see what he thinks."

"To what, transferring?" Vanessa eyed me, dropping her empty cup into the dishwasher. "For real?"

"It's that, or I stay here for another year, and I'm not sure I can, Vee. He's broken me."

Vanessa reached for me, and I allowed myself to cry, her hands stroking my back as she soothed me.

"Look at it this way," Vanessa said kindly. "At least no one knows."

I nodded, wiping my eyes on the back of my sleeve.

"Plus, you know, he's hot and all, but he is your uncle. So maybe you can apply for a transfer and spend the summer getting an apartment and a job sorted, you know?"

Despite everything, I felt a flicker of excitement amongst the dark clouds within me.

Why should I stay here?

My college wasn't outstanding by any stretch; certainly no different to any other college. Of course, my dad would be supportive, and yeah, my sister might miss me a tiny bit, but I was only young once.

One person seemed to know about being young once

better than most, so I decided to visit him after finishing work.

Gramps.

FRANCO

I busied myself every day; working late, drinking with the guys, hitting the gym, and generally passing out with any spare time I had.

I was burning the candle at both ends, but I didn't give a shit.

I'd been to Ella's house one time, and she hadn't come out of her room once. Christopher said she had woman problems, but I knew better.

She didn't want to see me.

I didn't give a fuck, considering how she'd cheated on me on her vacation. It mattered to me that she would do something like that without once thinking how it would make me feel.

So as far as I was concerned, I didn't want to see her either.

The weeks passed, and I couldn't avoid a visit to see my brother and dad, so I found myself sitting on the couch I'd fucked Ella on, pushing the memory away. She'd made her bed, so she could fucking lie in it.

I could hear someone walking around upstairs, and my heart dropped when I saw Maria skipping down the stairs.

"Daddy, why can't *I* move to California?" Maria pouted, plopping herself down beside me.

"Why, who's moving to California?" I laughed, sipping my beer.

Maria gave me a strange look, glancing at Christopher, then my dad.

"How does he not know?" Maria asked, her brows knitting together.

"How do I not know what?" I demanded as Christopher and my dad exchanged a look. "Well?"

"Ella's moved to California." Christopher frowned. "It's big news, and she said she wanted to tell you herself. I was surprised when you didn't come to the airport—"

My head spun, but I tried to remain calm.

"Airport?"

"I gave her some money," Dad said with a cough. "She's a young girl; she's bright enough. Good for her, I say."

"Did no one think to tell me?" I whispered, my stomach twisting. "Seriously?"

"Calm down, bro. She's your niece. I'm sure she'll call you." Christopher laughed, picking up his phone. "She's always texting me photos, and it looks so nice."

"Oh, to be young again." Dad sighed.

"She'll probably meet a stupidly hot guy, and I'll be left here, miserable and alone," Maria complained, but I couldn't speak.

Was this a fucking joke?

"We thought you two had fallen out," Dad said, turning to me with watery eyes. "She didn't want us to say a word to you, but she promised she'd tell you herself. Did something happen?"

Yeah. I fucked Ella, and we fell in love.

"She thought I was a bit overprotective, that's all. You know, with guys she was with?"

"Honestly, you probably stifled her," Christopher said, shrugging his shoulders. "It's probably a good thing she's gone. Still, she'll visit, huh?"

I lifted my phone out of my pocket, my fingers swiping across the screen in record time.

FRANCO:
Cali, huh? When were you going to tell me, Ella?

I stared at the phone, but the message remained unread. Ella was probably too busy partying to give a shit about her phone, but fuck it.
Did she really think so little of me?
She didn't reply.
Not that night, nor the following day.
I called Christopher, who told me he'd spoken with Ella ten minutes before I'd rang, so I knew she was alive.
She was ignoring *me*.
I was so fucked with her attitude. She was behaving like a bitch.

FRANCO:
After *everything*, you ignore me? Well, you know what? Fuck you. You're the one that did this to us, and you've left without a single word. Goes to show that words mean fuck all, Ella. Take care of yourself.

I deleted her number, making sure my drunk ass couldn't call her.
Out of all the women in the fucking world, it had to be

her. Then she cheated on me and fucking moved across the country without a word.

I unscrewed the whiskey bottle, taking a deep slug from it.

Well, fuck Ella Russo.
See if I give a shit.

TWENTY-TWO

ELLA

PERIOD PAINS SUCK.

It was a hot ass summer's day, and I was curled up in my bed, dosed up on pain relievers. I'd always suffered from bad periods, but this one was worse than usual.

Luckily for me, Todd was out of the apartment today, something about seeing a man about a dog.

Living with a guy was a little different from what I'd expected to happen when I moved to LA, but it sort of just happened.

We'd both been to view the apartment, and the landlord thought it made sense to offer it to both of us as we would be attending the same college, UCLA.

Todd was always out, and when he was in, he was a clean freak, so it had its plus sides. He never brought anyone back either, so quite often, I could lounge around looking like shit, and there was no one there to judge me.

Another pain shot through my stomach, and I groaned, turning my face into the pillow.

I couldn't even sleep.

I dragged myself to the bathroom, deciding to run a bubble bath.

That's what I wanted, a hot bubble bath.

And chocolate.

Where was the chocolate?

I paused, dunking tonnes of bath cream under the running water before heading to the kitchen.

Every time I went to the store, I bought chocolate so that we never ran out.

Except for this time, I hadn't, and there was no fucking chocolate.

Annoyed, I slammed the cupboard door shut, stomping back to the bathroom.

My phone rang from inside my bedroom, and as usual, I jumped.

I'd been living here for two months, which was only eight weeks, but I still wondered if Franco would call me.

My heart ached at the thought of him, and the pain in my chest far outweighed the ones in my stomach.

Painkillers can't heal this, though.

Franco.

I missed him beyond comprehension, but I knew leaving had been the right thing to do. I met some new friends and even got a voluntary position shadowing a teacher in school to get some experience under my belt.

The time with Franco lived in my dreams and any spare gap I had in my mind.

Standing in line for groceries?

I'd think of the way he kissed me for the first time.

His lips on mine, the way he'd groaned when we'd allowed ourselves to indulge in the forbidden taste of one another.

Never had two people been more right for one another.

The sex—don't even get me started on that.

I needed to stop checking his Facebook profile too.

It became part of my ritual, waking up and checking his profile before brushing my teeth for the day ahead, and it was the last thing I looked at before bed.

I'd even saved his profile photo so that I wouldn't ever forget what he looked like.

As if I could.

I rarely called home, but when I did, I wouldn't ask about him. Dad never said anything either; I think he knew something wasn't right between Franco and me.

I eased myself into the bath, resting my head over the roll-top side.

As far as apartments go, I'd lucked out massively.

Every room was painted white, the windows all covered with funky slat blinds that reminded me of a rustic cottage-type feel. The floors were solid wood, and we even had a fireplace in the main room.

It was small, but I fell in love with it.

Grandpa's money had been so helpful those first few weeks, but I soon got a job in a cool student bar not far from college, which helped out.

All in all, I didn't have any time to think of Franco, but somehow he made it into my head.

Nights out with the girls were the worst, especially when they made out with random guys, and I tried not to remember what it felt like to do that with Franco.

I'd kissed a few guys, but it just wasn't the same.

Maybe I'd be single forever, and that would be my payment for falling in love with someone I could never have.

Then kissing someone else.

I knew kissing Julian was a stupid ass mistake, but I couldn't get over Franco fucking that girl, either.

I closed my eyes, trying to focus on the odd drip that fell into the bathwater, inhaling deeply.

How would I ever move on?

I had no option.

The apartment door opened, and Todd sighed heavily, dropping his bag onto the floor with a clunk.

"I'm in the bathroom!" I called as he muttered something incoherent back.

Moments later, knuckles grazed the door, and Todd yawned.

"Are you in the bath?"

"Yes."

"Do you want some curry? I'm making chicken madras."

I nodded my head, realizing that he couldn't see through the door.

"Yes, please, with rice?" I asked hopefully.

Sometimes Todd would do something odd like serve the curry with a slice of bread or stir fry with a side of beans.

The man knew how to cook, though, but he was quirky.

"No, with a great steaming turd," Todd answered cheerfully.

"I'm on my period, and I need chocolate, Todd. We're out." I pouted, wiggling my toes in the water.

"Marvelous. I'm not going back out; it's too hot."

"Okay."

I knew I'd needed to go and get some. The sheer thought of it made me ache.

Silence.

"You can have the big piece that's in my stash if you watch the game with me." Todd offered his voice fading as he walked away.

"I hate baseball!" I complained, wondering what chocolate he had.

"Reeses."

How the hell did Todd know that's what I was thinking?!

"Fine!" I yelled, sinking further into the hot water. "Thank you. You're the best roomie ever."

"I'm the only one you've ever had," Todd yelled back from the kitchen.

I grinned, wondering if I was single forever, would I get to keep Todd as my roomie?

Probably not.

Maybe I should get a cat.

Sometime later, I nodded off on the sofa, waking when Todd sneezed beside me.

"God!" I grumbled with a yawn. "I'm going to bed."

"You didn't even watch the whole game," Todd complained. "You stole my chocolate and passed out!"

I shrugged, making my way to my bed. I was so tired; there was no point trying to fight it.

I cranked on the AC and stripped out of my clothes, laughing at my vast pants. For lack of a better name, they were my period pants, but they were loose around the waist and comfortable-exactly what a girl needed.

I checked my phone, my heart dropping when I saw only a few tags on Facebook from some girlfriends.

I couldn't expect Franco to chase me, but then again...maybe I could.

We loved each other.

A pang echoed in my chest as my head hit the pillow, and I opened WhatsApp, selecting his name, which of course, didn't have a profile photo.

The anonymous silhouette of a person represented him, and it was nothing like the real thing.

My fingers hovered over the text box, the cursor flashing at me mockingly.

I couldn't.

What could I say?!

I'd been an idiot for kissing Julian, but I felt like leaving had been for the best.

In hindsight, I realized it had been too intense between us.

I'd never replied to his texts, and knowing Franco, he wouldn't forgive that so easily.

I closed the text box down, gritting my teeth with frustration.

I had to stop thinking about him.

TWENTY-THREE

FRANCO

"PASS THE CHILI SAUCE," Dad said, watching me.

I reached across the table without thinking, handing him the bottle.

"That's ketchup, son."

I frowned, glancing at the bottle.

"Sorry. My bad."

"You're not thinking. What's up?" Dad asked, exchanging a glance with Christopher.

"I dunno. Tired, I guess," I mumbled, running a hand through my hair.

"You look like shit. Why don't you take a vacation?" Christopher suggested as I lifted a cigarette to my lips. "Mexico did you good."

I scowled at the mention of Mexico. I didn't want to think of Ella, and everything made me think of her.

Shit, looking at a brick wall made me remember kissing her against walls so many times.

As for the pantry?

I'd rather starve than go near it again.

"Can't afford it." I lied, lighting my cigarette, inhaling deeply.

"I'll pay." Dad shrugged, a gleam in his eye.

I fixed him with a stare, blowing smoke out slowly.

"I'm good."

"Go visit Ella in California," Christopher said. "I don't like you two not getting along. Just go surprise her."

"No thanks." I snapped, causing my brother and Dad to raise their eyebrows.

"What's that guy's name she's living with? Tom?" Dad rubbed his chin as Maria piped up.

"Todd, and he's so gorgeous. I bet you anything they're together."

What.

The.

Fuck.

I swallowed my envy and fury down, sucking so hard on my cigarette. I burnt my throat, causing a choking fit.

"Ella lives with a guy?" I coughed, reaching for my beer.

"Yup. Weird, but she seems happy enough."

"Does she?" I asked, a lump in my throat.

"Yeah. Ella's working in a bar, and she said she's meeting loads of new people. She's volunteering in a school; it's all working out," Christopher chirped. I wanted to strangle him.

Working in a bar?

My Ella?

I closed my eyes, shrugging my shoulders.

"She got her haircut!" Maria thrust a phone into my face, the image of the woman that stole my heart looking back at me.

She had it in a long bob, and her dark eye makeup brought out her insane eyes.

Ella's hands wrapped around another girl, and her smile was so fucking wide.

Why was she so fucking happy when she didn't have me in her life?

"Good for her."

"Dad, can I visit Ella?" Maria pleaded, her eyes wide as she steepled her hands in a praying motion. "Ella said she'd meet me off the plane."

Christopher scoffed.

"I don't think so. My two gorgeous girls on their own? Nope."

"Dad! It's Ella!" Maria argued, and I stubbed out my cigarette, tuning them out.

Christopher went to grab more beer, and Maria followed him, giving him a million reasons why she was mature enough to go on a flight across the states.

"Franco. Take your niece to see Ella," Dad ordered, tipping whiskey into the glass before him.

"What the fuck? No. I'm busy with work."

"You're a miserable bastard at the best of times, but you're driving me mad lately. Just go."

I stared at him, and the twinkle in his eye made my head reel.

"Ella is my niece."

"So? Go see her."

My heart thudded against my chest, my limbs stiffening.

"Make sure she's really happy, Francesco. For me." Dad smiled before leaning over to steal a cigarette from my battered packet.

I clenched my jaw, ready to argue when Christopher came out of the house groaning.

"I guess I could, but does she want her old man turning up?"

Dad winked at me, and I dropped my head back, staring up at the sky.

"I'll take Maria," I muttered, ignoring the soaring feeling in my stomach.

I was a fucking soppy cunt. That's what I was.

"Yes, Franco!" Maria screamed, throwing herself at me. "Thank you so much!"

Christopher nodded, leaning back into his chair.

"Good man."

What the fuck had I just agreed to?

ELLA

I swallowed, staring at the people spilling from the doors, grinning as they greeted family and friends.

Todd leaned on my shoulder, yawning.

"Can you see um?"

"Not yet," I whispered, my body trembling.

I'd not spoken to Franco in over four months.

I couldn't believe he was here, in California.

"You okay? You're shaking." Todd pointed out with a frown.

"Yeah, probably the after-effects of last night." I waved my hand when my heart stopped.

The beard was new.

But the eyes that scanned the crowd honed in on mine like a bird tracking its prey.

If it was at all possible, they darkened at the sight of Todd beside me, and I inhaled sharply, moving out of Todd's grasp.

"They're here?" Todd frowned, following my gaze.

Franco wore a cream shirt; his sleeves rolled up to

reveal the tattooed forearms that sent me dizzy. He held a case covered in pink flowers, one I recognized from home. He had his carry-on thrown over his shoulder, and the moment our eyes met, I knew it wasn't over.

"Ella!" Maria yelled, her eyes running over Todd appreciatively.

"Hey," I whispered, wrapping my arms around my sister as Franco eyed Todd with an unfriendly stare.

"Hey, bud. I'm Todd, Ella's roommate."

Todd held a hand out, and I pleaded with Franco with my eyes, swallowing heavily.

"I'm Franco," he muttered, shaking his hand firmly.

"Whoa, quite the grip." Todd laughed, waving at Maria. "Hey! Little sis, right?"

Maria reddened, holding her hand out.

"Maria."

"I don't know if Ella told you I'm her chauffeur," Todd declared, jutting his thumb to the airport doors. "And I'll be out of your hair for your stay."

"What?" Maria gasped, glaring at me. "Why?"

"We only live in a small apartment. We're on top of each other with just the two of us, so I'm staying with a friend so you guys can have space," Todd explained, grinning at me.

"On top of each other, huh?" Franco practically growled.

"Not like that," I stammered. "We're just friends."

"Yeah, she's too good for me," Todd added, not helping himself out at all.

I shot him a look before jamming my hands into my jeans pockets.

"Um, shall we go? Todd is gonna drop us off."

"Great. Let's go." Franco rolled his eyes, pushing past me.

His scent, a mixture of freshly washed clothes and *him*, made me almost reach out for him instinctively.

But as he strode off, Todd shrugged his shoulders at me.

"He isn't overly friendly."

"No." My eyes followed Franco's broad back, my heart shattering to pieces once more. "He's not."

"He hasn't even spoken to you." Todd glanced at me with concern. "You sure you'll be okay?"

"Oh, you know how it is. We've got some things to iron out." I forced a smile, my heart leaping into my throat when Franco turned, raising his eyebrows.

"Can we go? Or are you two gonna keep chatting like girls?"

Ouch.

Franco was back.

TWENTY-FOUR

ELLA

I ATTACKED the pasta that stuck to the bottom of the pan, annoyed. I'd been too distracted by Maria showing me endless TikTok videos and boring me to death with all of the different dances she wanted me to see.

"I love it here," Maria said with a sigh. "Do you think Dad will let me come here for my final year?"

I snorted, rolling my eyes.

"No."

"But—"

"You're coming back with me, sweetheart."

Franco's voice boomed through the apartment, his hair still dripping as he walked out in just a towel.

My breath caught in my chest as I averted my eyes, dropping the pan back onto the counter with a loud clatter.

"Are you alright?" Maria asked, wrinkling her nose up at the bowl of pasta and sauce I pushed towards her.

"Yes. Just eat that and give your mouth a rest."

"Charming." Maria scowled, sniffing the pasta. "This smells burnt."

"It's that or nothing." I pointed out, leaving a bowl on the counter for Franco.

The tension in the apartment was beyond awkward, and despite having been here one night, he'd still not uttered a word to me.

I slumped next to Maria as she flicked through the channels.

"Is Todd single?"

"Maria. He's twenty." I shook my head, twisting the pasta around my fork. "So get that out of your head."

"So? He's four years older. It's nothing." Maria retorted.

Franco came out of Todd's room, dressed in just grey joggers, his hair damp.

Oh.

My.

God.

"Is this for me?"

I nodded without turning around, mumbling that yes, it was.

"It smells rank. Did you burn it?"

I cut my eyes at him, ignoring the glare he gave me.

"Leave it. I don't care."

"Well, you've gone to so much effort…" a smirk played on his lips, but when I met his eyes, it disappeared.

"Franco, is four years too big an age difference?" Maria whined, making a face at me.

Franco stared at her, leaning forward on the kitchen island to poke at the burnt fucking pasta.

"How can you burn pasta?" Franco muttered, shaking his head. "What do you mean, Maria?"

His voice had dropped, and Maria gulped, knowing she'd probably asked the wrong man the wrong question.

"Between people in love," I answered quickly, as Maria shot me a grateful look.

"Huh." Franco nodded, his eyes locking onto mine. "You're sixteen, just a girl, Maria. Someone at twenty is a man. He'd expect different things from you."

"Oh? Like going drinking with him and that?" Maria nodded thoughtfully. "But if you're in love… it wouldn't matter about expectations. Surely."

"Of course it does. He'd expect you to be faithful for a start. He'd expect to trust you. You're too young to sign up for that shit."

I tried to swallow the pasta in my mouth, but it paused halfway down my throat, prompting a coughing fit.

Most unattractive.

"You alright there, Ella?"

I gulped at the water on the table before us, waving dismissively.

"I'm fine," I croaked out.

"He likes you anyway," Maria muttered, easing back into the sofa as both Franco and I stared at her in dismay.

"What?" I demanded, briefly glancing at Franco.

"This tastes like shit." Franco pointed at the pasta.

"Don't fucking eat it then." I snapped, nudging my sister. "Who likes me?"

Maria rolled her eyes. "Have you kissed him?"

"What the hell are you on about?" I breathed, dizziness taking over.

If she meant Franco, I was doomed.

"Todd. Who else?!" Maria peered at me. "What's wrong with you?"

Franco watched me with amusement, pushing the bowl away with a grimace.

"Yeah, have you kissed Todd?" Franco asked, seemingly innocent to Maria, but fuck, his stare pierced my soul.

"No," I answered honestly, rolling my eyes. "He's my roommate."

"Whatever," Franco muttered.

"Can we go to the little store across the street? I saw the cutest gifts I want to get Sabrina and Chloe." Maria cleared her bowl, smacking her lips together. "Come on; I even ate that shit."

I studied her, trying not to notice how womanly she was becoming. Curves in places that could cause accidents, as Dad would say, olive skin and thick dark hair that curled naturally.

She couldn't go on her own.

"Fine. I'll load the dishwasher, and then we'll go. Are you coming, Happy?" I addressed Franco, who scowled at me.

"To a gift store? No, thanks."

He emptied the pasta into the garbage, pushing the bowl my way.

"Thanks for...whatever that was."

"Don't be a dick."

Maria skipped off to my bedroom, no doubt to get her purse.

I leaned down to load the bowls, fuming that I'd managed to burn fucking pasta.

Fingers gripped my wrist, brown eyes burning into mine as Franco muttered in my ear.

"Or what?"

His scent sent me insane, but I couldn't lose myself over him again.

I tugged my arm away, slamming the dishwasher shut.

"Don't. I know you hate me, and that's fine. But my

sister doesn't deserve to be in the middle of this. So get a grip."

Franco glared at me, his nostrils flaring.

"I'm fucking over this. Don't flatter yourself, Ella."

"Fuck you," I hissed back, turning away so he couldn't see the tears in my eyes.

"Been there, done that," Franco said quietly. "You're not a one-man kinda girl, Ella, so don't give me your shit."

I whirled around to him, speaking through gritted teeth.

"You said you loved me!"

Franco chuckled, shaking his head so subtly I could've missed it if I'd blinked.

"You said the same, Ella."

We glared at one another, and my eyes searched his, my fingers twitching to smack him across his handsome fucking face.

"You fucked someone else! So don't blame this on a stupid kiss, Franco!"

"I'm ready!" Maria chirped, looking up to see the two of us glaring at one another. "Is everything okay?"

"Yeah." Franco allowed his eyes to drag over me before biting his lip.

So fucking sexy.

Yet a stubborn prick.

"Bye, girls. Have fun."

Franco grinned at Maria as he passed her, walking into Todd's bedroom and closing the door.

Maria frowned at the closed door, her hands on her hips as she swiveled towards me on one heel.

"What was that about?"

I shrugged, pushing my feet into my sneakers.

"Franco being Franco, I guess. If I were you, I'd swap your heels for pumps."

"But you're not me, and I love having some height," Maria argued, and I rolled my eyes.

This fucking family.

FRANCO

This shit was becoming too much to bear.

Ella was ignoring me, but everything she did drove me crazy.

The way she tilted her head when she laughed, or how her smile lit up her eyes. Earlier today, I'd nearly walked into a pole watching her suck a fucking straw.

I'd ignored her and the way she'd looked at me, the pure hurt shining in her eyes.

Then earlier today, when we'd had it out in the kitchen.

Fuck.

I'd grabbed her without thinking, and she was damn lucky I didn't bite her lips off when she'd spoken to me through gritted teeth.

Who the fuck did she think she was?

But then she'd reminded me that I'd slept with someone else. It threw me off, but then I felt terrible.

As if I'd do that to her.

But it had been four months.

My dick ached at the thought of her, but I forced myself to think of something else.

There's only so much wanking one can do.

I stuck a game on the TV, trying to take my mind off the image of Ella riding me in the parking lot.

Why the **fuck** was I thinking about that?

I groaned, knowing it was too much to ignore.

I went to the bathroom and climbed into the shower.

I'd already had one today, but this was the cleanest way to blow my load.

The same shower Ella used.

I reached down, stroking my dick as it hardened, my mind filled with images of Ella dripping wet in the shower.

I remembered the way we kissed and how tight she'd been when we first fucked.

The noises she made when I'd made her cum, her body melting around mine.

I pumped my dick faster, tightening my grip around the end as I bit my lip, my palm flat against the tiled wall.

"Fuck," I muttered as I released myself over my stomach, the water filling my eyes and mouth as I lost it for a moment in time.

"We're back!" A voice rang through the apartment, and I chuckled, washing myself.

Good fucking timing.

TWENTY-FIVE

FRANCO

"SABRINA WILL *FREAK*! Shawn Mendes is God."

Maria beamed, tapping away on her phone. "I'm going in the shower. I'm dripping in this ridiculous heat."

I arched a brow at her as Ella adjusted the air conditioning.

"You get used to the heat," Ella said with a grin. "I did. I love it."

As she stretched, I averted my eyes, still horny as fuck despite what I'd just done.

She had that effect on me.

"Hey, asshole."

I frowned, looking up at Ella as she dropped to her knees on her rug, sadly facing away from me.

"Hey, slut."

Oh, *that* got her attention.

Ella whipped her head around, her palm connecting with my cheek with a stinging slap.

"How *dare* you?"

I gripped her wrist, tugging her up to me.

"What you gonna do about it, short stuff?" I smirked,

my heart thudding in my chest when she exhaled, her sweet scent wrapping around me.

"Get your fucking hands off me. A slut? Really?"

"You know I don't think that of you."

"Yeah? So why say it, prick?"

God, I love her temper.

"I just wanted to feel your touch."

Ella blinked, a harsh laugh escaping her lips.

"Well, I hope you enjoyed it because I'm not touching you again." Ella snapped, her eyes flashing with fury.

"My. Such a temper."

Yet, she didn't move back.

"Fuck you."

"Come here," I commanded, tugging her to me, my thighs holding her torso in place.

"What—"

"I didn't fuck her. I haven't fucked anyone since you," I mumbled, my eyes searching hers. Trailing my finger down her jawline, she moaned, her eyes closing.

"Don't lie."

"I'm not, baby."

I couldn't help it; the pet name slipped from my lips too easily.

Ella's eyes widened, shining with tears.

I would walk through fire just to be this close to her.

Tell me this isn't love.

"I kissed him so I didn't have to explain why I couldn't. Why I didn't want to," Ella breathed, looking up at me.

Part of me felt relieved, but I still wanted to rip the dick's throat out.

Our lips were centimeters apart.

LOUD KNOCKING ON THE DOOR.

Ella jumped away from me, her cheeks flushing as she headed to the door.

"Fucks sake," I muttered, sweeping my hair back.

I was *so* close.

"Hey!" Todd's voice boomed through the room. "How are we doing? Sorry, I need to grab some stuff from my room if that's cool?"

Maria stepped out from the shower, freezing like a deer in headlights in her skimpy towel.

Todd stared at her before clearing his throat, his eyes dropping to the floor as he rubbed his neck.

"Get dressed, Maria." I barked, glaring at Todd.

Maria nodded, turning and hurrying into Ella's room.

"Hey, Franco." Todd swallowed, giving me a half-wave.

"Pick your jaw up off the floor, man. She's sixteen." I snapped, earning myself a glare from Ella.

I shrugged, which only made her roll her delicious eyes.

"I wasn't—" Todd began to protest.

"Sixteen," I repeated, cracking my knuckles.

"Right. I'll just grab my stuff."

"Do you have to be so rude? This **is** his apartment too!" Ella shot me a look of despair, but she bit her lip which rendered her words useless. "Don't look at me like that."

"Why?" I smirked, holding my hand out to her.

Ella took it, and I tugged her to the sofa, pulling her into my arms.

"You hurt me so badly," Ella confessed, burying her head into my chest as I wrapped my arms around her.

"You fucking hurt me too."

I held her like that, the two of us inhaling each other for our sanity.

My lips brushed her forehead, but the sound of damp feet on the floor stopped me from taking it further.

"Hey, Todd," Maria breathed, sending me a scathing look. "Oh good, you've made up. About fucking time."

"Watch your mouth," I growled as Ella sighed, pulling away from me. "Why don't you make dinner tonight, Maria?"

Maria gave me a death stare, dropping her phone to the sofa beside her.

"Fine. I'll see if Todd wants to stay for dinner."

I went to protest, but Ella shook her head.

"He's four years older than her!" I hissed, but Ella rolled her eyes.

"He's gorgeous. Let Maria have a crush."

"What did you say?"

"Oh, God! Don't start," Ella groaned. "You know what I mean."

I was frustrated. I wanted to kiss her so bad.

Like she knew, Ella gazed at my lips, her tongue wetting hers.

"Hey, I've asked Todd to take me to the store," Maria declared, eyeballing me.

"I'll take you," I argued, but Ella folded her arms, glaring at me. "Fine."

Maria beamed at Ella as she flounced back to Todd's room.

"I don't like her in there with him." I scowled in the direction of the room, but Ella's fingers brushed against mine, distracting me.

"Let them go to the store, Francesco," Ella breathed without looking at me.

ELLA

Franco didn't fuck the skanky woman.

He was touching my hand, away from prying eyes.

My heart felt revived, new blood pumping through my body because of him.

"Do you want anything from the store?" Maria asked, gazing at Todd.

Poor Todd didn't dare look at her with Franco glaring at him.

"No."

"No, thank you," I purred, watching as Todd practically ran out of the door, followed by Maria.

For a moment, we stood side by side, our fingers lacing together as we turned, facing one another.

"I'm sorry," I whispered, my hand reaching up to cup his cheek. "I'm sorry for leaving you."

Franco exhaled, his hand sliding around my waist as he walked me until I was up against the wall.

Our bodies pressed together, but the sweet relief that was Franco's lips remained too far from mine.

"Don't leave me again." Was all Franco muttered, his mouth on mine, our fingers clawing at each other's clothes.

We fell onto the sofa, his hand dragging my jeans down, his fingers inside me…

"Oh my god!" I groaned, arching my back.

"You're **mine**," Franco whispered in my ear, entering me roughly.

My legs wrapped around his waist, his name leaving my lips countless times.

We fucked one another, both of our hips rocking against the others, my mouth sinking into his shoulder as he owned me.

"And you're *mine.*"

My head hung off the sofa, but he gripped me firmly, his mouth sucking on my hard nipple as I neared my release.

Hard, fast strokes sent me to heaven, and I cried as I came around him, tears leaving my eyes.

Tears I thought I'd cried.

"Don't cry, baby," Franco whispered into my ear as he groaned, emptying himself into me.

This time I felt it hit my inner walls, coating me with his delicious semen.

I didn't give a damn about anything.

All I knew was that I couldn't be away from him anymore.

I was in love.

We're risking it all, but I'd do it again in a heartbeat.

"I love you, Ella." Franco kissed my lips, lifting me into his arms. "But I think you're all dirty and need a shower."

"You too. I love you so much."

Franco kissed me as we moved into the bathroom, slamming the door shut behind us.

God, I hope Maria and Todd take their time.

TWENTY-SIX

FRANCO

FEVERISH KISSES COVERED MY NECK, Ella's sweet mouth moaning against me as we wrapped our arms around one another.

"Come home, Ella."

I couldn't leave her here.

Not without me.

Ella moved back, her eyes wide, eyelashes damp from the water.

"Franco…"

"Ella. Baby."

Our mouths met again, and Ella dropped to her knees, fisting me into her mouth.

"Fuck."

I couldn't concentrate when she did this, and it had been so long since she'd wrapped her mouth around me.

"We're back! Hello?" Maria called, the door slamming shut behind her.

Ella gripped my hips; the sight of her on her knees, hair soaked, and mouth filled with my dick was enough to make me cum there and then.

"I'm in the shower." I bit out, throwing my head back as Ella dragged her nails over my balls.

"Ella?" Maria yelled, and Ella stared up at me, a twinkle in her eyes.

"She went out."

Ella widened her eyes at me as I smirked, gripping her head in my hands as I fucked her throat.

The stream of water hitting the bathtub filled the room, my grunts lost in their wake.

Ella owned me.

Gathering her hair into a fist at the nape of her neck, I lost myself, the sight of her tits bouncing beneath my balls, her shapely ass making me bite my lip so hard I tasted blood.

"Uncle Franco," Maria purred as I shot my load into Ella's mouth. "Todd said he wants to show me a cool place near the beach tonight after dinner. Can I go?"

Ella repeatedly swallowed, pumping my dick into her mouth as I relaxed, leaning down to lift her to her feet.

"No," I called out, dropping to my knees. "I'm having a shower, Maria. We'll talk after."

Smirking at Ella, I lifted her leg so that her foot rested on the corner of the tub, burying my mouth into her cunt.

Ella almost ripped my hair out, thrusting against my mouth as my fingers joined the party, pumping in and out of her as my tongue danced with her clit.

It made it sexier, knowing that Ella couldn't make a fucking sound, not without Todd and Maria hearing her.

Her taste made me dizzy, the sweet yet musky scent of her arousal in my throat, my tongue lapping at the juices as my other fingers dug into her ass cheeks.

"Franco," Ella hissed, and I looked up, the water temporarily blurring my vision.

The swell of her tits led to her arching against me, her breathing ragged.

"Come for me, sweetheart."

Whether it was the instruction alone or the consequence of my voice vibrating against her, Ella gasped, yanking at my hair as she doubled over, trying to drag me away from her throbbing cunt.

I resisted, my tongue flickering at her clit as I withdrew my fingers, causing a second avalanche to rock her body.

"Oh!" Ella moaned, and I covered her mouth with mine, lifting her against the wall, entering her with ease.

Rocking my hips against her, I enjoyed the tightening of her pussy around me, the way her breath caught as her orgasm gripped us both.

"Do you have any idea what you do to me?" I muttered into her ear, reaching yet another peak. "I can't stop, Ella."

"Don't." Ella sucked on my bottom lip, my fingers lifting her up and down on my dick.

"I won't."

ELLA

Franco groaned against my skin, emoting himself inside of me once more.

My skin hummed with his touch, my core dancing with fire as he slowed, pulling himself out of me.

"I love you," I whispered.

Franco looked down at me, a smile curling on his lips.

"You fucking better."

"I do."

Franco stepped back in the shower, the water saturating his hair as I watched greedily.

"How am I going to get out of the bathroom?" I hissed, unable to tear my eyes away from the curve of his stomach muscles.

"Just leave after me. Lock the door behind me and make out you're taking a shit."

I made a face at his crudeness, and he burst out laughing.

"Or tell her you've been fucking me. Whatever you prefer."

Franco kissed my mouth before climbing out, leaving me alone in the stream of water.

I let the water soak my face, holding my breath before I groaned.

Franco left, and I wrapped a towel around my waist, hastily locking the door.

Seconds later, a pounding sounded at the door.

"Ella? Jesus, did you morphe through the wall?"

"Hey, Maria."

"What are you doing in there?"

"Showering!" I called back, glad she couldn't see my face.

Silence.

Was she putting two and two together…

"I need to talk to you," Maria mumbled from the other side of the door.

I perched on the toilet, leaving the shower running, so she thought I'd just got in.

"About?" I called back.

"Can I come in?"

"No!" I breathed, considering throwing myself back in the shower. "I'm on my period."

"Oh. Come and find me when you're out."

"Sure thing!"

I was a wretched human being.

I gave it another five minutes, then an extra three for good measure. Then, finally, I opened the door, steam billowing out around me.

Franco was on the sofa, swiping through his phone beside Todd, who looked like he'd stolen something from me.

"Just gonna get changed." I sailed into my room, leaning against the door to find Maria looking up at me from the bed, a frown wrinkling her brow.

"You had time to wash your hair?"

A hand swept along my damp head guiltily.

"Yeah, it doesn't take long."

"Usually, you're in the bathroom so long I have to get Dad to kick you out." Maria grinned, letting me know she wasn't overly concerned about my duration in the bathroom. "I miss you, Ella."

I threw her a smile, hunting through my underwear drawer before slamming it shut on my hand.

"Fuck!" I yelped, dropping my towel as I reacted.

The door flew open, revealing Franco and Todd, their eyes bulging at the sight of me naked.

"Get some ice," Franco commanded over his shoulder, scowling at Todd.

Todd blinked, his cheeks flushing as he darted toward the kitchen.

Maria jumped up, holding the towel in front of me as she glared at Franco.

"Uncle Franco! She's *naked!*"

Franco shook his head, turning around at her words.

"Shit, these guys!" Maria gasped, turning to examine my hand.

"Ice!" Todd muttered from the door.

Maria took it from him as I glanced down at my hand, nausea sweeping through me.

Ugly purple, blue marks had appeared already, the indentation of the drawer evident on my skin. ,

Tears filled my eyes at the pain, but Maria wrapped the ice around my hand, wincing when I hissed.

"Can you help me get dressed?" I mumbled, nodding to my clothes.

Maria helped me, avoiding my hand as best as she could, even dragging a hairbrush through my hair before tying it up into a loose bun.

"Are you okay?"

"No," I admitted, holding my hand to my chest. "That fucking hurt!"

A soft knock at the door told me Franco was there, and Maria rolled her eyes.

"She's fine, Uncle Franco."

"Ella?" Franco murmured, and I knew he wanted to see for himself.

"It's okay, come in."

Franco dismissed Maria, who was only too happy to skip over to Todd, who looked like he'd seen a ghost.

"Well, that was eventful." I laughed as Franco closed my door.

"Let me see," Franco commanded, lifting my hand into his. "My poor baby."

His lips skimmed the bruises, his eyes meeting mine.

"I mean, a naked Ella is always a pleasant sight."

I rolled my eyes, pointing towards the door.

"Poor Todd."

Franco narrowed his eyes, pushing his lips out.

"Fucker."

Franco tugged me onto his lap, laying back on my bed.

"Wanna watch a film?"

"Yes." I buried my head into his neck as he tugged the duvet around me.

"I'll get you some painkillers. What do you wanna watch?"

Franco tugged his phone out, bringing up Netflix as he handed it to me.

I scoffed, dropping it to the bed.

"I can't hold it."

"Oh, my poor girl." Franco kissed my forehead, crossing over to the bedroom door.

My eyes followed him, my heart aching in my chest at the reaction he conjured from me every damn time.

"Hot chocolate?"

"Yes, please."

Our eyes met as he smirked, and I knew what he was thinking.

He had many ways of making me feel better.

"Anything else?"

"Just you."

TWENTY-SEVEN

ELLA

"I CAN'T BELIEVE this is my last night here," Maria said with a sob. "I want to live here."

I met Franco's eyes across the table, the hurt lurking beneath the soft brown that gazed back at me.

Everything had happened so fast.

One minute I was moving on without him; the next, he was here, and we'd made up. Now it was time for him to leave.

His dark hair curled at the ends from the warmth, his jawline sharp enough to cut glass. The waitress had nearly fallen over herself countless times, often stopping to see if 'we' needed anything.

It was clear it was aimed at my man.

"Uncle Franco, that waitress is hot for you!" Maria winked, nudging me. "You need to get a girlfriend. Or a wife."

I stared at my wine glass, swallowing down my frustration at not being able to tell the world.

"And you, is there any hot Californian guy you've got your eye on?" Maria turned her attention to me as I rolled my eyes, refusing to answer. "Don't you have any friends you could set her up with?"

Franco scoffed, glaring at Maria.

"No."

"You know, if you weren't related, I'd say you would be perfect for one another." Maria grinned as my insides turned to ice. "But you are, so we need to find you both someone else."

"I don't want anyone else," I said with a shrug, as Franco stared at me with surprise.

Maria frowned, sucking on her straw before she gulped down her juice.

"What?"

"Anyone," I corrected myself with a casual grin. "I don't want anyone."

Maria nodded, a confused look on her face.

"So, are you going to let me go out with Todd tonight?" Maria asked hopefully, her eyes locking into Francos as she nudged me.

Maria had a crush on Todd, and selfishly I wanted her to go.

I wanted to spend the last night with Franco without my little sister bugging me.

"To a bar?" Franco drawled, his foot stroking my calf muscle as I shivered.

"No, silly. It's a party, but a chilled one."

"A party?" I echoed, shaking my head. "No, Maria."

I loved Todd, but the thought of my sixteen-year-old sister loose at a party in California with grown men was enough to put ice on my night of fire.

"Come!" Maria suggested, her hands steepling together in a pleading motion. "Please!"

"Our flight *is* in the afternoon." Franco sighed, stroking his jaw as he bit his lip. "I suppose we could."

I stared at him, unsure if he'd forgotten what a night alone felt like.

"A party?" I repeated, glancing at Maria.

Her curls bounced as she nodded with excitement.

"Please!"

"No taking off with boys," Franco ordered, pointing the finger at her.

"I won't, but I'm going to set Ella up with someone so she isn't lonely when we leave." Maria clapped her hands gleefully as I felt the color drain from my face. "Todd said you liked his friend, Dillon?"

Franco's eyes flirted with mine, the brown in his irises now a dangerous black.

"Um, no—" I said hastily.

"Did you guys make out? Chill, Uncle F, before you start." Maria pointed at Franco, who glared at me silently, the possessiveness radiating from every pore.

Dillon.

The Greek foreign exchange student had a massive love affair with America, vowing never to leave.

He kissed *almost* as good as Francesco.

Who was I kidding?

No one kissed like Franco.

"Oh? What's he like?" Franco growled, moving his foot from my leg beneath the table.

"He's male," I offered feebly, as Maria jumped to her feet, waving across the restaurant at Todd, who had just arrived.

"What the fuck?" Franco mouthed to me, and I waved my hand at him dismissively.

"Ages ago. Meant nothing," I hissed back, forcing a smile when Todd slumped into the seat beside Franco, his eyes locked on my little sister.

"Sorry, I'm late. Did you order already?"

"Yeah, but it's okay. The waitress has the hots for my uncle," Maria giggled, staring at Todd from beneath her dark lashes.

As if on cue, the waitress appeared, all gooey eyes and sultry smirks. She gave Todd an appreciative look before staring daggers at Maria and me.

Todd ordered some food, and I tried to ignore the furious look on Franco's face.

It didn't matter if I'd kissed someone in high school; he was beyond possessive.

"I was telling Franco about Ella and Dillon," Maria continued, oblivious to the furious look I gave her.

"Oh, boy. He thinks he's going to marry you." Todd chuckled, accepting a beer from the waitress gratefully.

"Well, he's not," I scoffed, totally ignoring Franco.

I didn't need to look at him to see the fury or the aggressive way he drank his beer.

"I thought you were into him?" Todd grinned, gulping at his beer. "Sure looked like it to me."

"Did it?" Franco asked, his voice surprisingly calm. "I've never seen that side of you, Ella."

His eyes met mine as I flushed, knowing full well he'd seen all of me and more.

"Dillon is like a beacon for women. Looks a bit like you." Todd mused, dumping me further into the shit.

"Like me?" Franco gritted out, shaking his head in disbelief. "Huh."

"Any more hot friends?" Maria innocently asked as Todd gazed at her, a pained look in his eyes.

"Depends who for."

"Ella, of course." Maria batted her eyelashes at him as I jabbed her with my elbow.

"I'm not interested in any of Todd's friends. Or anyone

else, for that matter," I huffed, gulping down my wine as Franco watched me.

"In fairness, you said you were with Dillon to get over your ex," Todd recalled thoughtfully.

"Todd!" I snapped, my eyes wide. "Can you please shut up and stop telling my little sister about my private life?"

Todd chuckled as he held his hands up.

"Alright, sorry…"

"So, this party. Where's it at?" Franco asked, a twinkle in his eyes as he winked at me. "I can't wait to go."

I glared at Franco as Todd exchanged a puzzled look with Maria.

"Maybe you should stay and pack," I suggested, pouring the remainder of the wine bottle into my glass. "You don't want to forget anything."

"I wouldn't. I'm too careful," Franco smirked, his eyes locking onto mine as he tilted his head back, his Adam's apple bobbing as he inhaled the beer.

I can't stop fucking staring at him.

"How's your hand?" Todd asked, clearly trying to change the subject.

"Not great, but what can you do?" I shrugged, lifting the wine glass to my lips. "Whose party is it?"

"Denver's."

"Todd, if Maria goes with you, then I have to go. Which means Franco has to go. Do you think it's a good idea?" I arched a brow at him, smiling smugly.

There's your warning, boy.

Todd shrugged, glancing at Franco.

"Hey, you might like the women—"

"I won't." Franco cut him off, sending butterflies amok in my stomach.

The meal continued in awkward silence, and when we arrived home, Maria dragged me off to get ready.

"Todd's too old for you," I warned her as she rolled her eyes. "He lives in California."

"Does he have a second head I don't know about?" Maria asked innocently, sliding a pair of ripped black jeans over her legs.

"Maybe. If it means you keep away from Todd," I said, staring at my closet.

The wine had made me more chill, but I also wanted something that gave Franco easy access.

I settled on a black leather skirt with a sleeveless roll neck top, thigh-high stockings, and lace-up boots.

"Ooh, rock chick. I like." Maria nodded her approval before coating her lips in a deep scarlet color that made her olive skin glow.

We left the bedroom some twenty minutes later, and my eyes nearly fell out of my head when I saw Franco leaning against the wall.

His hair was slicked back; a cigarette pushed behind his ear as he sipped on a whiskey, his eyes glued to his phone as he frowned. He wore skinny black jeans and a white shirt; the sleeves rolled up to drive me fucking crazy, no doubt.

His lips fell into a natural pout, his eyes locking into my boots as they trailed up my body slowly.

Todd whistled from beside him, but he was gazing directly at Maria.

If he weren't careful, Franco would slice him open.

"Looking gorgeous, ladies," Franco smirked, his tongue wetting his lips as he stared at me.

Maria giggled, her cheeks flushed with excitement as we hailed a cab, her nervous chatter filling the small space. Franco sat up front, his eyes on mine in the wing mirror, shaking his head subtly from side to side.

I shivered, pleased with my outfit choice.

If it drove him insane, then mission accomplished as far as I was concerned.

We arrived shortly after, and it was evident the party was already in full swing; the door to the house was thrown wide open, the music blaring over the lawn as bodies danced.

"Ella," Franco called from the cab as he settled the bill, beckoning me to him.

Maria linked her arm with Todd, and I pointed at him, reminding him who he had on his arm.

"Yes, dear." Todd laughed, heading into the house with Maria.

I strolled up to Franco, tilting my head as he cupped my cheek.

"You look fucking edible, and I fully intend to feast on you tonight," Franco muttered, his thumb dragging my bottom lip down. "But how the fuck am I meant to keep an eye on Maria with you looking like this?"

Without thinking, I lifted onto my tiptoes, my lips brushing against his as his tongue dove into my mouth. I lost my breath as I pulled away reluctantly; our eyes locked on one another as he groaned.

"With great difficulty." I winked. "But you need to know something."

Franco arched his brow.

"What's that?"

"I'm not wearing any panties," I whispered into his ear, inhaling his delicious scent.

"Fuck, Ella!" Franco growled, capturing my hand before I managed to escape. "Might have to make this a quick one then."

I laughed, sure he was joking.

He is joking, right?

Surely he wouldn't—

But then he tugged me down the side of the house, pushing me into an alcove beside the trash cans.

"Here?" I squealed as he unzipped his jeans, pressing me into the darkness, away from prying eyes.

"Here," Franco growled.

"Yo, buddy, I'm trying to take a leak!" Yelped a voice as we froze like rabbits in headlights.

"Yeah? Use the fucking restrooms like everyone else." Franco shot back, but the moment was lost.

I couldn't even contemplate having sex next to some guy pissing, panties or no panties.

Rearranging my hair, I met Franco's pissed-off gaze with a smile.

"Come on, Franco. Plenty of time for that."

Except there wasn't, was there?

He's flying home tomorrow, and I can't even bring myself to think about it. The Franco-shaped hole in my chest was starting to reappear, and there was nothing I could do about it.

Franco walked beside me; his hands jammed in his pockets as he stared at the floor, chewing on the inside of his cheek. He did that when he was worried about something, and without thinking, I reached out, my hand on his chest.

The stones crunched beneath our feet as we came to a halt, and I scanned around us for any sign of Todd or Maria as his hand covered mine.

He exhaled, his breath fanning my face as I smiled, lifting his knuckles to my lips.

"We need to talk about what happens after tomorrow."

It was a statement more than a question, but Franco nodded, his gaze fixed on my lips on my hands.

"Not here. Later?" Franco huffed, his brows furrowing as he nodded toward the door.

"Okay."

My heart fluttered when he gave me a subtle wink, his hand moving to the small of my back.

The party was in full swing, and when I saw the number of people inside, I knew finding Maria would be difficult.

The room stank of weed and alcohol, and I ignored the appreciative looks we both got as we moved through the crowd, our fingers laced together.

My heart stopped when I saw Dillon leaning against the wall, talking to Todd and my sister, his gaze meeting mine through the crowd.

Fuck.

Like a lion sensing another predator, Franco stiffened beside me, reluctantly dropping my hand when we reached the others.

I turned to him, licking my lips as my throat constricted with nerves.

I never wanted these two to meet. Hell, I never expected them to.

"Hi." I waved a hand over Franco, who stared at Dillion with a blank expression, his jaw clenched. "This is Franco. Franco, this is Dillon."

Dillon pushed away from the wall with his foot, nodding at Franco with a curious gaze.

"Hey, Uncle Franco, isn't it?"

Oh god.

"Yeah, but he's only like, five years older than Ella, so… they're like besties." Maria broke the silence, her eyes rolling. "So if you wanna get with my sister, you're gonna have to go through him first."

Shut up, Maria!

Dillon glanced at me, reaching out to kiss me on the cheek as he whispered in my ear.

"Who told her I wanna get with you?"

Franco looked like he was going to explode, and I stepped back, creating some distance between us.

Dillon looked perplexed, and I just felt fucking awkward.

"Say it so the whole class can hear, son," Franco growled, crossing his arms.

Dillon chuckled, running a hand through his jet-black hair.

"I don't want to get with Ella."

Thank you, God.

Relief swam through me as my shoulders relaxed, meeting Todd's confused eyes.

"I wanna marry the girl. How do I get your blessing, man?"

I froze, knowing Dillon had crossed a line.

A fragile line.

"Are you fucking kidding me?" Franco muttered, staring down at Dillon. "Ella, tell this fool."

Tell him what?!

"I'm seeing someone," I said, my heart hammering in my chest when Maria gaped at me.

Todd frowned, screwing up his face in confusion.

"You are?"

I nodded as Dillon narrowed his eyes.

"Who are you seeing, Ella?"

"That's not relevant." I shrugged, avoiding Todd's curious gaze.

"Nah, it is. Only last month, you and I—" Dillon folded his arms, shaking his head. "Fuck, Ella. You're breaking my heart."

Please don't react, Franco.

"Well, it's relevant to me!" Maria shrieked, reaching

out to steal the drink in Todd's hand. "Who? Do you know?"

She looked at Franco expectantly, and he remained silent, a full Russo scowl on his face.

"Guys. Don't ask me anything; I won't tell you. It's early days…shall we get a drink?"

I suggested brightly, praying I'd made it believable.

The alternative didn't bear thinking about.

I dragged Maria behind me, checking Franco was following us.

He was.

"Hold Franco's hand too," I commanded my sister, trying to see over the sea of heads in the direction of the kitchen.

"Yo, you're the bar girl."

I stopped, noticing a customer from work leering at me through glazed eyes.

"Hey. Excuse me." I went to move past him, but his eyes fell to my sister; his lust-filled gaze made me want to vomit.

"Well, hello there, beautiful."

Maria giggled, the sort of giggle you'd expect from a naive fucking sixteen-year-old.

"Back off," I warned, pushing past him as I dragged Maria with me.

"Hey, I'm easy; you'll do." The guy smirked, laughing along with his dickhead friends that had appeared from nowhere.

"She said, back off." Franco squared up to him, the terrifying look in his eyes telling this man he wasn't playing.

"Alright, what are you? Her man? Do you get to fuck them both?"

Crack.

Maria screamed, and I held her to me as Franco punched the guy once, sending him flying into the crowd of people.

"Shit!" I hissed, scanning the room for Todd, instead meeting Dillon's eyes. "Help!"

Dillon flicked me the middle finger, turning away with a bitter smile.

What's wrong with him?!

I reached down, dragging Franco into my arms. My hands pulled him to me, my head buried in his back as I pleaded with him to walk away.

Franco would never walk away from a fight, never.

Insulting Maria and me was probably the worst thing that could've ever happened, but I knew this crowd, and they'd think nothing of jumping him. No matter what Franco was, he couldn't fight fifty guys.

"Franco, please!"

Maria was crying beside me, and rage took hold of me as I shoved Franco toward the exit.

"Ella, I'm here. Go."

As Todd held his hands up at the crowd, my body heaved with relief, ushering Maria and me out as Franco stormed away.

"It's cool. We're cool." I heard Todd muttering, and I gripped Maria, my heart in my throat.

"This was a bad fucking idea," Franco muttered, refusing to slow down.

"Francesco! Slow the fuck down!" I begged, forcing a smile for the sake of my terrified sister, who looked like she'd been through hell.

"Why did Uncle Franco hit that guy?" Maria wailed as Todd pulled her into his arms.

"Because he was a disrespectful prick!" Franco spat.

I hated seeing Franco like this.

It scared me; it made me think he would out us to everyone without a care in the world.

"You can't go around smacking people!" Todd snapped at Franco, smoothing Maria's hair. "Nothing would've happened to her!"

Maria cried harder, and I held my hand up to Todd.

"Don't," I commanded, my eyes reinforcing my words.

One step out of line, and Franco would kill a man.

"Whatever is going on with you two," Todd muttered, waving his finger between me and Franco, who was now at the end of the drive, his hands in his hair. "You need to sort it out. It's fucking weird how you are."

I stared down at Maria, who looked thoroughly miserable. Her mouth wobbled as she took a deep breath.

"You love Uncle Franco, don't you?"

My mind went blank.

"Of course, we all do!" I gushed, but she shook her head, glancing up at Todd.

"No. In a different way."

Holy shit.

TWENTY-EIGHT

ELLA

DENY IT.

"Maria, listen to yourself!" I snapped.

My head swam with dizziness.

My sister was staring at me with wide eyes, and I knew then that she *knew*.

I feel sick.

Franco closed his eyes, inhaling deeply.

"Fuck it."

No. Noooooooooo.

"Francesco, shut up *now*," I commanded, my eyes almost bulging out of my head. "Let's go home."

I fought back the tears on the way home, aware that Todd was only there because of Maria.

I was glad he was there for her despite everything because I was lying through my teeth to her.

She's my *sister*.

Lying to your family is criminal.

I mean, everyone told white lies, right? Some more so than others.

But this?

I'm in love with my uncle.

I didn't care, though. I couldn't help how I felt around him, and I was eternally grateful he felt the same way about me.

As we walked up to our apartment, I felt a tug on my arm.

"Ella?" Maria whispered from beside me.

"Mm?"

Please don't ask me if I'm with Franco.

"I love you."

I glanced over at her, my mouth opening and closing as she nodded.

"I mean it, I do. But you and Uncle Franco ..." her face contorted with disgust, and my heart sank. "It will kill Dad and Grandpa."

Maria dropped her head, moving back before giving me a sad smile.

"I know, but—"

Maria put her hand up, shaking her head.

"Don't. I know you're denying it but stop. It's obvious what's going on. *I—ugh.*"

Maria shook her head as she walked into the house after Todd, leaving Franco and me outside.

I rushed to the door, ignoring Franco's exasperated sigh.

What the actual fuck? My sister knows!

Locking myself in the bathroom, I threw up into the toilet, tears streaming down my face.

This is horrendous.

My sister will tell Dad, and his heart will shatter.

His daughter and his brother?

I retched again, a feeling of despair crippling my empty stomach.

A soft knock on the door echoed through the silent

room.

"Ella?"

Franco.

A sob took over me as I tried to hold it in, the lid of the toilet clattering shut as I rose. I threw water on my face, causing my makeup to stream down my blotchy cheeks.

"Ella, open the door."

I stared at my reflection, a harsh laugh escaping my lips.

I look every inch the disgusting woman I am.

Hooking a towel from the rack, I dried my face, giving Franco the fright of his life when I opened the door.

His eyes softened when he saw me, but my sister sat glaring at him from the sofa.

"Don't be upset."

My eyes searched his, my lower lip trembling.

"Are you serious? Of course, I'm upset."

My words come out in harsh, ragged gasps.

Franco pinched the bridge of his nose, exhaling deeply.

"I know. Maria is upset too, though," he reminded me gently, his eyes locking onto mine. "We have to fly back tomorrow; we all need to get some sleep."

I nodded, moving past him without touching him. Instead, I inhaled his scent, avoiding my sister's eyes.

"Get some sleep, Maria."

"I'm sleeping on the sofa." Maria folded her arms, ignoring my pleading gaze. "Goodnight."

Franco watched me walk into my room, a look of utter desperation on his face.

Our last night together.

Spent like this.

But it wasn't about that now; it was about the fact my sister *knew* I was seeing Franco.

It was the end of everything, And when I looked back at Franco, his eyes told me that he knew.

FRANCO

The cat was out of the bag.

My head would be served to me on a fucking stick, and I was powerless to stop it.

I'm not a pussy, but some beatings still scare the crap out of me.

My brother and my father were top of the list.

Todd, who scowled at me throughout, left after a whispered goodbye with Maria.

"I know you're pissed—"

"It's disgusting," Maria hissed, waving me away. "I honestly don't even know what to say to you. Leave me alone."

I nodded, backing away into my room. Well, Todd's room.

Fuck.

I couldn't sleep.

How could I, knowing Ella was twisting and turning in the room beside mine?

I decided to text her.

FRANCO: Talk to me.

ELLA: I don't know what to say.

Nor did I.

. . .

FRANCO: I'll talk to them when I'm back. Try not to stress, baby. I love you.

ELLA: They're going to kill us. But I love you too. Do you want me to come back with you?

FRANCO: Fuck no—let me talk to them first. Get some sleep. I know it's hard.

ELLA: I love you so much.

FRANCO: Remember that when the shit hits the fan. Love you too.

There was no real way to deal with this other than with honesty. My heart sank at the thought of breaking my dad's heart, not to mention my brothers.

They'll think I'm sick. I didn't care, though; I loved her.

I didn't want them to disown her. Me, I understand.

But Ella losing her family for me? I couldn't bear it.

The rest of the night dragged by agonizingly slowly, and I tried to sleep.

I really did.

But the night has a way of making it all seem so much worse than it usually was, but not in this instance.

You couldn't get much worse.

Eventually, daylight rolled around, and I heard Maria moving around.

"Morning," I greeted her, striding to the kitchen for a juice. "I know you think it's disgusting—"

Maria arched a brow at me, her eyes puffy and red-rimmed

"Can you blame me? My sister and my *Uncle?*"

I winced, nodding.

"I get it, Maria, but it just happened."

Maria laughed bitterly.

"No, Franco. Falling over and grazing your knee *just happens.* Catching a cold *just happens.* Having a relationship with your niece doesn't *just happen!* It's incest!" Her voice shook, her fists bunched up at her sides. "It's ruined our family."

I bowed my head, accepting the tongue lashing.

"Yep, you're right. But it doesn't change anything. So if you don't want to talk to me, that's fine, but don't fall out with Ella."

At that moment, Ella left her room, her face swollen and blotchy.

"I'm sorry, Maria." Ella sighed, walking over to her sister. "I don't expect you to understand, but I want you to know that we never did any of this to hurt you."

Maria remained silent, zipping up her bag.

Ella looked at me desperately.

"We love you."

"I don't *want* your love. It's *sick*." Maria snapped back tearfully. "How could you do this to us? To *Dad?* After *everything?!*"

Ella swallowed, and my heart dropped seeing her in such pain.

"You aren't just my sister, Ella," Maria said, her lip

curling up with disgust. "You're *his* niece. It's wrong. Todd knows too! Everyone is going to know you're sick."

Ella glared back at Maria, the two sisters' eyes to eye.

"If it's sick, then I'm sick. I love him, and I'm sorry it's making you feel this way. But I don't give a damn what anyone else thinks."

"You should! How can you love *him* more than us, Ella?"

Wow.

"Todd's taking me for breakfast. Which is crazy, considering he knows I'm from a fucked up family. I'll leave you two to do whatever it is you do being closed doors. But you're telling Dad, or I will."

Maria ripped open the door to reveal Todd, who stared at us both awkwardly.

"Let's go." Maria pushed past him, tugging the door shut behind her.

I turned back to Ella, striding over to pull her into my arms.

"Is it really so wrong?" Ella sobbed, her fists clutching the shirt on my back.

"Not to us."

"They're going to kill you; let me come with you."

I pulled away, searching her eyes.

"How will that help anything? You live here now; there's no point in you coming back just to face their anger. You know it will be rough; let them cool off before you come back. Please."

The thought of my brother and Dad laying into Ella was too much.

"I love you, though."

I stroked her face, kissing her tear-stained cheeks.

"Then it's worth it, Ella."

Our foreheads pressed together as we inhaled one

another, desperately trying to find the calm within this shitty storm.

"I know, but I'm scared."

I kiss her forehead, pulling her into my arms.

"I've got you, alright? Breathe, baby. Let me deal with it, please."

She nodded against my chest, and I knew without a doubt that she was worth everything and more.

She was my One.

TWENTY-NINE

ELLA

TODD STAYED AWAY THAT NIGHT, and I cried myself to sleep, knowing what Franco would be going through at home.

Through every crisis, we'd had each other's backs, and this was the worst thing we'd ever faced.

The deceit, the lies, the sneaking around.

The unfathomable idea that we had crossed every line.

My phone rang, and I stared at it in horror.

DAD

Oh.

My.

God.

My hand trembled as I reached for the phone, my heart smacking against my chest as I slid the phone to 'answer.'

"Dad?"

"I swear to God, Ella, this had better be some kind of sick fucking joke."

His voice told me he wasn't playing, and the sobbing in the background gave me an insight into his reaction. "Your sister just told me that you…that you and *your uncle*, Ella…."

His voice choked, and I could barely hold the phone to my ear.

"Tell me it isn't true. Tell me you're not that kind of girl and that you'd *never* do something as disgusting as that. Ella! Tell me!"

"I'm so sorry, Dad!"

Silence.

Then he spoke coolly, his voice cracking toward the end.

"You've ripped this family apart. I hope you're happy."

I was left with silence on the other end, and I let the phone fall to the floor, my lungs aching as the breath tore through my body, leaving me doubled over in pain.

My sister and my father despised me.

Franco.

I needed…Francesco.

I picked my phone up, barely able to see through my tears.

Please pick up.

The phone rang until the voicemail kicked in, and I groaned with frustration, nausea gripping my stomach once more.

I didn't feel bad about loving Franco; I'd always known I loved him. I just didn't realize he felt the same.

Once I knew he did, I knew there was no one else that would compare.

But this was horrific.

Thank God I moved.

Otherwise, my dad would have thrown me out, and my Grandpa—

My hand flew to my mouth; my guilt trebled at the idea of how my poor Grandpa must be feeling.

I paced the apartment in the dark, staring at the blank screen on my phone.

I contemplated calling Vanessa, but I didn't have the energy to fill her in on my sister's reaction and the phone call with my dad.

I poured a glass of wine, sliding down the kitchen wall until I slumped onto the floor with a pitiful bump.

This was one of those situations where the only company you have were your dark thoughts, the ones that told you how much of a bad person you were and how awful your decisions have been.

Could I have made better choices?

No.

Not when every time Franco looked at me, I shivered; every touch from his fingers sent me to oblivion.

I wanted to go to the movies with him or for dinner; hold his hand in public.

I wanted to kiss him goodbye before he went to work, promising a home-cooked meal later. I wanted to have children, paint bedrooms with him, travel worldwide, and discover every new experience with him by my side.

Maria's words echoed through my mind, and fresh tears spilled down my cheeks, leaving a trail of warm, itchy skin behind.

How can you love him more than us?

I didn't—I just loved him differently.

I took a deep glug of the wine, wincing at the strength, but anything that distracted me away from my mind was welcome right now.

I topped up the glass, draining it until I wasn't sure I could stand unaided.

But what I did do was crawl to the wine rack and open another bottle.

Franco would call soon.

I just needed to be patient.

My mind drifted to Maria and Todd, and my drunk ass concluded he *might* have been inappropriate with my little sister.

Feeling bold and pretty drunk, I fired off a text, telling him I thought as much.

Todd can fuck off too.

He's probably told the world I had been fucking my uncle, and I'd have to go undercover.

The thought made me grin, imagining myself with a short blonde wig and a rad new image.

I could turn into a goth, and no one would ever know.

I'd need a new name.

Shella? Valentina? Mella?

I liked the A at the end of my name.

I loved my name.

My mother chose it.

Mom.

Something in my gut told me that as much as she may have been disgusted, she would understand.

She'd see how happy he made me.

I knew it wasn't right, but I didn't care.

"I'm sorry, Mom. I've ruined everything; Dad said so. I've been selfish."

Silence.

My phone flashed up, and I saw Todd's name on the caller ID.

"Meh, fuck off," I slurred, tipping the remaining contents of the bottle into my now empty glass. "Fucking perve."

I yawned, calling Franco once more, cradling the phone in my neck as I laid down, staring at the ceiling.

Voicemail.

"Where are you?" I mumbled into the phone, closing my eyes. "I need you."

FRANCO

"I'm not following."

Christopher stared at me, turning back to Maria, who scowled.

"Ella and Franco. They're *in love.*"

My brother laughed, his smile frozen on his face as he frowned at our Dad.

"Maria, what are you talking about?"

"She's right."

Three pairs of eyes turned to me.

"What is she right about, Francesco?" Christopher narrowed his eyes.

I swallowed.

Here we go.

Feet spread apart, Franco. You're about to get knocked out.

"Ella and me."

I braced myself, puffing out the air I didn't even know I was holding in.

Christopher frowned, his eyes crinkling up in the corners as he glanced back at Maria. Her arms crossed, her nails digging in her arms.

"You should see them together. It's *disgusting.*"

A mist descended in my brother's eyes, and he stepped forward, tilting his head toward me.

"You and Ella, Franco? My *daughter?*"

I raised my hands, preparing to explain myself the best I could, when he smashed his fist into my jaw.

I fell back, but he didn't stop, hitting me again, this time in the stomach.

I doubled over, winded but knowing I deserved every blow my brother gave me.

"You pervert! How long!" Christopher roared his hands around my throat.

His eyes were wild; his teeth gritted together as he shook me.

"How fucking long!"

"Christopher!" Dad thundered, his fingers attempting to haul Christopher off me.

"Since I got back from Mexico!" I yelled, shoving him back. "I get it, alright! But I can't help how I feel!"

"Spoken like a true pervert." Christopher snapped, reaching for me again.

I jumped to my feet, meeting my brother's eyes.

"You know I've always looked out for her. You know how close we are. She's five years younger than me; how am I a pervert?"

"Because you're her uncle!" Maria screeched, her hand stinging against my cheek.

"Christopher! Don't." Dad clamped his hand on Christopher's shoulder.

"I'm sorry, Dad. I know it's wrong, but—"

This was it, the moment my dad disowned me.

I thought of Ella and clung to the fact that I was doing this for her, for us.

"You love her?" Dad huffed, shaking his head at me. "If you love her, then nothing any of us say will make a difference."

"That's all you have to say?" Christopher snapped, shoving me in the chest. "My brother and my daughter? Your *son* and your *granddaughter?*"

Dad's watery eyes dropped to the floor, his lips pursing together as he shook his head.

"It's a bad thing, falling for someone you shouldn't. A family member, no less." Christopher snarled, grabbing me by the throat and slamming me against the wall.

"I'll kill you, Franco. I'll fucking kill you."

THIRTY

FRANCO

"YOU'RE NOT GONNA CHANGE ANYTHING!"

This fucking brother of mine isn't calming down anytime soon.

"Better than me than any of those fuckheads, and you know it."

Christopher looked like he was going to swallow his tongue.

Or rip mine out.

"Maria, go upstairs," Dad said with a weary sigh. "*Now*, please."

Maria began to protest, but Dad gave her a look that told her to get her fucking ass upstairs.

"I hate you!" Maria sobbed, shoving past me.

Christoper stepped closer.

"I'm going to make you dig your own grave, and then I'm going to bury you in it. Alive."

You know what?

He means it, the nasty fucker.

I can't blame him. For a hot minute, I put myself in his position, and I want to tear the skin off my face for him.

But.

There's always a but, isn't there?

I love her. I love her so fucking much, and despite it killing my family, I know I'm hers for eternity.

"Go outside and calm down, Chris."

Dad's tone took me back to when we were kids, and Christopher moved back, but he pointed the finger at me, his teeth bared.

"I swear to **god**, Francesco, if Dad weren't here now, I'd fucking kill you."

"I know. I'm sorry, what do you want me to say?!" I snapped back, tearing a hand through my hair.

My jaw ached to fuck, and the sound of Maria sobbing from upstairs completed the soundtrack to my fucking day.

"I want you to tell me this is a joke, a *sick fucking joke*."

"Yeah? Well, it's not."

"Have you slept with my daughter?"

"Out! Now!" Dad interrupted, and I dropped my gaze, refusing to meet his eyes.

Anyone with half a fucking brain cell could see I'd not only fucked her; I'd done it countless times.

The screen door nearly ripped off its hinges when Christopher stormed out, Dad following him.

"Stay here, Francesco."

Well, I was hardly going to follow the bear with a sore head, was I?

I watched as Christopher threw his hands in the air, his face twisted in anger.

Why the fuck am I still here? Fuck this shit.

Whether it was cowardly or not, I left.

I turned around, walked straight out of the front door without once looking back.

So what if I'm her uncle?

I didn't change her diapers, for fucks sake.

We grew up together.

I couldn't imagine not being with her now.

"Francesco!" Dad roared, and I halted, knowing he was too old and damn weak to be chasing me through the streets.

"Dad, I *know*. You think I'm sick—"

Dad strode up to me with determination, his fingers gripping my wrist, bringing me toward him. Dad was someone to be reckoned with in his prime; even now, respect seeped out of my pores for him.

He'd battled on without Mom, and when Christopher's wife—Ella's mother—died, he never left his side.

His gaze softened, his breath wheezing as I guided him to the steps on the porch.

He winced, his hand still gripping my arm as he lowered himself down.

"You okay?" I asked, wondering why he hadn't disowned me yet.

"I've been better, and you know it."

"I know it's wrong, Pops, but I swear, I love that girl. So fucking much."

To my surprise, Dad nodded.

"I know."

"I mean, in a different way than how I should." I clarified, waiting for the *'yep, you're a dick'* speech.

The corners of his mouth twitched, and he glanced at me, chuckling.

Fuck, my old man has lost it.

"Jesus, Dad, it's not funny. Chris just nearly killed me!"

Dad raised his eyebrows, nodding again.

"Yeah, he did. You're still wrong, despite it all, you *know* that, right?"

I frowned, staring at the lawn.

It needs cutting.

"Despite what? I'm not stupid, Dad—"

"No?" Dad snapped, whipping his hand over the back of my head. "So why don't you know when to fucking shut up?"

That slap took me back some years.

"Ow!"

I glared at him, and he waited, pushing his lips out, still fucking nodding.

"I'll just sit here until Chris calls me to start digging, huh?"

Was Dad wired wrong? What did I have to listen to?

All I wanted to do was get in the car and go back to the fucking airport.

I miss my girl.

"You can't be together *here*, Francesco."

"Why haven't you lost your shit?" I asked, my eyes locking onto his.

"Because you can't help who you fall in love with, son."

A harsh laugh escaped my lips, and I snorted, wiping my mouth with the back of my hand.

Dad's lost it.

"You watch too much daytime tv," I muttered, kicking the dirt with my sneakers. "Dad, I'm going. Chris will be out in a minute, and unless you want to watch me get buried, I need to leave."

I rose, dusting my jeans off.

Where the fuck is my brother?

"Ella isn't your niece. Not really." The paper-thin voice said from behind me.

What?

I stumbled, twisting around and frowning.

Either he's lost it, or I have.

"What? Say that again."

My heart was his now. He held it in his fist, metaphorically speaking. It pulsed and bled over his livery white skin, dripping on the floor.

I couldn't breathe, the idea that Ella wasn't my....

What the fuck?!

"I said," Dad cleared his throat, shrugging his shoulders. "Ella *isn't* your niece."

I laughed, unable to contain my disbelief.

"Of course she fucking is. I've seen photos of her as a baby with Chris, you...." My words trailed off.

I racked my brains; sure, I'd missed something.

Every birthday was accounted for in the family albums.

Trips to Disney together. Vacations as kids.

Dad must be bullshitting.

Ella would've said something.

Unless…

Ella didn't know?

Oh my fucking god.

I closed my eyes, my head swimming. Why would Ella not be my niece?

I'm adopted.

My stomach dropped, and I gazed into the eyes that mirrored my own.

I look just like Dad.

Dad grimaced, looking up at me with a sad smile.

"This isn't my place. Telling you this shit."

My eyes bulged, pain shooting through my sockets.

"Not your *place*? You just said Ella isn't my fucking niece!" I roared, barely noticing the screen door opening behind us.

Christopher gaped at Dad, astonishment owning his features.

"She is as good as one, so watch your fucking mouth." Christopher snapped, crossing his arms.

Dizziness swept over me.

"As good as one?" I echoed, my rage bubbling. "Someone better tell me right *now* what the fuck is going on."

"Christopher," Dad commanded, twisting to face my brother. "Please."

Christopher snarled, cutting his eyes at me. "It makes no fucking difference. *You* betrayed *me*."

"Is Ella my niece?" I breathed, swaying on the spot.

Please say no.

"Yes." Christopher barked. "Don't think you're getting off the hook so fucking easy because you're not. You had *no* right to do what you did."

We glared at one another, and Dad coughed, holding his chest.

"'Tell him!" Dad gasped, waving me away when I went toward him. "Just fucking tell him, Christopher."

"It's not right," Christopher argued. "Francesco deserves to feel fucking bad."

I stared at him, forcing him to look at me through sheer will.

"You know what, Christopher? It doesn't matter. I'll get a DNA test, Jerry Springer style. I'm in love with her."

"Don't you *dare* tell Ella!" Christopher moved like a coiled spring, taking me by surprise. Again, he grabbed my shirt, but this time I shoved him back, sending him toppling across the porch.

Maria ran out of the house, helping Christopher up as she looked at me.

My gaze remained on my brother, my chest heaving with rage.

Maria's eyes flickered back to her father.

"Dad?"

"Go *inside*, Maria!" bellowed Christopher, his eyes locked on mine.

"Don't tell Ella what?" Maria pressed, her swollen eyes moving across the three of us skeptically. "Seriously, Dad. Tell me."

"Yeah, tell us!" I demanded, avoiding Maria's murderous glare.

"Don't put yourself in the same sentence as me! There is no *us*, Francesco!"

I rolled my eyes, bored of this.

"Tell me, or I'm getting DNA."

Christopher glared at me, his chest heaving.

"Not that it makes any difference, but Ella isn't my biological daughter." Christopher spat, pointing his finger at me. "But I've had her since the day she was born."

The color drained from my face, my fists clenching beside me.

We aren't blood-related?

I fell back. The wind knocked out of my lungs with the shock of Christopher's confession.

Why the fuck didn't I know this?

Dad stared at the ground, and I knew I'd just uncovered some deep family secret.

"Are you fucking *kidding* me?"

"You're still her uncle, you sick fuck!" Christopher roared.

Maria was sobbing silently; a hand clamped to her mouth.

I'm not her uncle.

The words ran around in my mind, neurons firing in every direction, commanding me to respond.

I'm not her uncle.

Dad rose with difficulty and made his way to Maria. He looked between Christopher and me, moving to the door with a sad shake of his head.

"You two have to talk, no more fists. Or I'll be the one swinging, right?"

My chest felt lighter.

This changed **everything**.

We **could** be together.

"You are still her uncle, whatever you think. It's wrong." Christopher glared at me, tears in his eyes. "You can't tell Ella, Franco." His voice softened, and I glared at him.

"Why can't I? Give me one good fucking reason."

Christopher lifted his eyes to mine, swallowing as tears fell from his eyes.

"Before I met her mother…" he closed his eyes, biting his lip. "She was raped. I'm not Ella's father, no, but I always will be because she doesn't deserve any less."

THIRTY-ONE

ELLA

THE DOOR SLAMMED, jolting me from my drunken doze.

"Ella?"

"Urgh." I sat up, realizing I was still holding the wine glass.

Jesus.

Todd stood at the other end of the kitchen island, his gaze falling on me.

"Really? The floor?"

I rolled my eyes, lifting onto my elbows.

Todd dropped his gym bag on the floor, walking over to me. Crouching down, he sighed, his eyes softening.

"Water or coffee?"

I dropped my head into my hands, remembering that Todd knew about Franco.

"Ella."

"Wine."

"You don't need more wine." Todd pursed his lips, reaching for my hands. "Up."

Hauling me to my feet, he sighed.

"Now I know what the text was about."

What text?

I groped the island, guiding myself to the sofa.

Where is my phone?

"Did you touch my sister?" I tried to glare at Todd, but I almost fell off the couch.

Todd gave me a glass of water, rolling his eyes.

"She's *sixteen*, Ella. How can you even ask me that?"

I wrinkled my nose at the water, shaking my head.

"I saw the way you looked at her."

Todd dropped beside me, his eyes studying me.

He had a way of knowing what I was thinking without me even saying anything, and I knew he was doing it right now.

"She's gorgeous, Ella, but she's sixteen."

Todd dragged his hand across his stubble, a groan leaving his lips when I jabbed him in the stomach.

"You better not. I love my sister."

My words choked in my throat when I remembered the way my sister had looked at me before she'd left.

Utter disgust.

"She loves you too." Todd gazed at me, reaching for my hand. "I just think the whole Franco thing…."

I grimaced, dropping my head.

"Fucking my uncle. You can say it," I declared, eyeballing the location of the wine rack.

I needed more wine, and if Todd wasn't going to get it for me, I'd get it my damn self.

My strides were wide, probably too wide. I made it back to the island, giggling through my tears.

"Ella," Todd whispered from behind me, lifting my arm over his shoulder. "I'm going to take you to bed. You've drunk enough."

"I slept with my uncle. Do you think I'm sick?" I sobbed against him, my nose buried in his neck.

"Why did you do it?" Todd asked softly, nudging open the door to my room. He ignored my question.

He thinks I'm sick.
I'd better get used to people thinking that.

"Because I love him."

I did.

I'd *always* loved Franco, and it was a nightmare from start to finish.

"I can't ever be with him. My family hates me."

I gripped Todd's neck, bringing him down onto the bed, praying he could say something, anything to make me feel better.

"You're drunk, love. Just get some sleep; we'll talk in the morning."

"I don't have a family. I ruined everything." I wailed, refusing to release Todd.

"Nah, you haven't."

"I should've settled with Jackson, even though he was a knob."

"Jackson?"

"Or Dillon, I'm not related to him."

It was true; I could've.

"Not many men can resist you, Ella. You can have *anyone* you want."

I nodded, releasing him from my grasp. I fell back onto the bed when I realized Todd hadn't moved.

"Anyone," he repeated, his hand cupping my cheek. "You don't have to ruin everything to be with Franco."

"I've ruined it, too late." I sang, closing my eyes. "I'm going to hell."

Todd curled up beside me, his fingers lacing with mine.

"Plenty of people are, Ella. Everyone fucks up; it's what they do *after* that makes the difference."

I pressed my face into the soft pillow beneath me, the wine sloshing in my stomach as I wondered when the fuck everything got so complicated.

"Todd?"

"Mm?" He mumbled sleepily into my hair.

"What am I going to do?"

He groaned, pulling me into his arms, kissing the back of my head softly.

"Sleep. We'll talk in the morning."

FRANCO

This isn't fucking okay.

I was lying in bed, staring at the ceiling like it was going to open and reveal the answers.

I should feel happy, but instead, I felt hollow.

Is my Ella a product of rape?

I couldn't bear it.

Christopher had told me everything he knew, but it wasn't much.

What should I do? Turn up at Ella's door and tell her I had good news and bad news. Which did she want first?

Fucks sake.

I kicked back the sheets, huffing out an exasperated breath.

I could be with Ella now, bells and whistles really, Christopher be damned.

I want to marry the girl.

It felt like my future, the one I'd always secretly dreamt of, was finally within my grasp, and I had to let it go.

Yet how to tell her we weren't related?

My heart sank at the idea of her beautiful face crumpling with the news, but she had a right to know.

I'd support her, remind her every fucking day that her biological father's actions didn't reflect on her.

Ever.

That she was the best thing in the world, and I'd always known it.

God.

It's pointless being in bed.

These nights didn't happen to me too often, but I wasn't patient enough to wait for sleep.

I didn't wait for anyone or anything but Ella.

Ella.

I'd avoided her calls, her drunken voicemail breaking my fucking heart.

I'd already gone against my family once, once again wouldn't be too much of a surprise, surely?

I chewed on the inside of my cheek, throwing across the duvet. My skin was damp with sweat, and despite the windows being open, it felt like there was no air anywhere.

I didn't want to have to be the one to tell Ella, but I wanted her so much I probably had to.

I walked into the kitchen, pouring a glass of water, half-heartedly wondering whether to tip it out and fill it with whiskey.

In fact, fuck it.

That's a better idea.

I drained the amber liquid, enjoying the burning it created as it traveled down my throat.

I smacked my lips together.

Good stuff, whiskey.

I topped up my glass, noting it was enough to stun a

horse. Then, I crawled over to the sofa, hugging a pillow close to my chest.

I'm so fucking in love with her. It's insane.

Before long, my eyes closed, my brain projecting cruel images of me meeting Ella as some girl in a bar, her eyes sparkling with delight.

In my dreams, Ella looked at me with intrigue and fascination, her delicious smile making my mouth mirror hers, a stupid grin on my face when she asked me my name.

I wouldn't be Franco Russo, and she wouldn't be Ella.

A modern-day Romeo and Juliet, that's what we were.

But not in my dreams.

It's safe here.

So I slept.

THIRTY-TWO

ELLA

I WOKE to find my duvet wrapped around me, a large glass of iced water and painkillers beside my bed.

My head felt like someone had played a tune with a sledgehammer.

Badly.

I gulped at the water, the ice chilling my teeth, warning me that sensitivity was going to be the word of the day.

Sunlight shimmered through the window, and I scowled at it.

Fuck being happy and yellow.

I tugged the duvet over my head, twisting to find the bed empty beside me, the pillow I pulled into my arms smelling like Franco.

My eyes pinged open, sitting up abruptly.

Is Franco here?

I forced my rubbery legs out of my bed, staggering to the door like a resurrected corpse.

Todd laid on the sofa, his hands laced behind his head as he watched the television.

At the sound of my body falling into the wall mid-yawn, he sat up, his eyes wide.

"You alright?"

I recovered as I swallowed down vomit, scanning the room.

"Is Franco here?" I asked, possibly with a slur.

Todd's brows furrowed, shaking his head.

"No, Ella. He's not."

"But…" I closed my eyes, refusing to acknowledge the tears that stung them. "My pillow smelt like him, and I had water. Iced water, my—"

"Favorite. I know, I made it." Todd said flatly, a hand massaging his temple and cheek simultaneously.

"Oh." The disappointment was evident in my voice, and I turned, heading back into my bedroom. I remembered my manners, stopping to murmur a "Thanks" to Todd.

"It says on the calendar you're working tonight," Todd called after me. "Do you want me to call them for you?"

Urgh.

Work?

"No. I need the money."

"Ella." The disapproving tone in Todd's voice told me he wasn't impressed.

"What?" I yelled, falling back into my bed.

As far as I was concerned, I had at least eight hours of sleep to look forward to.

"It's two in the afternoon."

It can't be.

"No!" I wailed, dropping into my bed.

Todd chuckled, and I heard him moving around.

Cleaning again, probably.

"Is it *really*?" I stuck my hand out, feeling for my phone on the bedside table.

I relaxed when I felt the phone beneath my fingers, the cool glass soothing my panic.

No missed calls.
No messages.

The only thing the phone did, however, was confirm that it was two in the afternoon.

"Fuck my life."

"Here, I made you a sandwich,"

Todd said from the doorway.

I lucked out on the roommate lottery.

"Todd, you're like a woman. An old, fussy, wonderful woman." I took the plate gratefully, praying my stomach held it down.

My shift tonight was the only one I'd had since Franco and Maria had been here, and money didn't grow on trees.

Where did that saying even come from?

I made a mental note to Google it.

"I'd like to think if I *were* a woman, I'd be hot." Todd mused, crossing my room to open my blinds.

I hissed at him, and he chuckled, opening the window.

"Like Megan Fox."

"Mm," I agreed, chewing on the soft white bread. "She's beautiful."

"What about you?"

I pause, examining the sandwich. It had just the right amount of butter on too. *God bless Todd.*

"I'd be...hmm...Cody Christian."

Todd rolled his eyes, plopping down at the end of my bed.

"Yet your type is Dillon and…." Todd made a face. "Franco."

"Dillon is not my type," I scoffed, shaking my head. "Not anymore."

Todd sighed.

"Aside from that, you've clearly got a physical type. They're both dark-haired. Both hot. Confident. Except Dillon is a streak of piss. Useless bastard." Todd choked on his laughter, rolling his eyes at me.

"He's awful."

"Hey, you once said Dillon was a dream."

I picked at the crumbs on my plate, shrugging my shoulders.

"Dreams are a waste of time."

"Don't say that, love." Todd grinned at me, taking my plate. "Call in sick, and we'll order takeout and watch shit."

"I'll be broke at this rate."

"You know I've got money, shut up."

There was no arguing with Todd when he was like this.

THIRTY-THREE

FRANCO

THE POUNDING on the door sent me falling off the couch, slamming my head into the table.

"Ow, fuck!" I muttered, holding my head.

I sighed, pulling open the door to see Maria waiting, her arms crossed.

What the fuck is she doing here?

"Finally," she huffed, pushing past me in a cloud of some teen perfume.

Come in, why don't you?

"What do you want, Maria?" I glared at her, leaving the door open so she could leave as quickly as she'd arrived.

I didn't want her here.

Maria hopped onto the kitchen counter, swinging her legs.

"I wanted to apologize for my reaction."

I grunted, waving at the door expectantly.

"Great. Now go."

Maria narrowed her eyes, flicking her hair over her shoulder.

"Close the door because I'm not leaving."

"You aren't? Do I need to kick you out?"

Who did this kid think she was?

I'd allowed the slap to slide, but I had zero intention of talking to the little bitch.

"You wouldn't." Maria examined her nails, and I frowned.

"I would. Get out."

"Franco," Maria huffed, scowling at me. "I think you need to consider who you're talking to."

If I hadn't had been so shocked, I think I'd have dragged her out by her fucking hair.

The kid dared to flutter her fucking eyelashes at me, her gaze trailing over my bare chest.

Fuck, no.

"If you do, I'll tell my sister you made a pass at me."

Blood rushed through my ears, and I staggered back, her eyes locking onto mine.

"I would never touch you," I spat out. "You're sixteen and my niece!"

Maria rolled her eyes, jumping down from the counter.

"Ella was your niece. I mean, she's not now, but she was as far as you were aware, and you *still* fucked her."

I shook my head as she dragged her nails lightly down my arm, biting her lip.

"Why not fuck me?"

Jesus fucking Christ.

I shook her off, but she grabbed the back of my head, attempting to tug my head to hers.

Her strawberry-flavored lip gloss covered my lips, and I almost gagged.

"Get the fuck off me, you *stupid* fucking child!" I growled, throwing her away from me.

Tears formed in her eyes, hatred seeping from her pores.

Does she...have a crush on me?

Fuck!

That makes more sense.

Her extreme reaction...the desperation to tell our family...

What the fuck?!

"I mean it, Maria, get the fuck out before I do something I'll regret." I snapped, stepping back.

"Why is it always Ella?!" Maria screamed, hot tears falling down her cheeks.

Oh man, she's jealous.

Of Ella.

I mean, I got *why*. Ella was just a ray of fucking sunshine, complete with a killer attitude and beauty to match.

My heart ached thinking of her.

I wish she were here.

"Maria—"

"Everyone wants her! Jackson, you and even Todd!"

I stilled, tilting my head towards the front door.

If anyone saw us like this, they'd jump to the wrong fucking conclusion—*wait, what did she just say?*

So this is the problem. Maria thinks Todd has a thing for her older sister.

I don't have time for this shit.

"You're talking bullshit. Ella is with *me*."

"So?" Maria hissed, stepping closer to me. Her eyes were wide with fury; her teeth gritted together. "You're her fucking uncle, and you risked everything to be with her. Todd is hopelessly in love with her, and she doesn't even know. It's not fair!"

A sob choked in her throat, her hand covering her mouth as she sank into a chair, her shoulders trembling.

"Fucking hell, Maria," I breathed, waving a hand around. "Life isn't fair! Look at Ella and me; you think that's fair? No. Shit happens."

Maria's head snapped up, her eyes shining with tears.

"I'm *always* second to her, in every way! Now...now she's not even my real sister. Maybe that's why she's always been the favorite."

A fit of anger rose in me, and I knew if I didn't get her out of my sight, I was going to lay into her so badly the kid would be scared.

"She's your **sister**."

"The same way she's your **niece**?" Maria snapped back, cocking an eyebrow.

This bitch, honestly.

"No." I gritted out, dangerously close to the edge. I wanted to slap her damn face. "There's blood between you. You have the same mother."

At the mention of her mother, her eyes dropped, and she sniveled.

"All this time, Maria, Ella has looked after you, despite you being nothing but a little bitch to her." I roared, sick of her woe-is-me act. "She *always* puts you first. And what do you do?"

Maria shook her head, frowning as she mumbled something incoherent.

I don't want to hear her shit or lame-ass excuses.

"You tell her family something that wasn't yours to tell. Then, you try to kiss the man she's in love with and threaten to spread lies about me if I don't. What the fuck is wrong with you?"

Maria stared down at the floor, her cheeks pulsing with color.

"You don't fucking deserve her, Maria. Oh, and for the record, Todd isn't interested in you because you're an immature little kid, not because of Ella."

Maria jumped to her feet, pointing her finger at me.

"I'm not immature!"

I rolled my eyes, lighting a smoke and inhaling deeply.

"Get out of my house, Maria."

"No one will ever accept you," Maria hissed as she pushed past me. "You'll always be that weird couple who are related, and I'm not standing by either of you."

"I'm wounded." I laughed bitterly.

"Ella will be, even if you're not." Maria threw over her shoulder, letting the door slam shut behind her.

I stared at the door, realizing that despite her bullshit, she was probably right about one thing.

We'd never be accepted.

Did that matter?

I guess it does because everyone wants to be happy.

Ella deserved to be happy; she deserved the grand proposal, the white picket fence, and kids.

She deserved better.

But she wanted me, right?

I exhaled, watching the smoke drift across the kitchen.

What to do?

I caught sight of my phone and saw a text message from Ella.

ELLA

Don't shut me out.

. . .

She was right. This was her business too.

I called her, sucking in another drag from my smoke before she answered, her voice faint and tired.

"Franco?"

"Hey, baby." I closed my eyes as she wept and cursed myself for being such a dick. "I'm sorry I didn't call. It was a bit...hectic."

"Was it?" Ella whispered, and my shoulders slumped. "What happened?"

"It didn't go down well. Maria told your old man."

"Oh my god."

"He wasn't pleased, as you can imagine."

Ella was silent, but her ragged breathing told me she was listening.

"They know now, anyway."

There was a blanket of silence between us until Ella muttered, "and?"

Time to be an asshole.

Is it selfish of me to tell her that we're not related and why?

"Francesco, talk to me," Ella commanded softly, her voice breaking.

"If we want to be together, baby, we'll have to move away."

I was delaying, but I couldn't break the news over the phone like that. She's a product of such a vile act.

"What did they say?"

"Listen." I ignored her question, hating myself for it. "I'm going to come back to you. We'll talk then, alright?"

"Okay. When?"

She was desperate to see me.

I knew that feeling because I felt like I couldn't function without her.

Nothing made sense anymore.

Something so wrong was now possible, legally at least, but still frowned upon by society and our family.

Tough decisions had to be made, and I couldn't make them myself.

I needed my girl, and she needed me.

"As soon as I can. I'll text you, alright?"

"Hurry, Franco. I feel like my heart is breaking. My dad called…."

I closed my eyes, stubbing out my smoke.

I can't bear to hear her in this much pain, not when I can't reach out and touch her.

"Your dad will calm down, baby, trust me. Look, I love you. I'm coming to you, okay? Just hang tight."

"I need you."

My heart sank at the desperation in her voice, and I strode upstairs, already intent on packing.

"I'm coming, sweetheart. Stay strong."

"Todd's here. He's been great, but…" her voice faded, and I knew what she meant.

He wasn't me.

"I love you too, so much. I'll book a flight as soon as I can; keep your phone on you."

"I'll meet you at the airport."

"No, it's cool. I'll need a car. I'll let you know when I've booked a flight, gorgeous. Love you."

"I love you too, so much."

Thank God because I can't live without You, Ella.

I didn't want to have to try.

THIRTY-FOUR

ELLA
———

"TWO DAYS."

Todd grimaced, reaching out to squeeze my hand.

"Why can't he get a flight for two days?!"

"It's summer, honey. It's busy, everyone is flying out for the beaches and the stars, you know the drill."

Todd had been my rock since he'd found me in a drunken mess on the floor.

"I mean, it's cool, we can do another movie marathon, make pizzas—"

I gave him a wry smile, lifting my chin.

"No, I'm going to work. I can't hide from everyone forever."

Todd looked panicked, his tongue wetting his lips as he sat up.

"Nah, Ella, I don't think that's the best idea."

"Why?" I arched my brow. "I can't wallow in here all day long, every day. As much as I love being holed up with you," I added with a grin.

"Yeah, but, umm…." Todd raked a hand through his hair, wincing at me.

He had a way of speaking with his eyes, and right now, they told me he was scared of me getting hurt.

The question was, why?

"Our friends know about you and your un—shit, I mean Franco."

"Oh," I whispered dejectedly. "Everyone?"

Todd scrunched up his eyes, holding his hands up to me.

"It didn't come from me, Ella."

Dillon.

That bastard.

"I see." I exhaled, slumping into my seat.

"What's the plan when Franco gets here?" Todd asked, sighing when his phone beeped.

His eyes clouded over, a look of guilt splashing across his features which he tried to hide.

"I don't know," I answered honestly. "Who was that? Was it my sister?" I looked pointedly at the phone, my heart hammering in my chest.

Todd groaned, tossing the phone onto the table.

"Yep."

Part of me was grateful he'd told the truth because the knot in my stomach eased somewhat. If Maria was texting Todd, it meant she was okay, right?

"Did she mention me?"

Todd shook his head, giving me a sad smile.

"No. She's just talking about starting senior year."

My heart shattered at the thought of not being there for my sister, knowing how much she relied on me to keep her organized and sane.

Her anxiety and temper got her into so much trouble at times, and senior year was hard enough without facing it alone.

"Can you send her my love?"

Todd grinned, showing me his phone.

"I always do."

I smiled faintly, and Todd studied me.

"So you're going to do it? Continue your relationship with Franco?"

I nodded, avoiding his disappointed gaze. "I don't have much choice. I love him."

Todd frowned.

"But is it worth losing your family?"

I whipped my head to him, my heart in my throat.

"I can't help how I feel, Todd."

He looked away, and I couldn't help but wonder why he was suddenly so concerned.

"You disapprove, don't you?" I asked, heaving a sigh. "It's okay; I guess I have to get used to it."

Todd made a face before turning to me.

"I just want you to be sure. It's a big decision to make."

"What if it were you? What if you fell in love with someone that society didn't want you with?"

"My aunt is terrifying—I can't see it happening with her. She has fourteen chihuahuas." Todd shuddered, and I giggled, imagining Todd sitting amongst her and her dogs. "She's got two ex-husbands too."

"You know what I mean."

"Yeah, I know." Todd paused. "I guess if you love someone, it doesn't matter about who they are, right?"

I grinned, nodding.

"Exactly."

"But then again, some things are frowned upon for a reason, aren't they?"

Children.

I knew before he said it that it's what he was referring to.

A hollow ache within my core added to my overwhelming feeling of sadness, and I shrugged.

"Guess I'll never be having kids."

"You could always adopt?" Todd suggested, and I couldn't help but pull him in for a hug.

He always knew the right thing to say, and even now, he was trying to make a bad situation better.

"Have I told you I love you?"

"Yeah, get in line, love." Todd winked, kissing my forehead. "I'm going to the store for beer. Want anything?"

"Chocolate?" I asked hopefully, swallowing the lump that had formed in my throat.

Todd's support was everything right now, especially in a city where everyone knew my shit and was no doubt judging me regardless.

To know I had a friend like him made everything so much better.

"Of course, chocolate," Todd drawled, grabbing his wallet and keys from the side. "Beer and chocolate."

I grinned as he left, giving me that goofy smile that I loved so much. I snuggled into the comforter, checking my phone to see a text from Franco.

FRANCO:
Counting down the hours.

A tingle of excitement shot through my stomach, my teeth sinking into my bottom lip as I squealed with delight. The one man I'd always wanted was finally mine.

ELLA:

Me too.

Of course, everything came with a price, and the thought of never speaking to my family again made me want to vomit. I'd already deceived them, disappointing them beyond belief. They were no doubt disgusted with me. The only people I had left in the world were my family. I couldn't even entertain the look on my Grandpa's face when he'd found out.

I began to doze, my head jolting forward some hours later to find the tv was still on, and there was no sign of Todd.

"Todd?" I called out, my voice croaky and thick with sleep.

No reply.

I threw the comforter back, reaching for my phone in a sleepy haze.

Is he asleep?

It was barely nine pm.

Todd had been gone for just over an hour; the store was across the street.

I scrambled to my feet, heading for his room.

His bed was unmade, but there was no sign of him.

"Huh. Weird."

I checked the bathroom and even my bedroom, but there was no sign of him.

"Todd?" I called out again, panic uncurling in my stomach.

Maybe he'd seen friends and gone out for some drinks.

Yeah, that was likely.

I relaxed a little, pulling up his name to send him a text.

. . .

ELLA:
Hey, where's my chocolate?!

I dropped the phone back to the table, yawning. Friends was on TV, and I watched with amusement, passing at least another half an hour before I realized Todd hadn't replied.

I bit my lip, glancing towards the door.

This was odd.

I decided to call him.

The voicemail kicked in immediately, Todd's lovely voice greeting me to tell me that he wasn't able to take my call.

It was then that the feeling of dread returned, but it was heavier than before, more of a deadweight than anything else.

What could I do, call the police? Hey, my friend went to get chocolate and beer, and he didn't return?

Ha.

They'd laugh at me.

Still, I was worried.

I gnawed on the inside of my cheek, my heart thumping in my chest. Despite my rational thoughts, my heart and instincts seemed to be telling me something else.

Something was wrong.

Going with my gut, I pushed my sneakers on, opening the door to the warm air of Los Angeles. My legs trembled as I descended the stairs, my heart in my throat.

What the hell was wrong with me?

My senses were heightened like I was in a dream.

Or a nightmare.

"Jeez, Ella, pull yourself together," I scolded myself, turning the corner.

A crowd had gathered at the end of the block, and the feeling of dread swept through me like a wave.

Todd.

My steps quickened, nausea in my throat.

I pushed through the crowd, ignoring the puzzled looks and scowls.

"What's happened?" I breathed, staring down at the crimson stain on the sidewalk.

No.

"Some poor kid got mugged." A man to my left shook his head. "Poor bastard. He was only young." He did a double-take, looking at me. "Are you okay, Miss?"

Drums sounded in my ear, the floor swaying beneath me.

"Where is he?" I whispered as the woman beside the man peered at me.

"The morgue, I'd guess."

My hand flew to my mouth, but I was too late; the vomit hit the floor before I had a chance to warn anyone.

"Jeez, lady, you on drugs?" someone yelled, but I backed away until I hit the brick wall of my apartment building.

There, on the ground, were the keys to my apartment.

Our apartment.

THIRTY-FIVE

ELLA

MY HEART SLAMMED SO hard in my chest I couldn't breathe; the idea that my closest friend had been mugged and killed getting us treats made my stomach empty once more.

"Are you okay, Ma'am?"

I stared at the ground, wiping my mouth on my arm as I trembled.

No, I'm not fucking okay. Not at all.

Instead, I nodded, lifting my head to see a kind-eyed policewoman peering at me, her curls escaping from the rigid hat on her head.

"You don't look okay."

"I think I knew the man that died," I choked out, waving a hand to the scene behind me.

The policewoman frowned, pulling out a notepad and pen.

"What's your name, sweetheart?"

"Ella Russo."

"No one died here, Ella," the policewoman said softly. "But someone was attacked."

Todd's not dead?!

Relief rocked my body, my hands now gripping onto the policewoman's forearms as she steadied me, eyeing me like I was a bomb about to detonate.

"Todd? Is he okay?"

"What's your address?"

Scribbling away on her pad, the policewoman asked questions, nodding here and there, lifting her brows occasionally.

"All I know is that the victim has been taken to the ER. You'll need to be family to see him, but I'm assuming you know them if you live together?"

No, not really. Not at all.

Todd never talked about his family, and I'd never pressed. Other than his comment about his aunt the other night, he hadn't volunteered much about it.

"Um, yeah," I lied, my eyes focusing on the crimson stain on the asphalt ahead.

Todd!

"I have to go," I rasped out, fighting back fresh tears.

The policewoman nodded, a kind smile on her face.

"Do you have someone to support you, sweetheart?"

Franco.

I reached for my phone, nodding dismissively at the woman. I strode away, tears blurring my vision as I sobbed into the phone, hearing the voice that had the ability to soothe me instantly.

"Ella? What's wrong?"

I couldn't speak.

"Ella? For fucks sake, speak to me! Are you hurt?"

The fear in Franco's voice jolted me from my despair, my voice trembling as I finally spoke.

"Todd's been mugged." I choked out, waving at a cab desperately.

To my relief, it stopped, and I babbled to the driver that I needed to get to the medical center urgently.

The driver nodded, putting his foot down as he battled the traffic.

"Shit, is he okay?" Franco breathed, and I knew he was genuinely concerned.

"I don't know," I whispered. "I'm so scared; what if he dies? There was so much blood on the street…."

"Hey," Franco soothed, only making me cry harder. "Baby, listen. Breathe. I'm flying out tomorrow, I'll be with you soon, but I'm only at the end of the phone. So I'll stay on it until I board that damn plane if I have to."

"Thank you," I whispered, clutching the phone to my ear, the heel of my other hand curving into my watery eye.

"I love you, baby; it will be okay."

"Franco, what if he dies?"

The thought reminded me of my earlier pain, and nausea rose in my throat again. The cab crawled through the traffic, which was here whatever the hour.

"Don't think about that. Take it slowly. Did you manage to speak to anyone that saw what happened?"

As the cab took me closer to Todd, I filled Franco in, his calm voice reassuring me until my tears dried up.

"I'm here. I'll call you when I know something." I paid the driver, tipping him twenty bucks without thinking.

"Thanks, lady," The driver said, giving me a sympathetic smile. "I hope your friend is okay."

I nodded, still gripping the phone to my ear.

"I love you. Be strong," Franco whispered, and I pushed through the revolving doors, my heart in my mouth.

People were everywhere, in wheelchairs and stretchers, clustered together in waiting rooms that smelt of death and illness.

I swallowed and made my way to the reception desk, my hands trembling.

"Hi, I'm here to see Todd Daysron." Blood pounded in my ears as I gripped the edge of the desk, my knuckles turning white.

The man at reception nodded, tapping away on his computer.

"Are you family?" He asked, watching me carefully.

I stared at his salt and pepper hair that curled at the ends, at the pasty skin that revealed veins I didn't want to see.

"Yes," I lied too easily. "I'm his cousin."

"He's being operated on right now, but you're welcome to take a seat and wait." The man smiled kindly, revealing a set of crooked teeth.

"He's alive?" I sobbed, unable to hold back my emotion.

"Ella?" Uttered a voice from somewhere in the distance, but I didn't turn; I focused on the man with the salt and pepper hair.

"Right now, he is, yes."

The man's gaze flickered behind me, and I turned, my stomach dropping when I saw Dillon panting, his cheeks flushed.

"What the fuck happened?"

It didn't matter about us.

All that mattered was Todd.

I bit my lip, more tears spilling down my cheeks as I walked over to him, my relief at no longer being alone sweeping over me.

"Dillon…"

Dillon paled, his eyes searching mine as he shook his head.

"Is Todd…"

"No. He's not dead; the doctors are operating on him," I told him as he raked a hand through his hair, his eyes watering.

"Fuck! I was heading over to see him...and I saw the commotion. I spoke to a policewoman who described Todd, and I came here as soon as I could."

I nodded, staring past him at the wall that was littered with leaflets about domestic abuse, cancer, and all other kinds of illnesses and diseases.

"He was mugged."

Dillon closed his eyes, pinching the bridge of his nose as he exhaled.

"Bastards. He's not exactly a little guy, though. There had to be more than one guy."

"There was so much blood...." I clamped my lips together, trying to block out the memory of the street stained with blood.

Dillon's eyes softened, and he reached out to hold my hand.

"Hey, come here. I'm sorry about everything, I know you probably hate me, but this is about Todd."

I laced my fingers through his, nodding.

It didn't matter about Dillon.

I didn't care.

I was grateful someone was here with me; someone was holding my hand when I felt like I was going to be violently sick.

"Sit down, Ella." Dillon scanned the room, leading me to a seat by the entrance.

Warm air blew in with every person that walked in, and I ached with pain at the worry in the eyes of almost everyone here.

My heart felt like it was being stamped on, the thought

of Todd being beaten for money sending fury through my veins.

Why? Why him?

Dillon sat beside me, his head in his hands. Dillon was Todd's best friend, and without thinking of the bad blood between us, I reached out to pat his back.

"I can't lose him." Dillon turned to me, his eyes wild with fear. "I don't…I can't…."

His words ceased, but I didn't need him to finish the sentence.

I knew.

Todd was amazing. A true ray of light that would do anything for anyone. He didn't deserve this, not that anyone deserved to be mugged, but Todd was too goofy, too loveable to suffer like this.

Dillon held my hand to his cheek, and his tears cooled the skin that was alive with fury and fear.

"He'll be okay," I mumbled, ignoring the gnawing feeling in my stomach that told me he might not be.

"He has to be," Dillon choked. "There are cameras on that corner, Ella. We'll find who did this."

"We will," I vowed, a wave of dark anger rising within me.

It felt like days, but it was only hours before a nurse came out, calling out Todd's name.

We leaped up, and she frowned at the two of us, checking her clipboard.

"Are you both family?"

"Uh, no," Dillon said with a defeated grimace.

"Just me," I said, my fingers on her arm.

Dillon stared at me through red-rimmed eyes, but I gazed at the nurse. "How is he?"

The nurse beckoned us to follow her before she lowered her voice.

"He has no next of kin listed. So you're his cousin, right?" She checked, watching me.

No next of kin?

"Yes."

Fuck, lying was easy. I didn't care, though; I'd say I was his mother if it was feasible.

The nurse sighed.

"Well, could you contact the rest of your family?"

My heart hammered in my chest; my voice seized in an invisible fist in my throat.

"What? Yes. How is he?!" I snapped, unable to resist.

"He's stable. He's sedated, but his wounds are pretty deep." The nurse sighed, stroking my arm. "But we think he's through the worst of it. The mugger wasn't as fortunate if that helps."

Dillon's head snapped up, and the two of us gaped at the nurse.

"You have him? The guy that did it?" I asked, my voice shrill.

I'll kill the fucker.

"He died," The nurse said gravely, hanging her head. "When Todd is awake, the police want to have a chat with him."

I reeled, falling back onto Dillon, who held me upright, his hands digging into my shoulders.

"Why would the police want to talk to him? Surely it was self-defense?" Dillon voiced my thoughts as the nurse scanned the two of us.

"Look, I can't say much more. But at least Todd is alive. So let's be grateful for that. Are you going home? Do we have a number we can call?"

"We're staying," Dillon said firmly.

I nodded in agreement, and the nurse eyed me.

"You're welcome to wait, but if this guy isn't related, I'm afraid he can't."

"You can't stop me sitting in a waiting room," Dillon argued, stiffening.

"He's with me." I waved a hand at the nurse, lacing my fingers with Dillons.

"He's your boyfriend?" The nurse frowned, and Dillon squeezed my hand.

"Yes. Can he come in?"

In for a penny, in for a pound.

Dillon loved Todd too; if I was there, so was he.

Todd needs his best friends, I told myself.

Franco would understand.

The nurse led us to Todd's room, and my heart shattered at the sight of Todd hooked up to a host of different machines, his skin grey and pasty. His face was swollen, one eye half-open despite him being sedated.

Chocolate and beer.

I wept again, this time into Todd's hand, as Dillon sank to a chair beside me, his head in his hands.

"Fucking bastard deserved to die!" I hissed, but Dillon didn't respond. When I turned to him, I saw his shoulders shaking, tears flooding his cheeks.

"He needs to wake up, Ella. He has to."

You do, Todd. We need you.

THIRTY-SIX

ELLA

DILLON and I had sat on either side of Todd, our eyes watching him for any sign of movement. I felt like my eyes were too big for my head, swollen from crying.

Todd was perfectly still, but I focused on the rhythmic rising and falling of his chest, my head resting in the palm of my hand.

"At least he's healing," I said to Dillon, unsuccessfully suppressing a yawn.

Dillon nodded, his gaze moving from Todd to me.

"Did that nurse say he had no next of kin listed?"

I frowned, vaguely remembering something like that being said.

"Yeah, but maybe he just didn't fill it in or something when he moved here."

Dillon shook his head.

"He's never mentioned his family to me. Not once."

I looked at him with surprise.

"No?"

Dillon sighed.

"No. I bored Todd to tears with tales of mine, and he

never said a word. Although, I did ask a few times...." Dillon shrugged. "He just said it was complicated, and I dropped it."

We were silent then; both lost in our thoughts.

I'd never spoken about family for the fact I didn't want to talk about Franco.

Todd never pushed it, but he'd listened to me crying about my ex.

"Shit, I need to call Franco." I tugged my phone out, rising to my feet.

Dillon looked a little sad, but he nodded dutifully.

"I'll stay with him."

Pulling the door open, I stepped outside, calling Franco.

"Hey. How is he?" He answered sleepily, and I yawned in response.

"He's alive."

"That's great."

"But listen, Dillon is here, and I've kind of had to pretend he's my boyfriend so he can sit with Todd and me because I told the nurse I'm Todd's cousin." I closed my eyes, waiting for the red mist to descend over Franco.

To my surprise, he laughed.

"Why am I not surprised you did that?"

"I am family. I'm his cousin," I whispered, surprised that Franco was so relaxed. But even I believed my own lie. "I thought you'd be mad."

I clutched the phone, watching as doctors and nurses buzzed around me, their faces fraught with worry.

"Ella, you wouldn't have risked everything you valued in the world to be with me only to run off with some knockoff version of me." Franco sighed into the phone, and my heart soared.

"I love that you trust me," I whispered, turning to look

through the window to where Todd lay. "But Todd…the police want to speak to him because the mugger died."

"Shit," Franco groaned. "Fuck, that's bad."

Panic rose in my chest, and I licked my lips, glancing around.

"But it's self-defense, right?"

Franco paused.

"If he can prove it, I guess. It's his word against a dead man."

Tears blurred my eyes again.

The thought of Todd having to go through such an interrogation when he hadn't done anything wrong killed me.

"This isn't fair!" I wailed, rubbing my eyes.

I was exhausted.

"Baby, you sound tired out. Can you go home? Dillon will stay with him, right? There's nothing you can do until he wakes up."

Franco was right, but I couldn't leave Todd.

"I want to be here when he wakes up," I mumbled through my tears. My cheeks were itchy and warm, and I knew I probably looked like I'd been run over by a bus.

I watched as Dillon snuggled down into his chair, and I cried more.

"What time does your flight get in?"

"Midday. I'll come straight to the hospital if you aren't going home, but I'd much rather you went home and got some sleep."

"Todd's my best friend. He was getting chocolate for me and beer for him." I sobbed, and a passing nurse rubbed my shoulder, sending me a sympathetic smile.

Nurses were walking angels.

"Ella, please. Please go home and rest. Tell Dillon to call you. I don't want you cracking up, love; you sound like you're on the edge, and I can't do anything from here. Please, Ella."

I stared through the glass into Todd's room and thought about returning home to my apartment without him.

"I can't. Anyway, I'm his cousin."

"Haha, hilarious. At least try and get some sleep, hmm?" Franco grumbled, and I nodded.

"I'll try. I can't wait to see you."

I rested my head against the glass, closing my sore eyes.

"My phone is on all night, babe. Call me if you need me," Franco reminded me, and my heart snuggled further into my chest at his words.

"I love you."

"Love you more."

I was too tired to argue that no, he didn't. I spotted a vending machine and shuffled over to grab us some snacks and drinks.

Who knew how long we were going to be here?

Moments later, I was back in the room, and a kind nurse brought us some pillows and blankets, dimming the lights.

"Try and sleep while he does," she advised, closing the door behind her.

Dillon nodded off, his neck at the most uncomfortable angle.

He was going to ache when he woke up.

I laced my fingers with Todd's, resting my head on the space between his thigh and the edge of the bed, the soft blanket soothing me.

I wanted to be near him, even if he was asleep.

I couldn't be at our apartment while he was in here.

My tired thoughts of Todd with no family filled my brain as I descended into a strange sleep where I was aware of what was happening in the room, but I was also dreaming.

I was dreaming that I was talking to Todd, and he was laughing about the time I thought he was going to die in the hospital after being mugged.

I jolted awake, gripping his hand to find him sleeping peacefully, his breathing perfectly normal.

Dillon had his head thrown back, an arm thrust beneath it like a makeshift pillow.

He was a good friend to Todd, and I couldn't deny that.

Soon Franco would be here, and I'd feel better.

I just needed my best friend to wake up.

THIRTY-SEVEN

FRANCO

IT WAS pointless going to the apartment, so I drove straight to the hospital.

Traffic was heavy, as usual for Los Angeles. The air was thick with heat, and I whacked the air conditioning to ice-cold, wanting to avoid turning up smelling like I'd run here.

The fact that I was in the same city as Ella was a relief because I knew she needed me. Even if we weren't in this relationship, she'd need me.

Finding a parking spot was a fucking nightmare, and I honestly considered leaving the car in the street.

Eventually, I parked and stepped into the heat that stifled me for the minutes it took to jog into the building.

A pretty nurse smiled at me, her blue eyes friendly and welcoming.

"Uh, I need to see someone named Todd Daysron? He was mugged, so I guess ICU?"

The nurse pointed toward the end of the hall, stifling a yawn.

"Head down there, and you'll find the elevators. Follow the signs from there; you can't miss it."

"Thanks, Doll." I grinned, heading the way she'd sent me.

My sneakers squeaked on the floor; the hallway was pretty much silent otherwise.

I'd texted Ella to let her know I was here, but she didn't reply, something that worried me.

I reached an area with a reception desk beneath the neon sign of the ICU, and it was then that I saw her.

Hunched over beside the vending machine, clutching her stomach as she winced.

"Ella?" I called out, crossing the room in six strides.

Ella looked up at me, her eyes wide with fear.

"Francesco…"

She tried to smile, but something else happened, and she vomited onto the floor between us.

"Shit," she muttered as I waved at the reception guy.

He looked at me with disgust, like he wasn't paid to clean up vomit.

Like I gave a shit.

A passing nurse saw us, and together we sat Ella down, handing her a cup of water which she sipped on.

"Are you alright?" The nurse peered at Ella, who forced a smile, attempting to wave her away.

"I'm just tired; I'm so sorry about the mess."

Ella's voice was faint, and as she rubbed her eyes, I made a face at the nurse.

"Okay, don't worry about that; you're in the right place to throw up wherever you like." The nurse reassured her, glancing around us. "But I'm going to get someone to take a look at you, alright? Two secs."

The nurse gave us a quick smile and left, coming back shortly after with a handsome man in tow.

"This is Doctor Lamb, and he is going to ask you a few questions if that's okay?" The nurse turned back to the doctor, mumbling something about doing Ella's observations. The doctor peered at Ella and shook his head at the nurse.

"It's okay, May, I'll do them."

The nurse, May, threw us another smile before dashing away, clearly back to whatever it was she was in the middle of when she saw us.

"Thanks, May!" I called after her and caught a stern glance from the doctor, who folded his arms.

"Hey, there. If you'd like to follow me, I'll take you to a room?"

Ella looked mortified when a janitor came along, and she blurted out her apologies.

The janitor had earbuds in and didn't seem to care, so I pulled Ella against me, following the doctor.

"Hey, beautiful," I mumbled into her hair, her fingers grasping a fistful of my shirt as she wrapped her arm around my waist. "Always the drama with you."

Ella didn't reply, and I glanced down to see that she'd paled somewhat.

The doctor led us into a small room with a bed against one wall and a desk and chairs beside it.

Ella dropped into the chair, gazing at me through bleary eyes.

I swear if I didn't know better, I'd say she was drunk.

I tuned out as the doctor began asking questions, focusing instead on Ella.

She caught my eye a few times and tried to send me a reassuring smile, but she just didn't look *well*.

"Doc," I interrupted, earning another glare from the handsome fucker. "Her friend is dying in the ICU. She's spent the night there, and she's barely eaten or slept...could that be what this is?"

The doctor looked at me coolly.

"It could be a multitude of things, but right now, I'm just going to ask Ella to give me a urine sample so I can check it, and then you can go." Doctor Lamb moved his attention back to Ella. "There's a bathroom attached to this room if you'd like to leave your sample by the door."

Ella took the bottle he held out to her and shuffled to the bathroom.

An awkward silence fell between the doctor and me, but soon enough, Ella was back out, yawning.

"You do look exhausted," Doctor Lamb said. "I'll prescribe you some anti-sickness medicine once these results are clear. You're not on any other medicines, right?"

Ella shook her head, leaning into the crook of my arm.

"Okay, good. Your vitals all look great, so it's just the urine sample, then you're good to go. You're here with a friend, you say?"

Ella nodded, giving him Todd's details as he scribbled some notes down.

"Not allergic to anything?"

Ella shook her head.

"And there's no chance you're pregnant?"

Ella froze, her grip tightening around mine.

"No chance."

The doctor smiled and moved back to the sink, testing her urine.

Children? A baby?

All entirely possible now.

But that was wishful thinking.

Unless we moved far away, somewhere where no one knew us.

"I've missed you," I mumbled into her ear, kissing her temple. "You're probably just tired. Rundown and shit."

"Yeah, I need to get back to Todd; I only came for a snack. I can't believe you're here."

I held her, stroking her hair as she sighed.

"I can't believe this is how you see me. Smelling of vomit and looking like crap."

I stroked her hair, my other hand on hers.

"Nah. You've never looked more beautiful."

"Your urine is clear. Maybe your partner was right; maybe you are just a little run down. I'll prescribe you some anti-sickness, then try and get some rest. Being here and ill isn't good for anyone, remember that." The doctor said, nodding at me.

"Thanks, doc."

"Thank you." Ella smiled, and I led her out of the room.

Once outside, I kissed her forehead, stroking back her hair as I sighed.

"Let's go and see how Todd is; then we can get you home for some rest, okay?"

Ella nodded, pulling me close so she could bury her face in my chest.

"Do they all hate us? Back home?"

I wanted to soothe her, but I also didn't want to lie.

"They're not happy, Ella, but can we please talk about it once you're feeling a little better?"

"Okay," Ella answered in a small voice, lacing her hand through mine as we found Todd's room.

The prick from the party was pacing the room when we walked in, his eyes bloodshot and wide.

"Ella! I was so worried, girl; where did you go?"

Dillon.

"I wasn't feeling too well; then I found Franco…."

He completely blanked me, and I let it go because of the situation, promising myself I'd get my time.

"Well, no change with Todd." Dillon shoved his hands in his pockets. "Why don't you go home if you're not feeling well? I'll call you if anything changes here."

Ella glanced back at the bed and the poor fucker in it.

Todd looked the same color as the sheets, and he was hooked up to so many machines it was crazy.

"Are you sure?"

Dillon nodded, finally meeting my gaze. His cold gaze told me he still cared for Ella in ways I didn't like.

"Take care of her, man."

I resisted the urge to roll my eyes, instead choosing to blank him until I remembered he'd been decent enough with Ella while I was busy getting here.

"Always." I shrugged, waiting as Ella kissed Todd goodbye, her hair forming a curtain around them.

"Call me if anything changes," Ella instructed, following me out of the door.

Dillon yawned, nodding as he turned back to the bed.

Once outside the hospital, I helped Ella into the car, going as far as to put on her seatbelt.

"I'm okay, Franco!" Ella protested, pushing her hair behind her eyes.

"Let's get you home. You need some fucking sleep."

"With you around?" Ella smirked, and I rolled my eyes.

"I'm not touching you until you've had a bath and some sleep, baby."

Ella didn't respond, her head cradled in her hand as I started the truck.

Looks like I arrived exactly when I was meant to, after all.

THIRTY-EIGHT

ELLA

TRUE TO HIS WORD, Franco didn't touch me, not like that anyway. I had a shower as I felt like I'd fall asleep in the bath, wrapped myself in a terry cloth robe, and padded into my bedroom, where Franco had drawn the curtains and dimmed the lights. I rubbed my face cream on, yawning throughout.

This is ridiculous. Is this all of the stress finally coming to a head?

I was desperate to know about my family's reaction, but Franco refused to talk about it until I had slept.

I fell into bed, curling my legs beneath me as I exhaled, heavy eyelids forcing me into a restless sleep where nightmares taunted me.

Todd dead, Todd blaming me for his attack, Franco leaving me, my family disowning me...the list was endless.

The mattress sank beside me, and the familiar scent of Franco soothed me, my tired limbs searching for his in the dark.

"You should be asleep," Franco scolded me, wrapping his arms around me.

I snuggled into his chest, safe in the knowledge that at least one of my nightmares wasn't true—Franco was still here.

His fingers played with my hair, and his steady heartbeat guarded me while I slept, the familiar drumming the soundtrack to my dreams.

The following day, I woke to find Franco dressed, sipping coffee in the kitchen.

My heart skipped a beat at his smile, the way he knew how to greet me silently and still send me insane with lust and love.

I grinned back, skipping over to him with excitement.

"Someone feels better this morning," Franco murmured into my ear, his hands trailing the curve of my spine.

I did feel better.

Until I remembered that Todd was in the hospital, fighting for his life.

Franco must've sensed my fear, for he stopped caressing my neck with his mouth, his eyes locking onto mine.

"I called the hospital; they said there's no change, baby."

I felt the air leave my lungs. The idea that Todd still wasn't awake was almost unbearable.

Nausea swept through me again at the thought of losing him, and I scanned the room for my pills from the hospital.

"What are you looking for?"

"My anti-sickness pills."

Franco kissed my forehead, reaching behind him to pull the pills from a brown paper bag.

"You didn't sleep well last night. Bad dreams?"

I nodded, not wanting to get into it.

"You need to tell me about what happened back home,

Franco." I took a deep breath, nodding as though to confirm my words.

"Come and sit down, Ella."

I followed Franco to the couch, curling my legs beneath me as he held my hand, stroking it tenderly. I loved watching him fall in love with me, and he seemed to be doing it right now. The look in his eyes told me he was falling at that very moment, but something was holding him back.

I braced myself, but Franco looked pained, swallowing hard as he rubbed his chin.

"Your dad has something he needs to tell you, okay?"

What? I wasn't expecting that.

My brow furrowed, my eyes narrowing as I examined Franco. Beads of sweat appeared on his forehead despite the air conditioning; his eyes held a sorrow I wasn't familiar with.

"Franco, what the fuck does that mean?"

Franco shrugged, telling me how my dad had assaulted him, how Grandpa had taken Dad outside to calm down.

"I'm sorry," I wept, tears streaming down my face at the thought of Franco dealing with this alone.

All he did was fall in love with me.

"Dad told Chris—your dad—that he needed to tell me something, and it's not my place to tell you, baby girl." Franco's eyes studied me with such intensity I almost didn't dare push him.

My heart slammed against my chest, demanding an explanation, my words dried up in my throat.

"I don't understand what he would have to tell you—us—at that moment, Francesco!" I snapped, finally finding my voice.

Franco grimaced, holding my hands to his lips as it dawned on me.

Surely not.

"We're not related, baby."

It was like an explosion set off within me, a small moan leaving my lips as I laughed, shaking my head.

"That's not funny."

"I'm not laughing," Franco whispered, closing his eyes.

I stared at him, looking for any sign that he was joking, but there were none.

"Wait…" I said, licking my lips as I held his hands.

I have to be careful if Franco and I aren't related…

That means he's adopted. Or some crazy shit.

"Are you okay?" I asked, reaching up to move his hair back from his eyes.

But then his words hit me again, and I rolled them around my mind, again and again, dread in my stomach.

'It's not my place to tell you.'

Me?

We weren't related, not because Franco was adopted…

Oh my God.

Stars danced in my vision as Franco held me, his eyes scanning mine.

"I'm adopted?" I whispered, unable to think, unable to breathe. The words left my mouth, but it felt like someone else said them, someone who was curious yet calm.

I'm anything but calm.

I'm a storm.

My body trembled like I'd just got off a rollercoaster that I'd ridden twice in a row. Nausea played havoc with my stomach, and I mentally checked my dad's features against mine, finding no similarities.

Maria is so different from me, with her olive skin and beautiful, thick hair.

"Ella." Franco sighed, shaking his head. "I know you

want answers, but I can't give them to you. All I can tell you is that we *aren't* related."

I stared at him, wondering if he wanted a positive response to such life-changing news.

It's okay; we can be together.

But you're adopted, and your entire life is based on a lie.

"I need to call my dad," I gritted out, waving Franco's hand away. "If you can't tell me, he fucking has to."

Franco stared down at the floor, raking his hand through his head as he cursed.

"Please, Ella. Please, baby… .don't. Just be with me, and fuck any of that. It doesn't matter, right?"

I met his gaze, shaking my head as I called my father.

Or whoever he was.

"Fuck you, as if you'd leave it!" I hissed, tears sliding down my cheeks, hot and sticky and annoying the hell out of me.

"Ella?"

My dad's voice, stern and full of disappointment, filled my ear, and for a brief second, I was afraid of his judgment again.

My illicit affair with the man I loved turned out not to be related to me.

"Dad." I swallowed, wrapping an arm tightly around my stomach, hugging myself as I asked the question. "Am I adopted?"

A pause, and then an exhale.

"Dad?" I whispered, pressing my forehead against the cool glass that overlooked the busy street below.

The street where my best friend was mugged.

Part of me didn't want Dad to answer, and I allowed myself a brief fantasy of him laughing it off, asking where I'd heard something so ridiculous.

A woman pushed a cart on the sidewalk, occasionally

stopping to search the streets for cigarette butts, grinning when she found one. I watched her pocket it, then turned my gaze to the other end of the street.

Women stood in clusters on their mobile phones, designer shopping bags hanging from their arms. Chic bobs and oversized sunglasses dominated the face of the one facing me, and I felt hatred toward the world.

Why does one woman get the world, yet another searches the floor for a way to feed her vice?

"It's not fair," I interrupted my dad's words, none of which I was listening to.

"Huh?" Dad coughed, embarrassed.

"Life. It isn't fair."

I turned back to Franco, his hands clasped together as he watched me, his jaw tightening.

"I'm sorry, Ella," Dad said, his voice cracking. "I never wanted you to know—"

"That I'm adopted?" I said bluntly. "Clearly not. But hey, I'm in love with my uncle, and he's not my uncle, right?"

I was a bitch, but I didn't care.

Everything I'd ever known was a lie.

"So, who am I?" I choked out, wondering how cruel life was to hand me a new set of parents and how one had died slowly on me.

She wasn't even my mother.

That was enough to send me to my knees; Franco dashed over, his arms circling me.

It didn't comfort me like it usually did.

My mother isn't my mother? My dad... .isn't my dad?

"Who are my real parents? Is that why Maria hates me so much?" I was yelling now, but I didn't care.

Not anymore.

"Because I'm not her blood? I'm not a *Russo?*"

"You ARE a Russo!" Dad roared, making me flinch. "You are my daughter, and that is the end of that!"

"It's not, though!" I screamed back. "I want the truth, now!"

"No, Ella, please...." Dad cried, his sobs filling the static between us. "Be with Franco. If that's what makes you happy, then do it. I can't stop you."

"What aren't you telling me?" I stared at Franco, unsure whether I was asking him or my dad.

Franco said nothing, his gaze moving to the window behind us, his grip tightening on mine.

"You're not adopted, Ella." Dad's voice pulled me away from Franco, confusion coursing through me.

What the fuck is going on?

I focused on Franco's neck, watching the vein throb as his chest heaved, his plump lips parting to release a sad exhale of breath.

He's sad.

"Then what am I?"

I don't feel like I'm here.

Maybe I was not; maybe I was floating around in the sky, searching for butterflies and unicorns.

In the state my life was in at the moment, unicorns could well exist.

"Ella, come back home; let's talk about this." Dad tried, failing miserably.

"No. I don't want to come *home* when I don't even know what that is anymore."

Numbness owned me, depositing itself into my flesh like a disease, leaving my head reeling and my stomach churning. First, my arms were numb, tingling all over, then it was in my head, cheeks, and lips.

I can't breathe.

"Your mother is your mother, Ella; I'm just not your

father. That's the secret." Dad whispered his words allowing a wave of calm to wash over me.

"I'm still my Mom's?"

It was all I had to cling to.

The woman I'd adored more than anything.

Whose every word I can recall, her advice locked away in a dusty cabinet in my mind, brought out only when needed.

"Yes, Ella, and you'll always be mine," Dad said gruffly, but the phone slid from my hands, my fingers tapping the red button repeatedly until my screensaver flashed back up.

Dad was gone.

THIRTY-NINE

FRANCO

THE DAYS that passed were hard.

Ella withdrew into herself, barely talking and sleeping lots.

Todd woke up, and even this didn't pull more than a smile of relief.

"Let's go and see him," I suggested, desperate to get her out of the house.

"I don't want to." Ella shrugged, staring at the tv with a blank expression.

"Ella, I know you're upset, baby." I sighed, reaching over to stroke her cheek, still stained with tears. "But you can't hide away from the world."

Silence.

"Please, Ella. Look at me."

I wished she hadn't when she turned to me, her eyes filled with hurt and anger.

"Will you leave me alone? You have no idea how I'm feeling right now."

I didn't want to leave her, so I settled back into the couch, wishing she would curl up next to me or even speak without it being a response to my questions.

But she didn't.

Like a statue, she sat beside me, leaving an unhealthy gap between us.

My mind raced with solutions, but really, I knew she just needed time, time to process the fact that her father wasn't her biological father.

To come to terms with the fact that there was no blood between us.

Christopher called her daily, but she wouldn't answer.

He didn't call me; he only sent me one text message to check how Ella was doing.

The following morning I woke up to hear her vomiting in the bathroom, her sobs frightening me.

"Baby, are you okay?" I asked, knowing she was anything but okay.

Ella flushed the toilet, her pale face and dark ringed eyes concerning more than I liked.

"You're going to a doctor today," I told her, prepared for her argument.

To my surprise, she didn't.

She showered and got dressed while I watched her like a hawk, panic shooting from my brain all over my body, fear gripping my heart in a fist.

Ella was going through too much; I didn't need a doctor to tell me that. But I needed a doctor to tell me why she was still sick, despite anti-sickness meds.

I needed to hear her voice, see her smile, anything.

I sat outside while Ella went in to see the doctor, and I dropped my head in my hands, wondering when the hell this all went south.

I should be happy that Ella wasn't my niece, but I wouldn't wish the reason on anyone.

As far as Ella was aware, she had an unknown father, someone she hadn't asked any questions about, and I was grateful for that.

My blood boiled at the thought of whoever had done this to Ella and Ella's mother, but it was pointless getting pissed about that now.

I had to concentrate on Ella and hope she didn't push me away because that's what it felt like she was doing.

Pushing me away.

After what felt like forever, Ella came out of the doctor's office with more medicine and a nonchalant shrug.

"He said it's normal considering what I'm going through. He's given me links to counselors and advised me to start taking some anti-depressants."

Her voice was monotone, her gaze aimless.

"Ella, look at me."

"Francesco, I want to go home." Ella lifted her head, her eyes looking everywhere but mine.

"Okay, Todd should be back tomorrow—"

"No. I want to go home to Dad and Maria."

My chest ached, and my jaw tightened.

This was inevitable, but she was already in a dark place. How was she going to be when Christopher told her the truth?

I couldn't bear seeing her in any more pain.

"Alright," I agreed, reaching out for her.

Ella moved back, shaking her head softly, no words leaving her lips. But she didn't have to say anything-her body language spoke for her.

"I'll see Todd before I go."

"Before *we* go, you mean?" I corrected her as she shrugged.

"Yeah."

Ouch.

"I'll sort the flights."

I texted my brother, telling him the plan. He arranged to pick Ella up from the airport, and I decided to give them some space until Ella needed me.

We sat and watched mindless tv, not touching one another, both silent.

I didn't know what to say, and Ella was expressionless, unreadable.

Todd came back, and even he didn't get much of a reaction from her. Granted, he had healed well, but Ella didn't seem to register him when he came home.

"Welcome back, man." I smiled, glancing at Ella, who smiled at him faintly.

"You had me worried."

That's all she had to say?

She'd been *inconsolable*.

Barely able to breathe, and now this?

"What can I say? I'm a fighter. A tired one, nevertheless."

Poor guy.

Todd had to rest, and he had Dickhead Dillon by his side like a fucking nurse, getting him drinks and tidying the apartment.

I caught his gaze once, and he nodded at Ella, lifting his eyebrows questionably.

Fuck off. I don't know what's wrong with her.
She won't even talk to me.

ELLA

Numbness owned me.

My identity had been stolen, and there was nothing anyone could do to get it back.

I couldn't call the police, report a crime.

No.

Ella Russo was my name, but what is a name, exactly?

It's your identity, of course.

It's how you introduce yourself, how people remember you, what arrives on bills, letters, college applications.

My surname was supposed to be my heritage, my lineage if you like.

Russo— origin Southern Italy, hence the beauty my sister carried; the dark hair, the stubborn streak, the fire in her belly.

I thought I had that too, but maybe I learned it from my father.

He's not your father.

I felt like I was in a nightmare, floating around from viscous thought to viscous thought, trapped in my mind.

I'd already come to terms with the fact I was an outcast for falling for my fucking uncle, but then it turned out I didn't ever belong.

So how had my mother had me?

The question was at the forefront of my mind and the only thing I wanted to know.

It was the reason for going home.

My shoulders dropped at the word home.

I didn't have a home; because here in Los Angeles, my reputation was ruined; the girl who slept with her uncle; fell in love with him no less.

I couldn't be with him here, and I couldn't be with him at home.

I couldn't be with him at all.

I hated the way he looked at me now, a mixture of pity and love.

I didn't care for love.

Not anymore.

What has it ever done for me?

Nothing.

My mom loved me; she died.

Dad loved me; he lied.

Franco loved me; I ruined his life.

I'd risked it all and lost *everything*.

Todd didn't have any permanent damage, and I didn't stick around to hear the rest.

It wasn't that I didn't care…I did; I just didn't have any energy to spare. It was taking everything I had to *breathe*.

I flew home.

Well, back to Christopher Russo, the man who had looked after me since I was in diapers.

Walking through the gate, my heart flipped when I saw him, with navy chinos and a button-down shirt, his face grey and old.

I tugged my suitcase behind me, barely acknowledging Franco, who stopped, giving me space to meet Dad.

Dad glared at him, but when his gaze moved to me, it softened, his eyes watering as he swallowed down his emotions.

"Hey, baby."

"Hey," I answered, glancing around him.

"Where's Maria?"

Dad's eyes flickered with emotion, but he managed to mask it well.

"She's staying with some friends."

"She didn't want to see me?" I frowned, wondering if my sister had disowned me.

After all, she hated me for being so 'disgusting' with our uncle; did she know now that he wasn't my relative? Did that make a difference?

"Ella, she's confused . . ." Dad's voice drifted off, his gaze falling to the floor when I let out a bitter laugh.

"Maria's confused? Ha!"

A hand touched my shoulder, and I tugged it away, refusing to address Franco.

"I'll go," Franco said, his fingers drifting down my back as I shrugged, refusing to entertain the sadness in my stomach.

"Okay."

"Call me if you need me." Franco's hand squeezed mine, and the two brothers glared at each other as he walked away, his dark head disappearing into a sea of travelers that poured out of the exit.

I folded my arms as Dad grabbed my bag, avoiding my eyes.

"The car is out front."

The entire journey home, he said nothing to me.

Is he disgusted with me?

Of course, he is, Ella; everyone is.

The sooner I realized that, the better.

Pulling up to my house felt like the final nail in the coffin, the same curtains we'd had for as long as I could remember; the lawn now overgrown and filled with weeds—a sure sign that my dad was neglecting the things he cared about.

Maybe we had that in common.

The dull ache in my chest continued as I walked up the steps, pushing the door open and inhaling the home-sweet-home smell that used to comfort me so much.

"You don't look very well, Ella," Dad mumbled from behind me, closing the door with a soft thud.

I stared at the kitchen table, at the framed photos of us on the wall.

Who is that girl smiling back at me?

It was me, of course, but she was the version of me before she ruined everything she knew, the version of myself that had ambition, dreams, and hopes.

Now I'm a shell.

"I wonder why." I snapped, feeling bratty.

"Don't speak to me like that; you're hardly innocent in all of this."

There it was; Dad's true emotions.

"Right, so I slept with my uncle. He's not my uncle, dad; oh wait, you're not my dad. Sorry, should I call you Chris now?"

I whirled on my heel, ready for a fight.

I felt rage, my hands trembling as I lifted a finger to my father, to Christopher.

"Don't you *dare* speak to me like this. After everything I've done for you—"

I gaped at him, my eyes wild.

"Done for me?" I echoed, tilting my head to the side. "You *lied* to me. I'm not your daughter."

Pain filled my chest as my lip quivered, and his eyes reflected the agony I was feeling.

"But you are, Ella; you've always been mine."

I shook my head, tears blurring my vision.

"That wasn't your choice to make, and you know it. Were you ever going to tell me?"

Dad bowed his head, his hands gripping the counter behind him as he inhaled, releasing the breath so slowly I wondered if he had extra lungs.

"No, probably not."

The admission sent me reeling, and I fell into a chair, my head in my hands.

Everything was a lie.

Now everyone wants to tell the truth.

I looked up at Dad, and he made a face, the sort that told me he was close to breaking point himself.

It didn't matter anymore.

Nothing did.

I took a deep breath, spreading my palms flat on the table.

"Tell me everything."

FORTY

ELLA

DAD STARED at me through pained eyes, slumping to the seat across from me with a sigh.

I tried to brace myself, but nothing prepared me for the brutal honesty that only my dad could get away with.

"You can't handle the truth, Ella. Look at you."

His voice was hoarse, his fingers trembling as he reached out to me, our fingers touching for the first time in a long time.

"I'm fine." I bit out, tears filling my eyes and proving my lies.

"You're not. I can't break you further, Ella."

"It's bad, isn't it?" I swallowed, blinking the tears away.

What the hell happened?

Dad stared at me, nodding slowly. Fear crept in, pushing aside the bravado I was trying to muster. My eyes slid away from his, falling on a photo of Maria and me as kids.

Where is she?

"Just say it, Dad."

Dad shook his head, tears forming in his eyes.

"I can't."

I withdrew my hands from his, curling them into fists beneath the table.

"Please."

Dad dropped his head into his hands, dragging his fingers through his hair before lifting his eyes to mine.

"When I met your mother, she was pregnant. Only four months or so." He paused, his eyes crinkling at the sides. "At first, I couldn't tell, but then she told me, in the way that only your mother dropped bombshells."

He smiled, and I held my breath, waiting for him to tell me who I really was.

"She'd had a one-night stand, Ella, and she got pregnant."

I wasn't sure what I was expecting, but it wasn't this.

"My mom had a one-night stand?" I echoed, a laugh of disbelief leaving my lips. "I can't imagine her like that. She's only ever been with you."

Pain flashed in my dad's eyes, and he nodded, shrugging his shoulders.

"That was the only time she'd been with anyone else."

I leaned back in my chair, exhaling slowly.

"A one-night stand."

Which meant that we knew nothing of my father. Nothing.

"So when I say I'm your father, Ella, I mean it. I fell in love with your mother the moment I met her, and try as she might, she couldn't get rid of me. Not a day went by after that where we didn't see each other. Not a day."

"So what happened?" I pressed, lifting my eyes to his.

"We told everyone you were mine. I guess you were, to both of us. There wasn't any question because I never loved you any less."

A lump rose in my throat, and I nodded, a strange sense of relief washing over me.

"I thought I was adopted."

Dad shook his head.

"I watched your mother give birth to you. Never seen anyone love someone so much in my life."

A sob took hold of my body, and I snorted an ugly cry, hearing the chair scrape back across the floor, the familiar scent of my dad's cologne wrapping around me.

My dad.

"I love you so much, Ella."

"Why didn't you tell me?" I whispered, clinging to his arm.

His lips pressed against my hair as he choked out a response.

"Your mother didn't want you to know because she said I was the perfect father."

His voice cracked, and I turned, wrapping my arms around him, my face buried in his neck like it did when I was a child.

"You were. You are."

His body shook as he cradled me in his arms, and we remained like that until the sound of the door opening commanded our attention.

"I know neither of you wants me here, but you're going to have to carry me out in a box. I'm not leaving."

Francesco.

Dad sighed, stroking my hair as he gazed at me, my heart aching with love for him.

"It doesn't matter about the one nightstand. It doesn't matter who your father was—he didn't bring you up."

Franco frowned, his eyes moving from me to Dad, his mouth forming an 'O' shape.

"What?"

Dad nodded, stroking my face, his thumbs running under my eyes, wiping away my tears.

"Did you know?" I asked Franco quietly, my heart aching at the expression on my Dad's face.

"Uh, no." Franco shrugged, staring at my dad. "You're a good man."

Dad nodded, moving his gaze back to me.

"You don't look well, Ella. I need you well."

I dropped my gaze, exhaustion sweeping over me.

"The doctor gave me some pills…."

Dad and Franco exchanged a look, and I continued. "But I think it's just the stress of everything. Franco and I, now this."

I dropped my head into my hands, shaking uncontrollably.

"Todd."

My best friend.

Guilt swam through me at the thought of him struggling in our apartment with only Dillon to help him.

I'd been so wrapped up in my own drama I didn't even consider Todd.

"Hey," Franco murmured, crossing the room to crouch beside me. "Todd will understand; you know he will. You're under so much stress, Ella."

I nodded, reaching out to cup his cheek, my other hand wrapped in my dad's.

"I'm sorry," I whispered into the air, my dad's grip tightening on me as Franco's hand covered mine.

"You're so loved, Ella," Dad said gruffly, lifting my hands to his lips. "We all love you. So much."

"I know."

FRANCO

. . .

A one-nightstand?

Christopher stared at me, his jaw tense and his gaze hard.

He was protecting her.

Part of me was relieved, but another part of me hated him for telling me the truth too. Now I had to keep that secret from her forever, but I'd rather that than see her crumble any more than she already had.

"I need to go and lie down." Ella rose to her feet, wobbling slightly. "Can Franco come with me?"

The question was directed to Christopher, who paled, his eyes burning into me.

"No, Ella. I'm not ready for that."

Ella paused, turning to me.

"I'll come and see you later, okay? I just need to sleep."

"Of course, baby. I'll be here."

Christopher flinched when Ella fell into my arms, mumbling apologies through tired tears.

I kissed her head, cupping her face in my hands.

"You'll be okay. Don't apologize; I love you."

"I love you too."

I wanted to kiss her, but I knew Christopher would probably lose is shit, and Ella didn't need that.

I released her, watching as she made her way upstairs and out of my sight.

"Get out."

Christopher stared at the floor, his fists bunched by his sides.

"Fuck, Chris!" I snapped, shaking my head at him. "A one-nightstand? I've got to lie to her forever!"

When Christopher looked up at me, his eyes were cold.

"Yeah, well, you're good at lying, Francesco. Keep up the good work."

With that, he shook his head at me in disgust, pointing at the door.

"Out."

I swallowed, knowing my relationship with Christopher was doomed. There was no coming back from this.

All I could do was nod, turning away from his glare.

"I love her, Christopher."

He didn't reply; he just stared me down until I backed away, slamming the door behind me in anger.

Ella wasn't my blood relation, but Christopher was.

I had a feeling blood didn't matter anymore.

FORTY-ONE

ELLA

I WOKE up some hours later, feeling marginally better. The fog in my head had cleared somewhat, but something was missing.

Franco.

I'd pushed him away, and all he'd done was be there for me.

I couldn't help it, though; I hated what we'd done to our family, and now, finding out that we were allowed to be together and still not getting any form of a blessing from my father cut deep.

I sat up, rubbing my eyes as they adjusted to the darkness outside. Then, climbing out of bed, I realized I was still in my clothes from this morning.

Classy.

I plod downstairs, checking the time on the kitchen clock.

Two am.

Shit!

I made a cup of coffee, my eyes skimming the kitchen as I slumped into a seat.

Dad was asleep, for there wasn't a sound in the whole house. I couldn't hear him snoring, but a smile played on my lips when I heard him moving around in bed.

I love him so much.

Padding into the living room, I gazed out at the street, my stomach heating up from the coffee.

I'd grown up here, had a makeshift swing on the tree out front, the branches still bowed from my growing weight, then my sister.

Maria.

I hated that she wasn't here.

I knew she was angry, but if she loved me, she would still be here.

My heart ached, and I wondered how it still had the capacity to feel pain for the millionth time. How many times must it be hurt? Does it reheal every time?

Pressing my head against the cold glass, I sighed, my breath creating clouds before my eyes.

Through the glass, I saw a soft light glowing from my grandpa's house, and my heart thumped in my throat.

I'll have a heart attack at this rate.

"Are you up, Papa?" I whispered, placing the coffee cup on the counter.

Did he know I wasn't his?

I'm sure he does. But like Dad, he's never loved me any less.

Fuck it.

Swiveling on my heel, I tugged on my dad's warm jacket, inhaling his familiar scent.

I want to make this right.

The air was chilly, so different from the weather in L.A. Hugging myself, I crossed the road, tears already filling my eyes at the thought of seeing my Grandpa's lovely face.

Almost as though he was waiting for me, the door was

open, soft jazz music flowing through from his place by the television.

"Hey, Grandpa? It's me, Ella," I called out, wiping my feet on the worn welcome mat.

"Ella, come in."

I smiled at the sound of Grandpa's voice, and I headed into the family room, ready to throw myself into his arms and pretend this was all a bad dream.

I rounded the corner, doing a double-take when my eyes locked on the soft brown ones that I'd fallen in love with.

Franco was lying on the sofa, his hand behind his head, the other clutching a bottle of whiskey.

He smiled lazily, lifting onto his elbows as he gazed at me, almost as though he wasn't sure I was real.

"Hey, uh, I didn't know you were here…." I stammered, gripping the cuffs of my coat. "Hey, Grandpa…"

Grandpa rubbed his chin, glancing from me to Franco.

"So, now the cat's outta the bag, huh?"

My cheeks flushed, and I closed my eyes, still mortified that my *Grandpa* knew I'd been sleeping with his *son*.

"I don't know what you know, but I'm sorry." I blurted out, twisting my fingers around each other as tears slid down my face.

In an instant, Franco was up and by my side, taking me into his arms as he soothed me with his delicious voice.

"Sweetheart, don't cry."

This only made me cry harder, and I buried my face into his neck, wishing it was just him and me in the world.

"I'm sorry," I mumbled, my tears soaking his neck, mixing with the cologne I loved so much.

"For what?" Franco frowned, trying to tilt my head so he could see me, but I refused to move.

"For being such a bitch."

Franco chuckled, stroking my back as he sighed. "What did I tell you, Dad? She's hard work."

Grandpa coughed from behind me, but his words were like warm syrup over ice cream.

"She's worth it, though, son. Trust me; you'll never love anyone like you love her."

I pulled my head back as Franco released me, and I crouched by my grandpa's feet.

Moleskin slippers and his tartan robe carry his scent, and I rest my head on his lap, his callous fingers stroking my hair.

"Ah, Ella, come on, baby. It's not all bad; you are in love, no?"

I lifted my head, barely able to see through my tears.

Did he know?

How could he not know?

"I'm not your granddaughter," I whispered, biting my lip so hard it bled.

Franco exhaled loudly behind me, and I heard him swig from the bottle of whiskey.

Grandpa gripped my chin, holding it in place as he glared at me, fire in his eyes.

"I may be old, Ella, but I'm not fucking senile. Not yet, anyway. You're my granddaughter, alright. Always have been, always will be. Loved you since the day you kicked my hand through your mama's belly."

I choked back a sob, and his eyes watered, his fingers stroking my cheek.

"I don't give a shit about any of this, not a damn thing." Grandpa continued, nodding to Franco. "I've known since you could walk and talk that you two were meant for each other. I think Christopher knew too, truth be told."

I sucked in a breath as Grandpa cracked a smile, his wrinkles deepening as he nodded.

"I married my cousin, Ella."

I whipped my head around to see Franco nodding, a grim smile on his face.

"Would you believe back then our families were ecstatic? Of course, times have changed now, but back then, it was considered good to keep it in the family."

My head was spinning, my eyes scanning the room as though searching for something I wouldn't find.

"Seriously?" I whispered, glancing back to Franco, who shrugged, lifting the bottle to his lips.

"The whole family is fucked up," Franco muttered in between gulps.

Grandpa laughed, nudging me with his foot.

"Your dad will come around, trust me. You aren't even related. Get married already."

I felt light like I was walking on air.

"But put down that whiskey, or you'll be no use to our Ella," Grandpa commanded, waving his finger at Franco. "But I am old, and I'm fucking tired. So, I'm taking my old ass to bed, and I'll see you both for breakfast in the morning, capiche?"

I nodded, aware that Franco rose to help Grandpa to bed, and I tried to do the same, but nausea gripped me. I gulped down air, exhaling through my nose like I'd learned to do, keeping it at bay.

"Ella, you okay?" Franco barked, leaning down to me, his eyes swimming with concern and whiskey.

"Get him to bed, don't worry about me," I said, waving him away. "Go."

Franco bit his lip, the single-action sending my body into overdrive. A throbbing between my legs outweighed the nausea, and I turned away, still feeling odd for feeling like this in front of my grandpa.

"Night Ella, I love you, kiddo!" Grandpa called out, shuffling down to his room.

I pulled myself onto the sofa, the stench of whiskey making me heave.

Fresh air.

I hurried to the back door, throwing it open as my head span, stars filling my vision. I gulped at the air desperately, praying my usual tactic worked, but I gripped the counter, swaying.

"Baby, what's wrong?"

"Must be the shock," I tried to laugh, but instead, I threw up.

"That's it, you're going to the hospital," Franco declared, locking the door behind him.

"It's a bug!" I protested as Franco rolled his eyes at me.

"Ella, I think you might be pregnant."

I let out a strange moan as he shook his head, a warm smile twitching on his lips.

"I've got you, babe."

FORTY-TWO

FRANCO

"IF YOU THINK I'm pregnant, this is what I'm doing," Ella huffed, pacing in the bathroom.

I sat on the side of the bath, watching as she nibbled at her finger, her eyes wild.

She had to be pregnant, right?

My mind did its usual trick of jumping to the worst conclusion, and I imagined her being terminally ill or something equally horrific.

"Franco," Ella whispered, coming to a stop in front of me. Her lips parted, and she fanned at her face, eyes filling with tears.

I searched her face, waiting for her to give me the result, and when she didn't, I took the test from her, scanning it impatiently.

PREGNANT.

"Oh fuck."

Ella sank onto the toilet, the heel of her hands pressing into her eyes.

Blood rushed in my ears, but a stupid fucking grin dominated my face.

It wasn't about me, though; it was about how Ella felt.

Right now, she needed to be comfortable and sane.

"Baby, talk to me."

Falling to my knees before her, I pressed my forehead to hers, trying to pull her hands away.

"I'm okay; I'm just…." Ella trembled in my arms, her watery eyes lifting to mine.

"Scared?" I offered, sweeping her tears away with my thumbs, kissing her forehead tenderly.

This girl was everything to me.

"I don't want our child to be heckled in the fucking streets," Ella wailed, her lower lip trembling. "I'll die, Francesco."

I frowned, searching her eyes.

Is that all she's worried about? Not about giving birth or her body changing?

"Ella—"

"We can't stay here."

Ella whipped her head up to mine, and I couldn't help but nod with her. I'd be able to sell the house, but shit, where would we go where no one knew who we were? Los Angeles?

As though she read my mind, Ella cupped my cheeks, her eyes tracing the shape of my lips.

"Somewhere, no one knows us."

"You want the baby then?" I asked, running a hand through my hair.

This was fucking surreal.

Ella gasped, slapping her hands against my chest.

"Um, yes! Of course, I fucking do! What sort of question is that?!" Ella glared at me, and I held my hands up, unable to stifle my laughter.

"Alright, sweetheart, I was just asking you. Calm down."

Ella crossed her arms over her chest, her breath ragged.

"I'm so fucking worried about you, Ella," I admitted, my fingers stroking the bare skin on her arms. "There's so fucking much going on."

Ella's gaze softened, and she took a deep breath.

"But this...a baby, and us. So it's a good thing, right?"

A vulnerability hid behind her eyes, and I frowned, kissing her hard on the mouth.

Any doubt she had, I kissed away, her soft moan silenced by my gruff words.

"Of course it fucking is."

Ella wrapped her legs around me, and I inhaled her sweet breath, my hands spanning her back.

Her skin prickled with goosebumps, and I marveled at the idea of a mini-us growing in her stomach.

"Do you still want this? Us? Because if you don't, I understand." She broke the kiss, pulling her lower lip into her teeth as she watched me.

I couldn't answer her with words, and she must've taken my silence as a negative reaction, her eyes filling with tears.

"I'm sorry I pushed you away, but I do love you—"

"Ella," I interrupted her, my voice broken. "I've always wanted you. I want you, in every way, so stop this shit."

Ella gazed at me, exhaling as I held her tightly.

This was how it was always meant to be.

Ella and me against the world.

"I love you," Ella whispered to me, wrapping her arms around my neck.

Her sweet scent enveloped me, and her mouth brushed against mine, her tongue licking my lower lip, begging for entrance.

"Take this off," I whispered, tugging her shirt over her

head. Her white lace bra screamed innocence, but the way her tongue was thrusting into my mouth was anything but. Her hand cupped my length, gripping it through my jeans.

"Not here, baby." I lifted her into my arms, enjoying her delicious squeal as she gripped me with her thighs.

"Don't drop me."

"As if," I smirked against her jawline, kissing her throat as she arched against me.

"God, I want you," Ella moaned into my ear, tugging at my jeans. "I want you inside me."

"Such a dirty girl." I granted her request, tugging her bottoms off to reveal her delicious core. "If anything hurts, tell me."

"I'm pregnant, not ill." Ella laughed, sweeping her tongue over my ear, sending shivers down my spine.

"I haven't fucked a pregnant woman before; give me a break."

Sharp pain from my bicep made me hiss, and I looked up to see Ella glaring at me.

"Do you mind? Your bedside manner is shit."

"Sorry, baby," I smirked once more, knowing it drove her crazy.

I entered her slowly, her pussy gripping me like a vice. "I'll try and behave."

"Oh," Ella gasped out, her heels digging into my ass, pressing me into her deeper. "Fuck!"

"Mmm, like that, baby?"

Ella's eyes rolled back in her head, her hips lifting to meet my thrusts, her cries filling my bedroom.

"I swear, I'll never get tired of fucking you," I muttered into her ear, sucking on her neck as she became undone beneath me. "I want you to come, Ella. Let me make you feel good."

Ella moaned, digging her nails in as she rubbed her groin against me.

God, this felt so fucking good.

"Don't stop!" Ella commanded, uttering a series of gasps, her pussy throbbing around me. "I'm coming, oh...god!"

"Good, yes, baby. Fuck, you feel so good around my cock."

"Mmm," Ella mumbled, falling back into the bed, her hands pressing against the wall as I pounded into her, biting into her shoulder lightly as I emptied myself into her.

"Fuck!"

I scrunched my eyes shut, ecstasy flowing through my veins as I let loose; the frustrations of the past few days leaving my body, the soft chuckle from Ella made me kiss her hard on the mouth, igniting the complete adoration and love I had for her.

"I fucking love you."

Ella cupped my cheeks, kissing me back between words.

"I love you too, Francesco."

Fuck, I love it when she used my full name.

FORTY-THREE

ELLA

PREGNANT.

My fingers stroked my belly, my mind wandering beneath them, into my womb, peering at the dot that was forming within me.

The door opened downstairs, and Franco's voice rang out as he announced the pizza was here.

My mouth watered at the thought of mozzarella dripping from the thick tomatoey base, topped with chicken, mushrooms, and hopefully, lots of chilies.

And more cheese.

Swinging my legs over the side of Franco's bed, I made my way downstairs, not sure which vision I wanted first—Franco or the pizza.

"Large chicken pizza with extra chilies, right?" Franco nudged the box toward me as he ripped open his box, noisily smacking his lips together.

"I swear, I could live off this shit for the rest of my life."

I pulled a slice out of the box, my tastebuds screaming

with delirious delight as I inhaled the first slice in almost one mouthful.

I grabbed another, my teeth grazing my fingers as I shove it in, eating like a woman possessed.

"So. Good." I moaned, sucking the tomato sauce from my fingers.

We eat in silence before the pizza stupor hits us, five slices too late.

"I'll stick the leftovers in the fridge. Gotta love cold pizza," Franco said with a grin.

I nodded, jumping when my phone sounded in my pocket.
Maria.

I inhaled sharply, looking up at Franco, who was busy rearranging the fridge to fit the pizzas in.

I'd not spoken to Maria since I'd come home, so I answered her call eagerly.

"Hello?"

"Ella! I'm so sorry about everything!" Maria sobbed down the phone, her voice trembling. "I didn't mean to be such a bitch!"

"Maria, calm down."

But there was no calming her.

My sister apologized for everything she'd done and said and wanted me to know something.

"I don't trust him."

"Who?" I frowned, picking at the pizza box before me.

Maria was still crying, and Franco turned to the counter, his dark eyes holding mine.

Did she mean she didn't trust Franco?

"Uncle Franco. He's always looked at me weird, you know?"

I froze, my fingers gripping my phone.

There's *no* way.

"But I…" Maria's voice faded before she exhaled. "I want you in my life, Ella. I just can't say the same for him. He's broken my dad's heart."

"Your dad?" I echoed, swallowing hard.

Did she realize how harsh that was?

"Yes, my dad. I mean, we may not be full sisters, but we can still be friends, right?" Maria sniveled.

"Friends?"

Franco frowned, motioning to me to cover the phone so he could speak.

"What the fuck is she saying now?"

"Are you with him *now?*" Maria shrieked, her voice filled with hatred.

What the hell is with her?

"Yes, Maria, I'm with Franco."

My words were almost rehearsed, my voice barely mirroring my emotions.

"He's sick, Ella; he thought you were his niece!" Maria continued her tireless tirade of abuse, my eyes half closing as Franco shook his head.

"Come back to our house; you know you're welcome to stay over."

"Are you for fucking real?" I snapped, my anger finally resounding in my voice. "How *dare* you speak to me like this?"

Maria was silent.

"I'm still your half-sister, Maria, and out of the whole family, you are the *only* person I share any blood with. Mom's gone, and you're all I have left."

"You have your precious Franco," Maria sneered. "So not all hope is lost, is it? I'm always here, ready to be your sister whenever you dump his sorry ass. Until then—"

I trembled, an emotion so violent rushing through me I wasn't entirely sure I could identify it at first.

Waves of pressure racked my head, my eyes bulging as I grit my teeth, the pounding of my heart making me grip the countertop.

"Do *not* make me choose," I whispered, unable to see through my tears. "You have no right."

"Me or him, Ella, what's it going to be?" Maria sang, clicking her tongue.

How could she do this to me?

"I have to go."

I ended the call, staring at the back of the phone in shock.

"Ella, whatever she said—" Franco began, dragging his hands through his hair. "She's honestly vicious. I know she's your sister, but she's fucking cruel."

I lifted my eyes to his, tilting my head curiously.

Franco was always the middle man, kind to both of us despite clearly having a soft spot for me. When we argued, he tried to defuse it, but I never heard him speak about Maria in that way.

"Why is she? What happened?"

I swallowed, but Franco refused to elaborate.

"What is with everyone keeping fucking secrets from me?" I half screamed, slamming my hands down on the counter.

Franco stepped back, studying me as one would a wild animal that had escaped the zoo.

That's how I felt; like a caged animal, and I wanted out.

"She came over before I flew back to you." Franco sighed. "I threatened to kick her out—the bitch had slapped me at your house the night before, and I was damned if—"

I felt the color drain from my face, but the rage within me pushed it back, my cheeks pulsing with anger.

"Excuse me? Maria *slapped* you?"

I was horrified.

Where had my father been?

"Did you slap her back?" I asked, fearing the answer.

Franco scowled at me, screwing his face up with disgust.

"Of course not."

My heart ached for him.

He'd been here, alone, telling our family about our relationship, and my sister had the audacity to *slap* him?

Franco watched me, stroking his jaw.

"She was angry at me for being with you and for hurting her dad. She lashed out."

"Just like I will when I see the little bitch," I raged, crossing my arms over my chest.

It didn't make sense.

Why would Maria slap Franco?

I understood why she would slap him considering my father's reaction, but because he was with me?

"She's jealous," I whispered, the truth dawning on me. "Isn't she?"

Franco pursed his lips, his brown eyes moving to gaze past me, his brow furrowed.

There was something he wasn't telling me.

"Franco?"

He shrugged, rubbing the back of his neck with a groan.

"She's just a dumb kid."

"Tell me right now what happened," I demanded, leaning forward on the counter, so we were gazing at one another directly. "Now."

Franco nodded, chewing on the inside of his lip.

He was a good guy, and he hated us arguing. However,

I had a niggling feeling something was wrong, and I needed to know what it was.

"She came over, and I threatened to throw her out. She said if I did, she'd tell everyone I made a pass at her."

My mouth dropped open, a gasp of disbelief leaving my lips.

"What?!"

Franco looked at me desperately. "I swear to you, I've never *once* looked at her in that way. It's always been you, Ella."

"She blackmailed you?" I spat out with rage. "For real?"

Franco nodded, a grim look on his face.

"I threw her out anyway, but not before she told me Todd was in love with you or some shit."

I repeatedly blinked, laughing bitterly.

"She makes everything about her," I whispered, shaking my head. "Todd, you, me...everything ends up coming back to her."

"I mean, I wouldn't be surprised if Todd's in love with you because I fucking am," Franco confessed, his lips pulling into a slight smile in the corners.

"I wish I could doubt you, you know? But Maria has always been like this with me. It's so sad; I've only ever loved her."

"I know, baby."

Franco's fingers stroked my jawline, his eyes following his movements.

My fingers covered his, and my eyes closed.

Despite everything, I never doubted Franco.

Not once.

"I love you."

"I love you too."

FORTY-FOUR

ELLA

THE TIME HAD COME to break the news to my father.

I was three months along now, and I couldn't hide the soft swell of my belly any longer.

Franco told me no matter what; we had one another. But I knew how important my Dad's support was to him, me, to both of us.

Grandpa said we had to do it without him, but he also made sure Maria was out running errands because I wasn't sure I wouldn't murder her upon first sight.

So here we are.

My father stared into his hands clutched on his lap, almost as though he was searching for answers.

I studied my thumb, picking at the skin around the nail until it began to bleed, and Franco reached out to lace his fingers through mine. He squeezed my hand reassuringly, and I gave him a faint smile.

"So," I breathed, feeling ill at the thought of what I had to say.

How do you break the news of a taboo pregnancy?

Not only breaking the news but telling the man you thought was your father but wasn't—*God, this is fucked up.*

Licking my lips, I focused on Dad, deeply inhaling like it would calm my erratic heartbeat.

"We have something to tell you," I began, as something changed in Dad's eyes.

Hope, crushed by desperation, was replaced by confusion.

What did he expect me to say?

How do I tell him this?!

"I don't know how to tell you this…." I stared at the kitchen clock, focusing on it like I was speaking to it rather than my father.

Guess what, clock?

I couldn't breathe, my throat was thick—

"Ella is pregnant," Franco announced, his posture straightening like he was bracing himself for impact.

The room fell deathly silent, almost to the point where my ears rang.

Blood thumped through my veins, and I swayed with dizziness, wondering why Dad wasn't saying anything.

"Breathe, Ella," Franco murmured, stroking my trembling fingers.

Breathe?

It was like I'd forgotten how to. Finally, I opened my mouth, allowing a lungful of air to escape my body before I inhaled again; this time, the dizziness disappeared, and I focused once more.

Dad was staring at me, tears spilling down his cheeks as he nodded wordlessly.

When I was a kid, he'd look at me like this if I was mean to Maria; a rare event, but the girl pissed me off even then. The look was one of disappointment, and I wasn't sure I could bear it.

"Say something," I whispered, reaching across the table to grab his hand in mine.

Dad shook his head faintly, retracting his hand from mine.

"You're both fools."

A slice of hurt seared through my soul, cutting so deep I half expected to see blood dripping from my fingers.

Fools?

Dad stood, placing his fingers on the table as though making a point.

"This isn't right. I can't accept it. I won't."

I bowed my head, his words hitting me like a whip, my body jolting to every syllable in agony. "Don't tell your sister, for fucks sake. She already thinks you're going to burn in hell."

I flew to my feet, the chair behind me crashing into the wall.

Anger blazed through my veins, my words burning in my throat as I tried to throw them at him like missiles, wanting him to hurt as I did.

"You're supposed to be my fucking family!" My voice didn't sound like mine; it was like I was possessed.

Maybe I am. "He's not my uncle! He's *never* been, my uncle! And even if he were, I wouldn't change a *damn* thing because I *love him!*"

Tears blurred my vision, and I felt Franco slipping his arm around my waist, his lips close to my ear.

"Calm, baby. It's okay."

I pushed him, shooting a look of disgust in his direction.

"It's not okay! We're leaving, *Dad.* I had hoped you'd have come around by now, but it seems you're as messed up as Maria!"

Dad's eyes darkened.

"That's not fair, Ella—"

"*Fair?*" I half screamed, waving my hands in the air. "Do you think losing my mother was *fair?* Or the fact I had to deal with Maria and your heart break for *so long* I could barely grieve? I did *everything* for that little bitch, so I can say whatever I *like.*"

"Ella!" Dad roared, slamming his hand onto the table. "Not in my house!"

Silence fell; the only sound was the heavy breathing from my father as he shook his head.

"You're *not* my Ella," he said, staring at me as though for the last time.

My knees buckled.

"Christopher, come on—" Franco snapped, pulling me into his arms.

"And you're not my brother."

A moan left my lips as I turned, pushing past Franco and out into the yard.

"Maria is a little bitch! You think she's so fucking innocent and—ugh!" Franco went silent, and I ran back in, almost crashing through the screen door.

Franco was on the floor, my Dad on top of him, squeezing Franco's throat.

"Dad," I gasped, wrapping my entire body around his back, clawing at his arms. "Stop, please! He's right! Maria is awful!"

"You're a fucking disgrace!" Dad screamed at Franco, kicking him hard in the ribs. "I *never* want to see you again."

Dad's chest heaved, and I released him, running to Franco's aid. Franco got up quickly, brushing me off as his eyes burned into my father's.

"Yeah? That goes for me too, *bro.*"

"We're leaving, right?" I dragged Franco to the door, refusing to look at my father. "Now."

I fought back more tears, knowing there was only one way to end this insanity.

Franco wrapped his arms around me as we made our way down the road in stunned silence.

I knew Dad would be pissed, but this?

I swore there and then that I'd never forgive him for this.

Ever.

FORTY-FIVE

FRANCO

FOUR WEEKS LATER...

"I'm telling you, I don't care if you paint the room sparkly pink; it's gonna be a boy."

Ella did the hot thing she did, hands on her hips and a stern look that made me bite my fucking lip.

Four months pregnant, and she was hotter than she'd ever been before. Her cute black overalls snuggled her bump perfectly, the bright white t-shirt below highlighting her tanned skin.

"You've got a fifty percent chance of being right, so I'm not going to argue with you. I'm going with neutral colors."

Ella scanned the room, chewing her nail as she pressed her barefoot into the carpet. It sank in, the fibers sprouting between her toes as she wiggled them.

"This is so nice. I love it; what's it called?"

I lifted an amused brow, trailing my gaze up to her bare leg.

"Padding."

"That's it! Padding. Makes it feel all spongy and soft," Ella said with a grin before staring down at her bump. "Like I'm gonna be after this baby."

Her eyes clouded with insecurity, and I tilted my head, unsure how I could make her realize how fucking perfect she was.

"Listen, you're gorgeous, and you know it. Also, you need to go and have a little nap."

Ella frowned, looking at me with suspicion in her eyes.

"Oh?"

"Uh-huh," I said with a smile, crossing over to take her in my arms.

The swell of her belly pressed against mine, and I swept my hand down, caressing it as I kissed her lips.

"I'm taking you out."

Ella gasped, her eyes widening as she stood on tiptoe, kissing me back with such force it knocked me back.

"Really?"

Ella *loved* going on dates. She wasn't like any other woman I'd ever met—she was the cutest, sexiest woman in the world, and I needed to see her smile more.

"Uh oh, you've got that look in your eyes." Ella's eyes searched mine, her touch softening as her fingers danced in my hair. "The Russo look."

"I'm sorry, baby, I was just thinking about how much I miss your smile," I confessed, pulling her hair into a fist at the nape of her neck as she groaned happily. "And those moans."

My lips dropped to her neck, her soapy scent greeting me as I moved her shirt south.

"You said I needed to sleep!" Ella reminded me, her finger lifting my chin, so I was looking up at her.

"How do you make me feel like this?" I whispered,

dotting kisses along her jaw, nibbling on her ear as she giggled.

I could kiss her all day.

Fucking was great, but kissing Ella was just out of this world phenomenal.

"How do I make you feel?" Ella grinned, moving closer to me.

Ella's smile was a shooting star across the night sky, a rare sight but one you remembered forever.

"You make me feel lucky. Like I've won the jackpot or some shit like there are no bad days."

"So cliche, Francesco."

I studied her, shaking my head as I tried to understand how she made me feel.

"It's like...everything is in black and white, but you're color, you know?"

Ella nodded, and when she pressed her lips against mine, I saw fucking stars.

Millions of them.

My chest heaved with emotion, the idea that this perfect woman was not only with me, but she was carrying our child.

Of course, I felt fucking lucky.

I was richer than any billionaire.

"Are you scared?" Ella mumbled into my ear, stretching to reach me.

I dipped, burying my face into her neck as I inhaled her.

Ella scared me.

The way I felt for her scared me, but it always had.

"What do you mean?"

"About the future."

I closed my eyes, wondering what our future looked like.

No one knows, but we all had hopes and dreams.

"All I know is it's got you in it."

ELLA

The restaurant was overlooking the harbor, and Franco had booked us a table by the window, with a perfect view of the ocean.

We settled in our seats as the waitress lit the candle on the table between us, and Franco caught my eye, giving me his trademark smirk.

God, he's beautiful.

"Thanks," I murmured to the waitress as she left, lacing my fingers through Franco's. "This place is so cute. What made you do this?"

Franco eased back into his chair; his blue linen shirt against his olive skin made me melt into a puddle of obsessional goo.

Yeah. I was fucking obsessed with Franco.

"When we walked down here the other week, I saw the way you looked at it." Franco chuckled, scanning the menu. "You know you get anything you want."

A tingle in my stomach made me giggle, and I shot two fingers at Franco, who frowned.

"What?"

"Our girl agrees. Momma gets anything she wants, and so does our girl."

Franco rolled his eyes, but his smile was wide.

The fun debate started when we moved here, far away from anyone who knew us, but big enough so that there was no small mind mentality.

Incest was a label that you can't pick off, no matter how hard you try.

I gazed at Franco, who was ordering drinks.

How had I not noticed the server?!

"Uh, a peppermint tea, please."

"We don't have that, I'm afraid," the girl winced, tapping her pen on her cheek thoughtfully. "We have regular tea."

"Sure." I smiled.

"You're obsessed with that stuff." Franco laughed when the waitress left.

"No, just you."

"You're obsessed with me, Ella?" Franco teased, flexing his arms.

"Fuck, yes."

"Right back at you, baby."

It was so relaxing to be together without the dirty looks and whispers we'd had back home.

An ache in my chest reminded me how hard it was to think about home, so I tried to push it away.

"Stop thinking," Franco instructed, narrowing his eyes. "Seriously, relax."

"I know, I am," I said quickly, moving my attention to the window.

But I was lying.

All I could think about was my father.

Grandpa regularly called, asking how we were getting on.

I'd given up the apartment in LA, and Dillon had moved in my place pretty quickly. This alleviated my guilt for leaving Todd, but he was coming on leaps and bounds with his recovery.

But my father?

Not a word.

FORTY-SIX

FRANCO

THE LINE CRACKLED in my ear, the raspy coughs taking over my father's voice for a good minute or so before he adjusted the phone.

"Sorry, son. The old lungs aren't holding up much lately."

Nothing to do with the packs of smokes the doctor has been telling him to give up all my life.

"Dad, tell me you're not smoking."

"Of course, I'm still smoking; stopping now isn't going to save me, Francesco."

Christ.

My eyes fell to Ella, who was asleep on the couch, her hands cradling her bump protectively.

I want him to see this baby be born. He was the only family we had, dammit.

"Dad, you need to—"

"Have you called to lecture me?" Dad barked, conjuring up an image of his furrowed brow in my mind.

"No, but—"

"How's Ella?"

I smiled then, gazing at her beautiful lips that parted with each exhale, the way her fingers caressed her belly, even in her sleep.

"Still perfect, Pop."

"Baby doing okay?"

We were both skirting around the real question that hung between us; was Christopher ever going to contact his daughter?

"The baby is good."

"And what about that small ass town you took yourselves off to? What's it called again?"

"Oobatt."

"Sounds like it's in fucking Germany."

I snorted with laughter as I thought of the quaint little town we'd found ourselves in, with a decent hospital less than an hour's drive away. With its cherry-topped ice cream sign that proudly announced it served the best ice cream in America, along with the traditional barbers complete with a line of older men who sat out front. Then there was the scent of warm apple pie every time you strolled down Main Street; I didn't think it could be further from Germany.

How did they get that smell so fucking perfect? It made me hungry every damn time. Maybe they piped it in as they do with the cookie shit at Disney.

An image jumped into my mind of Ella and me taking our mini-me to Disney, watching the delight on their face when they met 'ole Mickey.

"Maria wants to go to college in LA when she finishes school," Dad interrupted my thoughts, a wheeze coming from the depths of his chest as I winced.

"To be honest, Dad, I don't give a fuck."

"She's been talking to that boy who Ella lived with. Seems a nice enough guy."

Todd?

"Huh, ain't it funny?" I shook my head as I watched my beautiful girl sleep, wondering why the fuck Maria wouldn't want to speak to her and miss out on her niece or nephew.

Because she was a bitch.

"No, it's not. You all need to make up before I die."

I stared at the ceiling, ignoring the sincerity in his tone.

Sure, he was old.

Maybe he smoked far too fucking much, but he was happy, and that had to count for something.

But death?

"I don't wanna lose you, Pops."

A heavy sigh, followed by more coughs, filled the line, and I knew it was important to listen to him right now.

"You're gonna, as sure as the sun fucking shines, Franco," Dad chirped, gulping his drink. "So get used to that idea. The doctor wants to send me for tests—I told him to get lost. Other than these blasted lungs, I'm as fit as a fiddle."

I was silent, a lump forming in my throat at the thought of my dad never meeting our child.

"Of course you are." I chuckled, turning my gaze to the sink full of dishes.

"You picked any names?"

"Uh, no, we can't agree." I rubbed my neck, laughing as I remembered Ella's face when I suggested the name Eleanor for a girl in honor of her name.

"I like the name Andromeda."

"Bit of a mouthful for a baby."

"Meh, babies grow. Name her after a fucking star, Francesco. Make her lucky from the start."

"You can help us choose when he or she arrives; stop

talking like you're not going to be here." I snapped, closing my eyes when silence fell between us.

"Well, that's my thoughts for a girl. I like Antonio for a boy." He continued thoughtfully.

"Tony?" I screwed up my face, shaking my head.

Typical Italian name.

"Fuck, I didn't mean Antonio—I know an Antonio, and he's a prick."

I stifled my laughter, knowing exactly who he was referring to.

"Okay, Pops."

"Abramo. It's the Italian version of Abraham, and it's a strong name. It will carry him well."

I swallowed down the lump in my throat as another coughing fit took over, this one lasting much longer than the last.

"Dad, I'll call Chris—"

"No!" Dad rasped. "I'll be fine."

This was the one thing about living in this little town, far from anyone we knew.

I couldn't be there for my dad when he needed me the most.

"You remember something, Franco—cough-cough—"

I rested my head against the wall, darkness uncurling in my stomach.

My dad was fucking dying.

"Don't change for nobody. Not for any of them. You do what feels right, and you'll never go wrong. Capiche?"

I couldn't bring myself to respond.

"I gotta go, son, but you make up with your brother. Family is family, and sometimes people need to come together. I love you."

"I love you too, old man."

"Less of the old, but fuck, I'm tired. Old and fucking tired. Be good."

The call ended before I could say anything else, and before I knew it, I'd dropped the phone onto the counter, the heels of my palms pushing into my eyes as though to remove the thoughts that were racing through my head.

Dad was right like he always was.

The whole reason we'd moved to this town was that it had a population of like, five hundred people, and not one of them knew who we were.

They assumed we were married, and once they realized they couldn't find us on social media, they shrugged us off as the new couple.

People were real fucking cute, though, bringing pies and cakes to welcome us in, dropping flyers of all kinds through the door like we didn't have access to the delivery apps that adorned every American phone screen.

"Baby?"

The sleepy voice from behind me soothed me instantly, and as Ella yawned, I took her into my arms, kissing her lips softly.

"Hey, you."

Ella frowned, searching my eyes. She knew something was wrong; this was how we were.

Our connection was almost ethereal.

"How's Grandpa?"

I shrugged, allowing my eyes to skim around the room like I wasn't screaming inside.

"Alright." I lied, forcing a smile I didn't feel at all. "You know what he's like. He gave us some name suggestions."

Ella gasped, clapping her hands excitedly.

"Ooh, go on!"

"Andromeda for a girl," I began, watching her carefully for a reaction. "Or Abramo for a boy."

"Wow, I love them both. I also think it's adorable that their great grandad will have chosen our baby's name."

"You like them?"

My eyebrows flirted with each other as she nodded enthusiastically.

"They're beautiful."

I cupped her face in my hands, resting my forehead on hers as we gazed at each other.

"Do you wanna go on another date, Ella?"

Ella grinned, nodding as she twirled around in the air.

"Yes, please! Somewhere that has spicy food this time."

Like our life wasn't spicy enough...

FORTY-SEVEN

ELLA

FRANCO GROANED FROM THE STUDY, and I grabbed the mug of coffee I'd made for him, circling my hands around it for warmth.

I was officially waddling now—but it just meant we were one step closer to meeting our baby.

Franco leaned back in his office chair, his fingers laced behind his head. His laptop screen looked complicated, nothing but digits and letters that made zero sense to me.

"Coffee, baby?" I purred, placing it before him.

His fingers danced up my spine as he rose from the seat, cupping my face in his hands.

"That depends. What else are you offering?"

He ran his tongue over my lips, his hands twisting my neck to the side so he could attack it with his mouth.

His stubble made me shiver, and I ran my hands through his hair when he suckled on my neck.

"Umm, that's good."

Franco pushed the wrap dress I'm wearing away from my shoulders, his lips and tongue tracing my collarbone.

"Haven't you got work to do?" I mumbled into his hair, inhaling his freshly washed scent.

Franco looked up at me, a smirk on his lips.

"Work can wait. My girl needs me."

Impatiently he slid the dress down to the floor, his hands caressing my bump as he did.

"You have no idea how beautiful you look. I want you to be pregnant all of the time."

I cackled, kicking the dress away from my feet.

"Isn't that a fetish? Pregnant women?"

Franco hooked his thumbs in my underwear, peeling it down my thighs.

"Just one. You," he growled, pointing in the direction of our bedroom. "In the name of comfort, go to our room. Otherwise, I'd be fucking you over this desk."

His gruff voice sent me delirious, but I did what he said, easing onto the bed with a sigh of content.

"Spread your legs for me, Ella."

I did, my legs quivering with excitement as he scooped his hands around my ass, pulling me down to his face. He exhaled over my clit, and I bit my lip, waiting to feel him.

"Your pussy is delicious, do you know that?"

"Mmm," I moaned, grinding my hips toward him.

"Impatient, Ella? Tell me what you want."

His finger slid along the center of my lips, lightly stroking my clit.

"I want you to devour me."

"Fuck, baby." Franco went all in, his tongue sweeping around my slit, his hot breath sending my nerves into overdrive. His hands lifted me to meet his mouth, my body bucking with desire as he sucked and nibbled on my clit.

My eyes rolled in my head as he found his rhythm, tongue fucking me while using his fingers to stroke my clit.

"Yes!" I cried, my thighs crushing him in place.

A soft pinch made me gasp, and teeth dragged along my inner folds, which were now dripping wet.

"You taste so fucking good, Ella."

I was riding his mouth, but Franco didn't wait for me to reach climax like he usually did. Instead, he moved over me, his perfectly sculpted abs resting close to my bump.

"I need to be inside you; tell me how you want it."

I tugged him down to my mouth, his palms flat on the bed on either side of me.

He tasted of me, but I didn't care; it turned me on more.

"Bend me over," I whispered, and he nodded, helping me to my feet.

I kneeled on the bed, arching my back, so my ass was perfectly presented to him.

Franco rubbed my sopping entrance with his solid dick and moaned as it slipped in without any effort.

"Tell me to stop if it hurts," Franco whispered, gripping my hips as he slowly pulled me back onto his full length.

He filled me slowly, sliding in and out of me repeatedly so that we could feel every single movement.

"You okay?" Franco slowed, and I pushed back onto him, turning to lock eyes with him.

"Franco, I'm fine, just fuck me!"

"Easy, sweetheart," Franco smirked, hissing as he slammed back into me.

"Yes!" I cried out, thrusting my hips in his direction.

If he were worried about the baby, I would do it myself.

In fact...

"Let me go on top," I demanded, wincing as he slid out of me. "I want to be in control."

Franco positioned himself on the bed, helping to guide

me into position as the tip of his cock pressed back into me.

"You're so beautiful, Francesco," I cried out, wriggling until I had him fully inside of me. "Kiss me."

Franco did, his lips against mine as we breathed one another in, then out, our tongues thrashing against one another.

I lifted my hips, gasping when I slid back down, the rhythm taking over once again.

Franco was gazing up at me, and my hands laced behind his head as I tugged on his hair.

"Ella."

My lips tried to lock onto his, but my hips moved as fast as they could, given the bump between us, meaning I was teetering on the edge of my orgasm sooner than I would've liked.

"I'm so close," I wailed, feeling myself becoming tired already.

Franco found my clit, and with expertise only he had, he stroked me so perfectly that my orgasm hit me like a freight train—taking my breath with it.

My entire body felt like it was on fire, and the only touch it craved was his.

Moments later, he filled me; the warmth deep in my core made me sigh with immense pleasure.

I didn't move for a while, and we kissed like lovestruck teenagers until we heard Franco's work phone ringing off the hook.

"Shit, I better get that. Please don't get dressed; I love you like this."

He lifted me with ease to the other side of the bed, and I cleaned myself up with the tissue beside the bed.

Still breathless, I rolled onto my back, sighing with happiness.

As much as I loved my life, I still missed my family.

The dull ache they'd left hit me at the strangest of times—this being one of them.

Like, who thinks of their family post fuck?

I didn't care, though.

If it meant I had nothing in the world but Francesco and our baby, I didn't care.

You made your own family.

Life was too short to dwell on other people's opinions on how you lived your life.

I heard Franco laughing as he made some shit excuse about not answering the calls, and I closed my eyes, drifting into a contented sleep.

EPILOGUE

FOUR YEARS LATER

FRANCO

"Stay still, you crazy child." Crouching to my knees, I fixed Abramo's tie, ignoring his hateful glare.

He had his mother's eyes, and he had already mastered the look of disapproval she wore so well.

"Don't like it." Abramo pouted, still glaring at me.

I sighed, glancing at Ella, who was staring at her reflection in the mirror.

"Only I would be going to a funeral pregnant."

A smile played on my lips as I ruffled Abramo's hair.

"Go and wait for us downstairs. We won't be long."

Ella sighed, pressing down her dress as she examined herself from the side.

"I'm not rocking this dress. Grandpa would disapprove."

I crossed the room, locking my arms around her belly, kissing her neck softly.

"You, Ella Russo, are fucking stunning."

"Fucking stunning!" Abramo yelled from behind the doorway, his little feet carrying him off down the hallway as he cackled.

Ella arched her brow at me, tutting.

"Francesco, you've got to watch your mouth. You know what Abe's like."

"Listen, that boy will follow me to the moon and back so that he can hear me swear. Little shit does anything to get me in trouble," I grumbled, winking at Ella.

"Oh, I love how you refer to our child, Francesco. I can't wait to have another *little shit.*"

I laughed so hard my lungs ached, and Ella rolled her eyes.

"Grandpa loved you in a trash bag, and you heard his instructions. So no arguing today; that's all he asked for."

Ella's eyes welled up, and I pulled her against me, kissing her head.

"He loved you, and he loved us. He met Abe and made happy memories. He was old but happy."

I swallowed, nodding at our reflection as though to confirm what I was saying was right.

"I know, but Dad will be there...and maybe Maria." Ella licked her lips nervously, and I tilted her head to look at me.

"You've got me. Right by your side."

Ella nodded, and I straightened up.

"It's time to go."

"Can I play there?" Abramo asked, pointing his chubby finger at the cemetery.

"No, son, you can't." I sighed, scanning the crowd for my brother.

"Why?" Abramo's lip curled with disgust.

Ella emerged from the bathroom, dabbing at her eyes.

"Because we have to be respectful at a funeral."

"Grandpa said go crazy."

"Abramo, just relax, please. Mommy needs you to be a good boy today, okay?"

Ella smiled down at our son, and he nodded like an obedient puppy.

"Okay, Mommy."

He took her hand, resting his other on her swollen belly.

"You better be a boy."

"Have you seen them?" Ella asked, her lip quivering. "They must be here—"

"Ella. Francesco." A deep voice called from behind us, interrupting Ella.

I turned, heaving a sigh.

My brother looked a hell of a lot older than the last time we met, but the hurt in his eyes hadn't faded. His eyes locked onto Abramo, and his gaze softened.

"You look like Grandpa," Abramo announced with a yawn. "I'm bored."

Christopher grinned, walking toward us slowly, crouching down to Abramo's height.

"Hey, kiddo."

"Who are you?" Abramo scrunched his nose up curiously as Ella shook beside him.

"This is your...." Ella began, staring at Christopher in horror.

"This is Chris." I cut in, nodding at Christopher.

Christopher finally made eye contact with me, nodding to himself.

"I'm Chris," Christopher repeated, his eyes watering. "What's your name?"

"Abramo," Abramo said confidently, still watching Christopher suspiciously as he rose to his feet.

"Ella, you look beautiful. Another on the way?" Christopher croaked out, his eyes falling to her belly.

"Yes." Ella turned to me, her eyes filling with tears. "I can't do this."

"Hey, look at me. I'm here. We're saying goodbye to the one person who loved us unconditionally. We promised him."

I slid my arm around her, meeting my brother's eyes.

"Excuse us."

Christopher opened his mouth to say something, but everyone began filing into the church silently, meaning he had to do the same.

He'd had years to come over and meet our son.

Years to make amends with Ella.

I knew there was no love lost between him and me, but Ella was his child, for fucks sake.

How could you not be there for your child?

I guided my family to an empty pew and laced my fingers with Ella's.

"Are you still doing your eulogy?" Ella asked me, her voice catching in her throat.

Dad had asked me to speak and even told me what to speak about. That old fucker knew what he was doing, but I wouldn't turn down a dying man's last wishes.

"Yeah. If you are okay with being here while I go up?"

I examined Ella, then Abramo, and she nodded, squeezing my hand.

"Of course."

People took turns speaking, and we listened to tales of him growing up as a kid, how he'd spent his life, and even us.

The time came for me to go up, and with one last squeeze of her hand, I made my way to the pulpit, deeply inhaling before I began.

The sea of faces that stared at me expectantly didn't help my nerves, but then I remembered who I was doing this for.

"My father asked me to do this today. I know many of you know about me, and who I fell in love with, and even how it happened." I shifted uncomfortably as the room fell eerily silent. "But one person understood, and everyone in this room loved him. My dad."

My throat throbbed with emotion as I stared down at the paper in my hands, my trembling fucking hands.

"He told me that you couldn't help who you fell in love with. When he married my mother, everyone celebrated their unity. They were cousins, but back then, it was acceptable. It was common to keep bloodlines pure. Not so much today."

I scanned the faces in the room, noting how intrigued people were. This was gossip, alright, just as Dad predicted.

Cause a fucking riot, son, he'd told me.

"Ella isn't my blood relative. She isn't my niece through blood, and therefore we can do whatever we like. But to some people, it didn't matter, and those people missed out on so much."

The door opened at the back of the church, and I watched as Maria walked in with Todd, her head dipping when she saw me. They scrambled for seats, and I found Ella, her eyes locked onto mine.

"They missed out on our happiness. Our first child.

Our love. He kept us going when the whole world was against us. He made me see that if you had the love of one person, you could do anything. My dad told me to tell you all today that you must've respected him if you're here. If you take one thing away from this, know that he was a good man. He believed in love, real love, not the sort society forces upon us. He loved us with all of his being, and he never once said he was disappointed in us. Not once. He named our son, and he created many happy memories with him."

Tears threatened to fall, and I blinked, letting them slide down my cheeks.

"So I ask you to celebrate the life and wisdom of this honorable man, and I hope you feel as lucky as I did that you got to meet him. Thanks."

I stepped down, blinded by my tears.

There was a stunned silence, and then the hymns began. People reached for their hymn books, eyes wide and blinking.

I hope I did you justice, Dad.

ELLA

My heart hammered in my chest as Franco spoke, my hand wrapped around Abramo's so tightly he frowned at me.

"Mommy, why are you crying?"

"Shh, baby. Daddy is talking," I whispered, jumping when the door opened at the back of the church.

My eyes reluctantly left Franco's, and I saw my sister walk in, holding hands with my ex-best friend.

I felt winded, but somehow I managed to turn around, finding Franco gazing at me as he continued.

I'm here.

I nodded, forcing a smile to let him know I was okay and fought my tears.

I loved him so much it hurt.

I knew it would have taken a lot for him to stand up there today, and my heart was bursting with pride for him.

Grandpa was always a joker, and I saw a lot of him in Abramo. But, of course, he did this to cause mischief, or maybe, just maybe, he was helping us make amends.

Franco finished, heading back to our pew with tears spilling down his cheeks.

"Baby," I whispered, pulling him close to me, my forehead resting on his wet cheek. "You made him proud."

"Bastard, making me do that." Franco laughed, wiping his tears with the back of his hand.

"Bastard!" Abramo sang, grinning like the little devil he was.

"Abramo!" I hissed, tugging him back into his seat. "Stop doing that!"

I closed my eyes, praying this would be over soon.

Not helping matters at all, Franco kept making faces at Abramo, causing them both to fall over laughing.

"This is the weirdest funeral I've ever been to," I mumbled to myself, joining the line to pay respects to my Grandpa's casket.

Everyone stared at us, but Franco held my hand throughout, kissing it repeatedly.

He was the only thing keeping me sane.

"Franco."

I whipped my head in the direction of the voice I'd grown up adoring, my heart sinking in my chest when I saw Dad gazing at Franco.

If he says anything disrespectful to him now, I'll lose my shit. I'll unleash pregnancy hormones like no one has ever seen before.

"That was...quite the speech." Dad pressed his lips into a thin line as he glanced at me. "Knowing that old fool as I do, that was a message to me."

I swallowed, moving forward in the line as Franco studied Dad.

"Have you got something to say, Christopher?"

Ouch.

Dad shuffled forward, gazing at the casket with sadness.

"Yeah, I have. But, unfortunately, I've been just as much of a fool, and for that, I'm sorry."

My heart soared, and a hand flew to my mouth, stifling my sobs.

I'd waited years to hear him say that.

Years.

"I just couldn't see past it, you know? My brother and my daughter." Dad glanced at me. "I told you, blood or not, you'll always be my daughter, so it always felt wrong."

Franco gripped Abramo's hand, moving toward the casket to say goodbye. I nodded at my Dad, my arms hugging my stomach.

"You missed so much."

"I missed everything." Dad agreed, smiling at Abramo. "But if you'll have me, I'm here now."

I couldn't speak, but Dad slid his arm around me, guiding me forward.

"It's our turn to say goodbye, Ella."

Blinded by tears, I stumbled towards the casket, feeling Franco steadying me from one side, my Dad on the other.

Placing my hand on the closed casket, I tried to compose myself, praying I held it together.

The varnished wood beneath my fingers was strangely

warm, and for a second, I felt like Grandpa was there.

"Thank you for everything," I whispered, pressing my fingers to my lips, then to the casket. "You were one in a million. Love you, Grandpa."

I stepped back into Franco's arms as Dad released me, placing his hand on the casket.

His shoulders shook as he cried, and Franco nodded at me to move forward, my hands lacing with my father's, my head buried into his shoulder as he held me.

"I'll make it right, Pa. You wait and see; I'll make it right. Say hi to Mom for me," Dad whispered, tapping the casket lightly. "God speed."

Together we move away, and Dad holds his arms out to Franco.

"I'm sorry."

Franco glanced at me before stepping forward, allowing Dad to hug him.

Franco wouldn't be able to forgive as easily as me, but I couldn't ask him to, considering everything.

"Yeah, you've been a prick." Franco shrugged, his gaze softening.

"PRICK!" Abramo screamed, causing the whole church to fall silent.

"Well." Dad laughed, looking down fondly at Abramo. "I think it's safe to say Dad's spirit lives on."

"That it does," I whispered, wiping away more tears.

I didn't even have the energy to grab Abramo from the pulpit, but Franco grinned at me, waving at him dismissively.

"Fuck it; it's Grandpa's funeral. Let him wreck the joint if that's what he wants."

Dad chuckled, and I let out a strange noise, somewhere between a laugh and a cry. Dad wrapped his arm around my shoulder, tugging me close.

"Let me make amends, Ella. Can I call you sometime? Maybe visit?" Dad asked hopefully, dropping a kiss onto my head. "I'm afraid your sister doesn't feel the same way." Dad sighed, glancing around the now-empty church.

My emotions were so intense I could barely breathe, so instead, I nodded, watching as my son played with his daddy in a church.

It wasn't normal behavior, but since when did we ever consider ourselves normal?

"To be honest, Dad, I don't care. Not all wounds heal, you know?"

Dad nodded sadly.

"Some take a lot of time, kid."

"I appreciate your apology."

Dad turned to me, following my gaze to his brother.

"I appreciate you talking to me. You don't know how much I've missed your voice."

"Little shit!" Abramo roared, giggling as Franco lifted him into his arms, frog-marching him past us.

"I think we should leave this place before he sets it alight." Franco laughed over his shoulder, his eyes meeting mine.

"You good, baby?"

I smiled at my Dad, walking over to the love of my life. Pressing my lips against his, I nodded.

"As long as I've got you."

Franco smiled, kissing me back.

"You're gonna be good for a long ass time then, beautiful."

Damn, I hoped so.

THE END

BOOKS BY

LINZ VONC

The Winterburg Series

Mine

Theirs

His & Hers

The Assassination of Alice Deacon

Running Winter

Standalone books

Theodore

Initials Only

Vacay

Jain

About the Author

Linzvonc is the author of countless stories which she published for free on sites such as Inkitt and Wattpad. (*Psst, some are still there!*) She dabbles with different elements of romance; sweet romance, teen romance, paranormal romance, dark romance and erotic romance. When she isn't writing, she's with her gorgeous family and connecting with readers on social media. Linzvonc loves to read, and this is why she started. To write the books she wanted to read! Linzvonc's dream is to one day be on Netflix, and in every bookstore in the world.

Libraries are usually where you'll find her hiding, by the way. That or a coffee shop. So if you see a woman typing furiously on a phone or laptop, check if she's got a nautical themed sleeve tattoo, big glasses and a glazed expression.

You just might have found her.

Printed in Great Britain
by Amazon